Praise for Phil Whitaker

'Whitaker is so genuinely inventive.'
—*The Spectator*

'Whitaker is clearly a writer to watch'
—*Daily Telegraph*

'Whitaker is an intelligent, sympathetic and eloquent writer.'
—*Sunday Telegraph*

'Phil Whitaker has gone where no novelist has
dared to go before.' —MARCUS CHOWN

'Funny, engaging, insightful, and even moving. Masterful.'
—PHIL HAMMOND

'Touching and sad, yet funny and entertaining.'
—MARGARET FORSTER

'A wonderful story. if literary thriller means
anything it means *The Face*. Buy at once.'
—*Time Out*

'Heart-stopping. *The Face* is a thriller unlike
any I've ever read.' —*Literary Review*

'A clever, beautifully judged piece of writing.'
—*Financial Times*

You

PHIL WHITAKER won the John Llewellyn Rhys Prize, Betty Trask Award, and was shortlisted for the Whitbread First Novel Award for his debut, *Eclipse of the Sun* (1997) after graduating from the UEA creative writing MA. He went on to win the Encore Award with his second novel, *Triangulation* (1999), and has published three other novels, *The Face* (2002), *Freak of Nature* (2007) and *Sister Sebastian's Library* (2016). *You* is his sixth novel.

PHIL WHITAKER

YOU

CROMER

PUBLISHED BY SALT PUBLISHING 2018

2 4 6 8 10 9 7 5 3 1

First published in Great Britain in 2018 by
Salt Publishing Ltd
12 Norwich Road, Cromer, Norfolk NR27 0AX United Kingdom

www.saltpublishing.com

Salt Publishing Limited Reg. No. 5293401

A CIP catalogue record for this book is available from the British Library

ISBN 978 1 78463 144 4 (Paperback edition)
ISBN 978 1 78463 145 1 (Electronic edition)

Typeset in Neacademia by Salt Publishing

Printed and bound in Great Britain by Clays Ltd, St Ives plc

The excerpt from 'Something Dark' by Lemn Sissay is copyright © Lemn Sissay
2008. It is reprinted by kind permission of Lemn Sissay and Oberon Books.

For PA and RG

It's not black, it's not white,
it's not dark, it's not light
Secrets are the stones that sink the boat.
Take them out, look at them,
throw them out and float.

Something Dark
LEMN SISSAY

PROLOGUE

Rendezvous

THE ROAD THROUGH the village is closed. They're digging up the drains – some problem with the sewage backing up or something, Christ knows. Red and white plastic barriers, portable but implacable, linked in a line from pavement to pavement, blocking the way. A rectangular yellow sign, leaning back on its spindly metal legs, black arrow and stencilled lettering redirecting traffic up the Farleigh Road. It'll be a way round the impasse, sure, but the sat navs won't like it, and the route will be clogged by the abnormal volume of cars. Some drivers – frustrated by the delay, feeling thwarted in their plans – will try doing their own thing. They'll hang a right down some narrow lane, embarking on some tortuous circumnavigation along the ancient droves that thread between the hedgerows hereabouts. Do-it-yourself detours from which some, perhaps, may never return.

I think: a car could smash through it all, crushing the lightweight barrier, sending bits flying like a skittles strike. What would the ground workers do then, gathered round the shallow shit-filled trench they've excavated? Look up, alarmed? Hold out puny hands, thinking they might halt the oncoming threat? Dive to safety once they realise it's futile?

But we don't, do we, we users of the road? Such violence would be unacceptable. We obey the imposition, accept our fate. We turn around and try to find our way, some other way, any way we can.

The High Street has never been so quiet. Everyone who lives there loves it, I'll bet. A break from the late-running commuters, defying the speed limit. A lull in the lorries rumbling through, their deep vibrations rattling family photos on the mantelpieces, and heirloom china on the shelves.

I phoned a couple of days back. The stop is the other side of the closure but I wanted to be sure. I'm making a journey on Thursday, I said, I have to catch a train. I shouldn't have fallen for it, the youth on the other end yabbering through an endless list of road names I've never heard of, telling me this was the diversion that would bring the bus round. I couldn't follow what he was saying. So I said to him: Look, fella, can you just tell me, is the bus going to stop here or not? Oh, yes, he said, the bus is definitely running as normal. You will definitely make your train.

Half an hour in the autumn chill, the FirstBus sign jutting from ten foot up the telegraph pole; the timetable mounted in its weatherproof frame below, making its empty promises. Me, interrogating every engine note as vehicles approach either side of the crossroads.

I should have ordered a taxi.

In the end a guy in a Toyota pulls up, passenger window winding down. He leans across, one hand on the steering wheel, peering up at me.

'You're in for a long wait.' He gives me a rueful smile, like he's been caught out before and knows how I must be feeling. 'Would you like a lift? You can pick it up at Hinton.'

He's called Sree, he tells me, as we pull away. He's about my age, I guess, around fifty, but his face has barely any lines. How come Asian skin weathers so well? I'm surprised, meeting him; there are so few ethnic minorities out here. I figure he must be a recent arrival but, when I ask, he says he's been in the village twenty years, ever since he and his partner left London. His other half is called André, which snags my attention; he sounds French, artistic. It sets me wondering about them: their history, how they met, what they do.

Sree chats on, checking his rear-view mirror, working up through the gears, warming to the opportunity to reminisce. They didn't intend to live here, he says, not when they first made plans. They were thinking of Bath. But the village was so much quieter then. And when they came to see the house on the High Street, with its views over Churchmead, the tower of the fourteenth-century church standing sentinel against the backdrop of the hills rising westward towards Falkland . . . well, they fell in love.

He has a friendly, cultured voice. I've got him down as an architect, or a doctor or something – a professional not a businessman, at any rate – but I don't ask. It only invites enquiries in return. I like him, though; I have a sense we could get on. He feels it, too, I'm sure. I'm chastened it should have taken this – this non-running of a bus – for us to have come across each other. I've been here three years already. I keep myself too much to myself.

'So where are you off to?' he asks, glancing at my hold-all, crammed in the footwell, and the curious canvas roll bag clasped upright between my knees.

I think about it. I could just tell him, be completely straight, but it would lay me open to questions – the well-meaning, life-affirming sort of questions we use to make connections. There would come a point when I would regret having said anything, where I would have to slap a layer of gloss on things, just to make them acceptable. Even with all the time in the world, it is hard for anyone to comprehend. Unless they've been here, too. Then they understand only too well. That's what these past seven years have taught me – that people make assumptions, interpret things according to their own lights. When superficial appearances make such perfect sense, it's the devil's own job to persuade someone otherwise. On the surface: a river sliding naturally – peaceably, even – downstream. But beneath the sky-tree-light-reflecting sheen? All manner of currents swirl, and limbless creatures prowl. It's something only I know. Me, and those of my clan.

The pause has become a silence. I'm seeming rude, to someone who has been only kind.

I tell him: 'Oxford.'

I listen to the word hovering in the air. My tone has the hint of a warning: that is all I am going to say. But I might have left the door ajar. I look across – his face in profile, his aquiline nose, the frank brownness of his eye. He's not that interested. He's just making conversation.

I turn my attention back to the road. We flash past signs welcoming careful drivers to Hinton Charterhouse. There's the FirstBus sign up ahead on the left, where in a moment Sree will drop me and I will wait a while longer to pick up the next hourly service.

'Yeah,' I say, as though talking to myself. 'I'm going to Oxford.'

❧

I am on my way to see you.

I am on my way to seeing you.

Two sentences, virtually identical. Those three little letters,

6

that innocuous i-n-g, spelling a whole world of difference. I'm no writer; I couldn't tell you the grammar. All I know is, one sentence is definite, concerned with something that is going to happen. The other is contingent, provisional, a work-in-progress, with no end in sight.

All I know is: I am on my way to see you, but it'll doubtless be one more wave from this distant shore. That's what Prof calls it: waving from a distant shore. Seven years I've been on my way to seeing you. And I have to carry on, stranded here on this stony beach, the pebbles painful under the balls of my feet, so far away you can scarcely make me out. My arm is achingly tired, but I will keep describing these arcs of love. The sea breeze cuts cold across the impassive channel; there is salt on my tongue. Gulls cry overhead. I have to keep calling, my voice hoarse from not being heard, the sounds I make too puny to cross even a fraction of the gulf between us, even were they not to be whipped away on the wind the second they leave my lips.

Who are you? Your childhood was happy, your family loving and warm, I know that much. You skipped through those early years, your skirts dancing round your knees as you made your way. You have a sister, two years younger, and she was your only bane. Sometimes you were inseparable, playing together, exploring and adventuring. Other times you felt overpowering antipathy, and you would take it out on her in a thousand subtle ways – excluding her from your games, letting her know she wasn't wanted, wounding her with words when no one else was around.

Then when you were twelve, an earthquake: buildings, their foundations, every structure rent and brought down. Your father announced he was leaving, leaving the home, the family.

You. Your sister. Mummy – devastating her, shattering her heart. Wonderful Mummy. The times you would find her, hunched over her knees, crying and inconsolable, no matter how hard you tried to console. You felt so desperate, so powerless to help.

To think, you once stood in that kitchen and pleaded with him not to do it. Daddy, is there *any* hope? Your vulnerable young body sheathed in a pretty floral print dress. Your hands entwined tight together in front of you. Your eyes imploring.

To think. Back then you believed it was him deciding to go. Bit by bit, over the months, over the next couple of years, the truth dripped out. How the man you once loved as your Daddy was a tyrant, a bully. How he had controlled Mummy, repressed her, rendered her daily life a misery. How he had forced her to go out to work, keeping her from spending the time she craved with her young children. How he belittled her, monitored every penny she spent, humiliated her in front of others for a pastime.

To start with, in this post-separation world, you spent every other weekend with him in the modern box he was renting, and a couple of nights each week after school. But the more you learned of him, the more you began to see his true character in how he treated you, too: his rigidity, the way he kept over-riding your feelings.

Gradually, you learned about his drinking, his fecklessness, his domineering ways; how Mummy had, for years, kept the family together, putting up with virtual slavery for your and your sister's sake.

Every time you were due to stay with him you would see the pain in Mummy's eyes, you could tell how anxious she was about your well-being, how searingly she was going to miss you while you were gone. To go felt like a betrayal, and the guilt of it skewered you.

You wanted less and less to do with him, you could hardly stand to go there anymore. Still Mummy would take you, holding you tightly before you left the car. Your hands, encircling her body in that last heart-rending hug, could sense in her tremulousness things that you couldn't name. You would insist you didn't want to go. She would say: you have to, we have no choice, the court ordered it. And it's important to see your father. Her voice would shrink and crumple under those last words, like paper on a fire. She would check in with you constantly while you were there – Skype, instant messaging, calls on the mobile – ensuring you were all right, letting you know she could come and fetch you at any point if it proved too much to bear.

The final straw, just after you turned fourteen. Your daddy wanted to take you – you and your sister – to Italy the following summer, to go round the galleries in Florence, and see the Siena Palio. Two whole weeks away from Mummy, fourteen days of unbearable pain for you and for her. You felt ripped apart even contemplating it; you thought you might be physically sick. And the prospect of it forced Mummy to tell you that from which she had so long hoped to shield you. How in the months before he left the home, your father had begun to spend more and more time alone with you in your room, the door firmly shut. How Mummy would come in and interrupt, to find him sprawled across your bed, a chilling grin on his face, with you sitting innocently beside him, focused on your homework, oblivious to the danger. With you in Italy, she would be a thousand miles away. She could no longer hope to protect you.

Those happy skirt-dancing days of your childhood, an utter sham. You broke off all contact with him. A two-line email. You never saw him again.

When you think of him now, on the occasions you are forced to, you feel nothing but cold fury. Fury and disgust. When you think of Mummy, nothing but admiration, and a love so visceral it hurts. You have surmounted those traumatic years, the both of you. Mummy has scaled enormous heights to carve some semblance of a career for herself. Cut off from all but token financial support, she somehow managed to feed and clothe you, and give you a home. As for you, you kept your head down, studied hard, achieved a clutch of As and A*s in your GCSEs at the local comp, and did a repeat performance in sixth form. It paid off: A-levels good enough to satisfy an offer from Oxford, where now you are training to be a doctor.

That is what I know of you. The story of your life thus far.

⁂

The bus, when finally one arrives, is comfortingly warm after the morning chill. It takes me down the valley, deciduous leaves piled in huge mounds at the feet of the densely wooded slopes rising to our right. Opposite, I catch glimpses of Wellow Brook winding between thickly overgrown banks, a venerable waterway, unchanged over the centuries except by imperceptible degrees. At Midford, we pass the remnants of the old railway bridge, lopped off at either side of the road, the line severed, a victim of Beeching's brutal disconnection of this community two generations ago. There's the old mill house, home now to a family with a trampoline, it would appear. The mill race shows evidence of children's epic dam-building, great mounds of sticks and branches and other debris heaped up and impeding the flow.

A quarter of an hour and I will be at the station. The train I'd booked a seat on has long since departed, but there will be another. I allowed myself leeway; I still have time to keep my side of our rendezvous.

We climb out of the valley, and I take in the views across this landscape that I have come to love. Up through Combe Down and into the city outskirts, past the Cross Keys, the Esso garage with its ever-escalating price of fuel. Scaffolding around a derelict house. A Union Jack fluttering from the flag-pole at the old St Martin's Hospital. Dropping down to Bear Flat, the Devonshire Arms clad in glorious russet Virginia creeper. The polar bear atop the porch of the Bear Hotel. Round the corner now, and views out over Bath itself, the perfect symmetry of the Royal Crescent in the far distance; a crane looming above the old quays, where new construction is underway. Down past the disused wharf houses on the banks of the Avon, the neo-Georgian SouthGate centre, and on to where I will catch my train.

Who am I? That depends, I have come to learn, on who is doing the looking. We can start with my name. Steven James Buchanan, that's what I was baptised. Steve to Ma and Pa; Stevie to everyone else. Everyone else except you and your sister. To you, I was once known as Daddy. For now, let us just say, I am your father. I am your father, and I am on my way to seeing you.

Tacoma Narrows Bridge

I F YOU ARE to come on this journey with me, you will have to trust. We will not be going anywhere together, not in a physical sense - that would be impossible, in any way, shape or form. We will dissolve ourselves instead into pure imagination, ranging over both topography and time, our consciousnesses scorching through the ether like twin spangled streams, unbounded by the laws of nature. Some of the places we alight you may recognise or remember. Others will be new - beyond the start of your memory, even of your life. Some, neither of us can know. These I will build from scraps and conjecture; extrapolations from what I was told.

How on earth can you trust me?

Come, let me show you something. Come with me to a sitting room. You're immediately struck by the dated decor - those broad-striped curtains, the footstool made to look like a Rubik's cube, the fatness of the TV set in the corner. It's OK, don't be alarmed. We have simply spanned time, materialising ourselves some twenty years ago. The room is one of those large spaces created from two separate receptions, the partition wall long ago demolished, the ceiling now supported by a hidden steel beam, the scars made good by plaster, paint, and skirting. It doesn't matter much, but you should know that we're in Oxford, in a Victorian terrace on Chatsworth Road. We're looking on a man, turned partially away from us. He's standing between a shabby blue sofa and an unlit gas fire across the other side of the room, jeans-clad as ever, cotton shirt under crew-neck sweater, leather moccasins on his feet. You feel a shock of recognition. At the same time, you're taken aback by my appearance, how much younger I look. What am I? About thirty, at a guess; you're too stunned even to begin to try to calculate. My hair is thick and dark brown – no hints of grey; no thinning, not even at the crown. Even at this angle, you can tell that my glasses are round-framed and tortoiseshell, as was the fashion of the time.

I turn towards us. What's that I'm holding? Forgive me; perhaps this is too soon. What I am holding – one forearm beneath, one hand wrapped round its front – is a baby, eight, maybe nine months old. Terry towelling bodysuit, yellow duck on its front. Round faced, pudgy armed, wispy haired. You.

A sudden tightening inside. I've flipped the baby round to face me, then hefted her in the air. High above my head. You watch, horrified, as infant-you soars towards the ceiling. Christ, what would a social worker say? Inevitably, gravity asserts itself. You hang motionless for an instant, then begin to fall. What the hell am I doing? The very next moment, my hands gather you, slotting in against your sides, tight into your underarms. I lower you gently to my chest.

You watch, spellbound. This tiny, younger you starts to giggle. Hysterically. Peals of delight issue in a continuous cascade from your infant lips. I am laughing, too, the skin round my eyes crinkling with love. It dawns on you that this must be a favourite game. Again and again it happens. Up, down, catch. Up, down, catch. You see how my eyes never waver, always tracking the path of my precious child, arms outstretched in readiness. It's the most wondrous feeling, whooshing up, your tummy caving inside as you crest the parabola. For that brief moment you are flying, absolutely free, nothing holding on to you at all. And every time, as you begin your descent, my pigment-stained hands clasp you and arrest your fall. Do you worry? Do you even know there's the possibility of disaster? In the world you know then, is there even the chance you will be allowed to crash, bruising and breaking yourself on the floor beneath?

Perhaps you have questions. Perhaps there are already things twenty-one-year-old you would like to ask the me of then, throwing and catching baby-you like a human ball. You can speak, but you will not be heard. You can touch, but your hand will slip through me as though I were made of air. We are in that room, but we are not of it. We are two future selves who have yet to come to be.

Away, let us leave us to our game. It was just a little thing. Something to give you confidence – hope, even. Something to help kindle the embers of your trust.

As we travel, you will constantly ask yourself a question: what is truth? In this post-truth world – in which professions are corrupt, politicians lie with impunity, once-major religions contract – there is nothing left in which to believe, there is no such thing as truth. All we have are the myriad truths that bumble around, one inside each one of us on this benighted planet. Those truths collide continually, sometimes bonding to form complementary wholes, just as often bumping and bashing and repelling each other like particles of identical charge, or multiple north poles. What, if anything, is there left for us to cling on to?

Yet there is such a thing as truth. I have to believe that. That which exists outside our heads, independent of our minds and all that they can do. That which actually happens. Recognising it, knowing it – that is the difficulty.

How will you do it? How can you discern truth in what I show? Always, nagging at you, the stalking doubt: am I merely giving you my version, painting myself in flattering colours, brushing over imperfections and blemishes, drawing you into a web of justification and jaundiced sight?

I cannot answer that – that is a question for you alone. All I can promise is to apply no varnish, nothing to dull the colour, or protect the picture that my brushes will describe. One thing may help, though. Take my hand. I know: it feels strange, acutely uncomfortable – it will for a long while yet, perhaps forever. But take it. Let me whisk you to one other place, show you one more thing before you decide whether or not you will come along.

Do you recognise it? A cavernous modern hall, huge panes of glass forming one entire wall, pillars of white-painted metal, each as thick as a sequoia trunk, rising at rakish angles to support the roof. We're light as air, you and I, hovering above hundreds of people, who are milling between the display stands below. Families, in the main: this is a place for children, for education, for eyes to be opened to the world. A cacophony of chatter assails our ears: kids exclaiming, parents explaining, everyone vocalising the wonder of it all.

I was never much into science, but it was something you loved. There you are, down there, purple sparkly jumper with the silver love-heart stitched to its chest. The way we wear things as seven-year-olds without a trace of self-consciousness. We're walking briskly, we two, away from the exhibition about human embryology, over towards the adjoining section. Hand in hand. We live in the West Country now, Oxford long behind, left when you were just four, your sister two. This place is @Bristol, its name a fitting herald of the online world that is evolving around us as we breathe.

Mummy and your sister are elsewhere in the vast hall, your sister's interest snared by the interactive stands demonstrating *trompe l'oeil* and all manner of other perceptual tricks. You and I are heading for engineering, though, returning to see once again the Tacoma Narrows Bridge.

Do you have any recollection? It made such an impression at the time. Look at you, a little girl with her dad, rapt in front of the screen, waiting till the video starts its inevitable next loop. Let's descend, softly as sycamore seeds, so we, too, can catch the show.

You peer over your own seven-year-old shoulder, watching what your child's eyes see. On the monitor, a film of a huge, girded structure, fabricated in steel and concrete, its fairway tarmacked like any regular road. A river torrenting below. It looks so solid, so substantial; the bridge should be indestructible to any but the most explosive force. But now, look at it: it starts to twist, buckling around its longitudinal axis. Rapidly, the amplitude picks up, it's warping now, great swingeing torques, oscillating wildly like a manic fairground ride, whole swathes of concrete and metal seesawing like they're made of naught but the flimsiest card. In spite of ourselves, we're laughing, child-you and I: it looks so comic, so counter-intuitive, it doesn't look possible. Bridges just should not do that. It's like something out of a black and white Laurel and Hardy.

Look. Panicked people have abandoned their cars mid-crossing – they're old fashioned ones, Fords mainly, this was the 1940s after all. Empty, the vehicles pitch side-to-side like sea-sick passengers in an Atlantic storm. The Tarmac starts cracking, disintegrating like a global-warmed ice floe. This is the bit you love the most. That guy, in his long great-coat and trilby, running forward, barely able to keep to his feet, thinking nothing of his own safety. He was a professor or something. At last he makes it to the nearest car, grapples with the door, opens it. Allows the dog trapped inside to leap free. Then the pair of them scarper, unsteady as drunken lords, back to the safety of solid ground. Finally, the shearing forces overwhelm. The whole central section of the bridge collapses, plunging into the water below, displacing an almighty plume of spray.

The wind, the wind. That awe-full destruction caused by nothing more than the wind. Yes it was strong, gale-force if I recall, but nothing that would have qualified for even a mention on the news. Nothing that should have troubled that man-made colossus. Do you remember the explanation, intoned in voiceover as we watched it all unfold? How, unanticipated by the hapless engineers, a wind of a certain, very particular speed established a fatal resonance with the bridge's structure, setting it vibrating like an instrument string. Untrammelled energy was channelled into its fabric, bringing about its eventual demise.

Come, let us leave @Bristol, leave your seven-year-old self to enjoy the rest of her day, all the marvellous sights she has yet to behold. You cast a glance behind as we ascend, up past the arboreal pillars, each of us starting once more to demate-rialise. Below us, you and your dad have moved on, are lost now back in the crowd. Impossible to pick them out; Mummy and your sister, likewise.

My words; this story – you will have your stalking doubt. And for all I will strive for honesty in my brushwork, which of us can be unflinching in telling our account? But truth. Truth will be like that wind. Truth you will know by its resonance. Be under no illusion. It will set things within you vibrating, sometimes violently so. Like for those folk on the Tacoma Narrows Bridge, it will feel scary. It will feel as though the ground under your feet is swaying, yawing, buckling, disintegrating. It will feel as though everything on which you have so long stood is about to come crashing down. Do not be afraid. For this is how you will recognise truth. And this is how truth will bring you, if you are brave enough to allow it - like that professor and that poor bewildered pooch - safe back to solid ground.

ONE

Origins

ARRIVING IN THE station foyer, I look to see when the next train is due before going to grab a coffee. A quick glance at the screen shows one is just about to depart. Suddenly I'm fumbling at the barrier, trying to get my wallet out, trying to get my ticket out, my roll bag sliding off my shoulder in the midst of it all, tangling my arm, everything conspiring to slow me. She's so kind, the woman there - she buzzes the gate open and lets me through on trust.

I run full pelt along the underpass, taking the stairs at the other end three at a time, and emerge to find the train standing at an eerily deserted platform, diesel thrumming, everyone else on board, the guard with his hand on the door. Shrill whistle. I run towards him, breathing heavily from the exertion, managing a few nonsensical words: *Is this Didcot?* He looks momentarily nonplussed, then seems to get what I'm asking. He gives me a nod and a grin and ushers me past, shutting the door behind me with a heavy clunk.

I find a seat without a reservation and slump in next to the window. I have to get my breath back; things are slowing down, time is catching up. This is such a short life. It won't seem that way to you, not the age you are now. Twenty-one. I remember how I was then, nearing the end of art school: nothing seems vital when you're that age, there'll always be a chance to change tack if you set off in the wrong direction. But believe me, it picks up pace, that clock, its hands turning more quickly with every revolution. Jobs and travel and dates and relationships, a decade chewed. Then maybe a career and a mortgage and maybe kids and then – whoosh – that's another fifteen, twenty years. And suddenly you're further from the start than the finish. And you begin to see it, that chequered flag in the middle-distance, in the niggles and the aches, and the changes in your body and face, and the evidence of what you can no longer quite so easily do.

We think there'll always be time to make things right. But there won't. There can't be.

I'm sitting facing back. It's easier somehow, looking out of the window; things unfold gently, none of the frenetic rushing-towards of a forward gaze.

The train gathers momentum, leaving Bath behind, heading for Wiltshire, and Oxfordshire beyond. Chimney stacks peek above a high embankment. A whiff of tobacco smoke as a guy goes past along the aisle. The guard comes on the loudspeaker but there's something wrong with the sound; I can't make out the first thing he's saying. Then suddenly we're out of the city, into open country, a long stand of tall trees beside the line, all grown at an identical slant, leaning like worshipful monks, evidence of the wind that has so long prevailed.

I check my phone. Nothing from you. There never has been, not in seven years. Every email I send, every text – chatty updates, interested enquiries, assurances of love – unacknowledged. Like coins down a wishing well.

I understand, though. I know what you have gone through. So I keep going, communicating every week or two. A marathon of waving from this distant shore.

What would you think to see me now, iPhone in hand? I've kept pace with technology, to a certain degree, anyhow.

Do you remember that old Nokia, how you used to laugh at its push-button Ludditeness, its inert screen, its jiggling space-invader-style icons? We went together to that shop. You - tech-savvy twelve-year-old that you were - enjoying showing off your knowledge of smart phones, helping your dad take his first step into the new era. I'd been thinking of getting one for a while. Then when I moved out, into that rented place on Drake Avenue, BT taking untold weeks to get the broadband connected - it pushed me to take the plunge, to get a phone I could do emails and internet with. Something to keep in touch with family and friends, those who were rooting for me in this strange new life I was embarking on. Something I could use to keep in touch with you and your sister when you weren't around. Bonus by-product: something you loved to play on - Temple Run, Flappy Bird, Candy Crush, all the faddy games so important to the young.

I put the phone away. There are voices from upfront in the carriage, a couple of families out for the day. Toddler chatter. A baby whining, on the verge of some need it hasn't words to express. Train journeys tumble in my mind. Playing noughts and crosses and hangman with you at a table we felt lucky to have found. That time we nearly missed the stop for the airport on our way to Disneyland Paris - you, Mummy, your sister, and me - me pulling the cord to halt the train just before it left the station, buying us time to get off, that inspector furious that I'd abused the alarm, me thinking it was worth it so as not to have missed our flight. These things happen. Days and weeks go by for me, you tucked away in your box, me living the life I have now for myself. Then a random sight, an inconsequential bit of music, and I'm ambushed. They're like crowbars, jemmying the lid off, splintering the wood, unleashing memories and the loss of you.

Enough of this. I get my phone again and send you a text, telling you I'm on my way, reminding you where the watching-the-world-go-by wall is, and saying I hope to see you there at three. Lots of love, Daddy.

Lots of love, Daddy.

꧁

Come on, let's do this.

I feel a sudden up-rush, I'm sucked out of my body, slooped through an air vent and out into the sky. The train whips past below. I catch one glimpse of myself behind the glass, sitting woodenly, staring out of the window, mobile in hand, eyes no longer registering. A hollowed out shell.

We have to be quick about it. I have to be back before a ticket inspector comes.

An incredible surge of speed. I'm going faster than sound, now, though nowhere near the speed of light. I do a couple of barrel rolls, testing my manoeuvrability. It's exhilarating, this abrupt freedom, this ability to be. The air roars furiously, a thunderous noise, as though outraged by my flight. My whole being is vibrating, I'm in sensurround, alive to possibility, my perceptions sharpened to crystal clarity.

Just for a moment, my euphoria dims: I'm alone in the sky. Perhaps it was too much after all; it was foolish to think you might be ready. But then, a thousand feet below, I catch sight of you, a shimmering vapour trail, forging a parallel course. Current thrills through me; you have decided to come. Of course you feel reticent – you have no idea how to approach me. Seven years you've lived with me as the enemy. It would be a big step for anyone to take, to bridge that gulf, let alone you.

I change trajectory by thought alone. Close on you in a graceful arc. Then we're alongside each other. I can sense your uncertainty; there's something reserved about your velocity, even though we're going at the same speed. I have to be careful, what nascent trust there may be is as fragile as a soapy bubble. I dive beneath you, loop round the far side, spin myself playfully back over the top, finishing up, in relative terms, where I started. I'm not showing off. My aerial acrobatics are intended to amuse. Distract. Reassure. Then it hits me, as it so often hits me: you are no longer the child still alive in my memory. You are twenty-one-year-old you. The larking, the clowning about – all the stuff that once-upon-a-time you so loved. Chances are that these now embarrass, even repel. How to relate to the you who for one third of your life I haven't known. I try to tune in, try to sense your mood. Still you're uneasy. I think I understand that. It was never going to be any other way, not really. But you have come. At least you have come.

We cross the Gloucestershire-Worcestershire border, coruscating streaks in the crisp blue October sky. Beneath us the verdant green of rural England cedes ground to the sooty sprawl of Birmingham and the Black Country. On over Staffordshire, the terrain becoming hillier as we approach the peaks of Derbyshire and our first destination. We're racing to the origins – every tale has somewhere to begin. Only this story has no single start. This is the story of you, her, them, and me, and it has multiple points of entry. And even these are just waymarks on paths that trace back through the generations. They stretch so far they have curved over the very edge of the world and are beyond what we can ever see.

If I were painting this, they would be present simultaneously, all these single start points, juxtaposed in a jumbled montage. Your eyes could rove at will, taking it all in. But pictures are susceptible to interpretation, their meaning is never clear. I have to use words, ponderous and slow and linear as they are. Even though words themselves are not exactly value-free.

Here we are. I pull up short. You slow to a halt a hundred yards beyond. We hover, briefly, mindful of each other. You maintain your distance. Trust will take time to build.

Follow me then, down among those drystone-wall-ribbed hills. Can you see our destination? That ramshackle farmhouse? The antiquated Ford tractor – bucket seat, no cab, tiny cowl; more of an engine on wheels – parked in its flagged yard. Only it's not antiquated, that tractor, not at this point in time. Not so many years from when we are now, all the harrowing, ploughing, and mowing here were done by horse; the muck-spreading, hedge cutting, and ditch maintenance, all done by hand. But the war that has recently raged to its conclusion on the continent – the VE Day celebrations are still fresh in everyone's minds – that war drained the tied cottages of their legions of agricultural labourers. Even the famous Land Army had its work cut out. The lack of person-power spurred great leaps in engineering. What you're looking at, that blood-red Ford 9N tractor, at this moment that is the last word in modern farm machinery.

There. Do you see him? Coming out from the milking shed. Knobbled knees below short trousers, V-neck pullover worn threadbare at the elbows. Some kind of hoop, he's rolling it along the ground, flicking it along with a stick, seeing how far he can make it go before a clod of earth or a pat of cow shit causes it to fall. You have no idea who it could be. You have never met him in your life. All these years you have believed him to be dead. That is Ted. That boy there, that is the child who will one day become Mummy's father.

He has tousled short back and sides. Sticky out ears. Front teeth that are splayed like subsided tombstones. Even at this distance, you can see his nails are grubby. He doesn't look much cared for.

Round the stone water trough he goes. You admire his skill with the hoop, he can even get it to turn rudimentary corners, provided he tweaks it just right. He looks serious, inquisitive, like an investigator, pushing the boundaries of what this simple toy can be made to do. Does he have much else to play with? There's nothing that looks remotely child-friendly anywhere in the yard. We haven't time to see, but you should know he has an older brother, Nigel, who is currently experiencing a growth spurt. Nigel is with their mother in Matlock, being kitted out with new bits of uniform for the coming year at school. But when they are together, Ted and Nigel, that hay barn there is their kingdom – the high-piled oblong bales become their castle; random sticks serve as arrows and swords with which to repel imaginary invading hordes.

There, did you hear it? That noise. Ted did. He stands stock-still, his hoop trundling away unperturbed across the yard. A sudden crump. Loud, but muffled in its quality. You listen carefully, as your child-grandfather does, too. The lowing of distant cattle. Skylarks, distracting predators from their nests. The drawn-out rattle of Ted's hoop as it finally runs out of steam, and settles on the flagstones like a spun coin.

Follow him, along the snicket between the stone barns, where the air feels damp and cool, into the front garden of the farmhouse with its tulips and dahlias and marigolds neat in the regimented beds. He's heading in the direction from which that unexplained sound seemed to emanate. I want you to brace yourself; this is not something you are going to want to see.

In through the front door, sticking close behind Ted's pre-pubescent shoulders, narrow and sloped as a wire coat hanger. Left to the parlour. Empty. Right to the dining room. Likewise. Down to the kitchen, its range pumping stifling heat even though it's summer, drab cotton underclothes drying on the hanging jenny. Deserted.

You hesitate as you see him approach the next door. Don't worry, there's no modesty to be preserved: the downstairs privy is in an outhouse round the back. That door, with its iron latch, its motley collection of different-width planks, that door leads to the room his father – your great-grandad – uses for an office. Where the paperwork for the running of the farm is held, together with the cash box, and a host of other private things.

Ted pauses for a moment. He's listening. The office is out of bounds; there'll be hell to pay if he's caught in there. The last thing he wants is to step in and find his old man, sat behind his wooden desk right in the centre of the room. But there is nothing but silence. Silence, and a peculiar sharp smell. His father must be up at Crams Land or Bugley Meadow, checking on the sheep. Ted pushes open the door.

I'm sorry, I didn't realise quite how messy it would be.

From the front, Ted's father doesn't look so bad, sagged in his chair but wedged in place, the shotgun like a massive peace pipe in his mouth, his arms extended where they'd been holding the stock, the butt of which is jammed against the edge of the desk. His eyes are still open. Imagine that: he didn't close his eyes. He stares sightlessly at Ted, his younger son, as though aghast at this intrusion into his private space.

The back of his head is spattered in a wide crescent across the far wall. I had no idea the blood would still be sliding down, these few minutes later. Bits of hair, matted black. Lumps of stuff that looks like offal, but must be scalp and skull and brain.

Let's get out of here. Sucked back across the kitchen, down the hallway, out into the garden. All the while, Ted is motionless, as though locked in a staring competition with his dead dad, trying not to be the first to blink. I know, you want to do something to help him, that little boy stood rooted to the spot, his mind like a derailed chain, suddenly unable to turn any thoughts in the face of that terrible tableau. But there is nothing you can do.

Come on, we must hurry. My train is belting across Wiltshire this very minute, and we've other places to go. That's all I wanted you to see. I'm sorry it was so unpleasant; I'm sorry if it shocked you – though even as I think that I remind myself you are no longer a child; you are twenty-one-year-old you. Doubtless you'll have seen far worse in films. Whatever, it was necessary – so you have the tiniest inkling of the impact on that ten-year-old boy. We've no time to hang around, no time to see what he did – whether he went to his father's buckshot-blasted body, or whether he hurriedly pulled the office door shut and retreated to his hay kingdom where he would curl up like a foetus among the sweet-smelling dried grass and remain for hours and hours even after his mother and brother finally returned home and the police cars came to strew the yard. Still less have we time to see Ted's story unfolding – being sent to live with a succession of grudging relatives, his mother deciding she could manage only the one child, now that the lease had to be given up and the farm become a memory. And that one child would be Nigel. No, we've got to leave him to get on with it, little Ted, as best he can. We'll see him again, though; there'll be time enough to catch up. And remember, this is just a waymarker – we'll never see the family story, the relationship traumas, the crowding defeats that culminated in that tryst with that dismal twelve-bore. Those are paths that stretch way off over the edge of the world, to places we will never go.

We're flying again, heading further north on our whistle stop tour. Is it respect for the dead? Sombreness for that little boy? Whatever, your speed is subsonic, your trail no longer scintillating. Our mood is sober; I know better than to try barrel-rolls to lighten it. You need to process, register, reflect on what you saw. I tuck in close, leaving a bit of distance, and parallel along.

South Yorkshire, West Yorkshire, on over North Yorkshire, overflying millions of our fellow citizens and the dramas and drudgeries of their lives. The air is cooler up here, the temperature falling as we cross the latitudes. Beyond the ribbon of the A1 I start to lose altitude, check that you are descending, too. The huddled settlements of Helmsley, Kirkbymoorside, flashing past beneath. My heart fills with love for you – your gritty pluck. You always were fiercely determined, would push yourself for hours on play equipment till you'd perfected the gymnastic manoeuvre you so wanted to do. Blistered raw hands, no matter – the goal was the thing. Come on, let's see this through.

Here we are, somewhere near Pickering. A perfectly ordinary merchant's house, double-fronted, slate roof, big blocks of grey stone. A house that says: we're prosperous. It even has coach lights either side of the porch, countering the day's-end gloom.

It's a squeeze, but we make it through the red-glossed front door – me squishing somehow through the brass letterbox; you, with your lithe youth, funnelling though the keyhole. Ah, that's better. It's warm inside, even here in the hall. We slide noiselessly along the dado rail, the Lincrusta wallpaper bumpily textured against us, and enter the drawing room.

An altogether cosier scene. Soft lamplight, a blazing coal fire in the grate, a Bakelite wireless warbling quietly to itself in the corner. A man, his wife, and their only daughter, are ranged round an occasional table, intent on their game. It's a brand new one, fresh from the factory, one of many gifts this girl was given for her recent birthday. It takes a moment to realise – the board is strikingly plain, the colours subdued to our modern taste – but the revolver, rope, and candlestick are giveaways, so the simple coloured pieces must represent Miss Scarlet, Professor Plum, Reverend Green. You had no idea Cluedo was this old, but it is – one of many new diversions for the middle classes as they adjust to the gradual easing of rationing, and the idea that life can be fun again.

The girl is excited. Her strawberry blonde curls jiggle as she bounces on her chair. I should tell you her name is Gloria. You peer over her shoulder to steal a glimpse of the Detective's Notes pad clutched on her lap. Not bad, not bad at all. We're some way into the game by now, and she's narrowed down the weapon (dagger) and murderer (Miss White). All that's left is to eliminate a couple more locations – the billiard room, conservatory, and library are still in the running – then she's won. No wonder she can hardly contain herself. It's a great effort for a lass of her age. She's not as young as you think, mind, this girl who will grow up to give birth to Mummy. Gloria is what we might term a micro mite, titchy in stature, which makes her look more like seven or eight, rather than ten. And there's something about the way she's dressed – that ruched sky-blue silk dress with its broad sash round the waist, its scalloped arm holes, the matching bow tied at the back of her head. She's playing games at home with her parents yet looks like she's fit to visit the Queen. A doll. That's what she makes you think of – you who lives in jeans and Fat Face hoodies and sweaters from Jack Wills. She looks like a living doll.

What's that? Ooh, the meanie! Gloria's character is Miss White (she's secretly thrilled to think she's the murderer) and she's been patiently advancing her counter towards the un-examined rooms. If luck is with her she'll have solved the mystery within a few more goes. But now her father's only gone and used his turn to whisk Miss White to the kitchen. Right over the other side of the board. Has he no heart? It'll take Gloria ages to regain the ground, to get back to where she needs to be in order to win. Someone is bound to steal her victory in the meanwhile.

Her jiggling abruptly stops. Her jaw muscles clench. Her mother glances at her sharply.

'Archie!'

The father, reaching for the lead pipe, freezes. He looks

up at his wife. Angie and Archie. Angie inclines her head pointedly in their daughter's direction.

You can't tell because you're behind her, but Gloria's face is rapidly reddening. Her eyes begin to brim.

Archie looks from daughter to wife. His expression is impeaching. Were we to get inside his head we might find some sort of half-formed argument: This is only a game; surely you can't —

Angie's eyes narrow. She's a wee one, too, five foot nothing in her stockinged feet. Fair of face, mind; what they call bonny hereabouts. Archie thinks about the consequences that will flow - the days of stony silence; the withdrawal of conjugal rights.

'Actually.' He lets go of the lead pipe, picks Miss White up and returns her to her former location. 'I think I'll accuse Colonel Mustard instead.'

One more moment to soak up the heat, then we must return to the cold. Before we do, though, notice the little girl, Gloria. Even though the setback's been reversed and she's on her way to victory once more, she's perfectly still - her excited jigging is done. She raises a hand, uses the heel of it to brush a tear from under her eye. Angie, from whom she evidently gets her blonde curls, reaches across and repeatedly strokes her thigh. Comforting her. Soothing her. Angie's treacle smile slides off her face when she looks back at her husband. Her eyes have a hardness to them, now, as though they are reconstituted stone.

Archie knows it's too late, that what he did cannot now be undone. Gloria will be allowed to win; Gloria is always allowed to win. But it will no longer feel like a triumph. It's been ruined. He's ruined it. He feels like folding his cards and leaving the pair of them to it. If he did that, though. He moves the yellow counter and his chosen weapon over to the corner of the board.

'Colonel Mustard, with the lead pipe, in the kitchen,' he says. He sits back in his chair and sighs, then summons for his wife a thin smile. 'Can you help with my enquiries, dear?'

That's it. We're off. Straight up the chimney, hot and choking and sparky. Out through the pots like shots from a gun. Blam. Blam. Soaring near vertically. Within seconds, they're far beneath us, Angie and Archie and Gloria, their home shrinking till it's no bigger than a house for dolls.

That wasn't so bad, was it? None of the blood and gore of that Derbyshire farm. But that was a different kind of violence we witnessed: subtle, deniable, incremental, bamboozling. But violence all the same. It was just one instance, just an example; I could have shown you ten thousand more.

I narrow myself, streamlining what shape I have to max-imise my speed. The buffeting is intense. Somewhere over the south of England I shoot straight through a huge flock of starlings, my incursion sending them murmurating in all directions. I check behind – see you, too, punch a hole through the shape-shifting black cloud. A moment later it closes behind you like a self-healing wound, as though you had never been.

We scorch along, catapulted into rarefied air. Our speed is incredible. We are speed incarnate, our existence weighed solely in kilometres per second. Below us, land gives way to sea gives way to land gives way to sea again. The Mediterranean, glinting like crinkled blue foil. Here and there, ships inscribe languorous Vs. Then a khaki island. Malta. Looking like it's floating. The shade-shift of the shallower waters that skirt its shores hinting at the sand sloping away beneath the surface of the sea.

Down to the harbour, cornering tight around the bridge tower of a Royal Navy destroyer berthed among the fishing vessels and cruise ships. Along the promenade, flitting just feet above the heads of the evening walkers. Gentlemen in hats; ladies with wasp waists and full skirts. The air is balmy; the hotel is whitewashed; the views over the Med superb. From the ballroom yonder, music – big band stuff. This is the fag-end of the fifties; Bill Haley and Elvis are blasting convention elsewhere, but their rebellious rhythms have yet to break through for the genteel classes. You feel exhausted, wrung out, all this ricocheting about in space and time. This is the last one, I promise, the last thing for now that I need you to see.

We enter through wide-flung French doors, and find ourselves a vantage among the glittering glass of a chandelier. The light is bright, it takes us a moment to adjust. Couples glide and spin below us, like molecules in liquid. Boy-girl, boy-girl. The dance floor is flowing. Dinner jackets and ball gowns, pearls and diamonds, Brylcreemed hair shining. It's a live band, remarkably, up on the stage, brass and strings and drum kit and double bass. Glen Gray, *VIP's Boogie*, if you want to know.

There she is, Gloria, her mass of curls marking her out. She's dancing with some sailor, his starched white uniform offsetting the shimmering blue of her taffeta gown. You can't help yourself, the thought is instantaneous: she's like a grown-up version of the Cluedo-playing child we've just visited. Ten years have passed, she's put on a few more inches, and filled out in other ways. It's a bit awkward, isn't it, looking down from where we are. But décolletage is all the rage. Think of it as marketing.

She's gay, isn't she, in the fifties' sense of the word. Her creamy complexion fair radiates excitement, possibility, *joie de vivre*. All evening she's been aware of the sly glances, the bobbing Adam's apples, the marking of her card. The centre of so much attention. She's not the best dancer – her moves are a little stiff, ungainly even – but with looks like that she'll be forgiven plenty.

Look at her partner, the sailor. He should be having a ball, shouldn't he, dancing with this beauty? Instead, his eyes are a little wide, his expression almost fearful, as though he's stolen some precious jewel and has just made out the distant wail of a siren. He's out of his depth with this one and he knows it. They came ashore, dozens and dozens of them, full dress kit, caps under their arms, leaving *HMS Decoy* moored in the Grand Harbour. They fanned out through Valletta in groups, hunting for entertainment, seeking spoils in the nightlife. Many will have wound up in bars and clubs, but he and his three confederates struck gold. It had been ridiculously easy to infiltrate this ball – even though their uniforms marked them out as aliens. They just strolled through the hotel lobby, gave a nod to the doorman, and into the ballroom without so much as being asked for an invitation. Respect for the military. And what a night it has been. Delightful debutantes as far as the eye can see. Some declined dance requests disdainfully, but for every one of those stuck-up Susies there was another girl who thought a swing with a serviceman would be a delightful change of scene.

And this one. Gloria. He can scarcely believe it. A mere look from her startled his stallion heart into a flat-out gallop.

Petite, blonde, curvaceous, her soft Yorkshire accent mellifluous to his ears after the coarse masculinity of two months at sea. The bewildering blend of her perfume, a scent he feels he could quite happily drown in. There is something about her, he can't put his finger on it. He wants her, yet she terrifies him to the exact and opposite degree. She is so poised, aloof even, her every remark – about her private education, and now this Maltese finishing school – seeming to stake out a picket fence between them. But the way she uses her body as they dance. He is acutely conscious of the brush of her breasts against his tunic, the warmth of her hand in the small of his back, the occasional contact of their thighs. It is as though she is talking in two languages, the verbal and the physical, and saying contradictory things.

As for her, what does she see in sailor-boy? She's danced with the heir to a tweed weaving dynasty, with a young surgeon, with a bright thing in publishing. What possible allure could an electrical rating from a *Daring*-class destroyer hold? He's hardly good-looking, even less so in his discomfiture. But it's the way she can tie his tongue, after all the suave chitchat of the confident dinner-jacketed bachelors, that is rather thrilling – a confirmation of her power. And she is hyper-aware of the resentful glances from her erstwhile suitors as she twirls around the hall. She has them on threads, the lot of them. She has only to twitch her fingers and they jerk to attention. She will decide who has what of her. She is in control.

Do you know why we're here? I admit, it isn't easy – he looks so different now he's grown to be a broad-boned young man. But just now Gloria makes some remark, throws her head back in a laugh (emphasising her décolletage), and he gives a grin to let her know he's found it terrifically amusing, even though he hasn't. You notice his front teeth, splayed and gappy. And those ears, sticking out as you recall. He made it somehow, did Ted, all the way through school and now to his national service years.

Dance over, they go for some air, this odd couple. Gloria looks back over her shoulder from the verandah. For a moment you fear we're discovered; she seems to be gazing directly at us. It's OK, remember: we are not of this time, we cannot be seen. No, that backwards glance is to check, in the periphery of her vision, that eyes are following her, as she wants them to be.

The chandelier tinkles as we exit its dewdrop cascades and glide out after them. It's dark now; dusk descends that much more precipitously this far south. The extensive gardens behind the hotel seem to vanish into the blackness. The music – a Count Basie number strikes up – is a good deal quieter out here. Initially we can't see them. They appear to have vanished, too, Ted and Gloria. Warm, humid air. Cicadas chirping insistently. The flickering silver of the leaves of a white poplar, as the half-moon appears briefly from behind cloud.

Ted's uniform gives them away, just a shadowy grey blur beneath the tree's canopy. Slowly slowly we advance, fifteen, twenty feet in the air, and insinuate ourselves between the branches. Down below us we can just make them out, the happy couple, her back pressed against the tree trunk. I know, I know. It's plain embarrassing. We don't like to think of elderly relatives as ever having been sexual beings. And it's hard to compute: you assumed people didn't behave like this, all that time ago. Perhaps, like every generation, you believe that sex as recreation – rather than re-creation – was invented just for you. But this is how it's been since the dawn of time, irrespective of the delicate fabrics with which we've tried to clothe it.

She's a tease, isn't she, Gloria? – she who will become your grandmother. Big long smooches, hungry lips, tongue probing, hands roving. Then pushing him away, saying we mustn't. Then a show of inward wrestling, for just the right length of time, before she's back at him, for all the world like she can't restrain herself, standing on tiptoes to reach him, pulling his head down with her hands behind his neck.

As for him. Well, he's intoxicated. That this unattainable beauty, this cultured creature, should want him. Then not want him. Then prove to want him so powerfully that it over-rides all the sense, breeding, and class that so securely scaffolds women like her in their station. That's too heady a mix for any young man. He's drunk on it, gorged on it. He has to do his seventeen times table in his head to stop himself ejaculating in his pants. I'm sorry, that's indelicate, but that's the sum of it.

We've seen enough. There's no need for us to dwell, it only gets more excruciating. No need for us to watch as she slides a hand to rest on the front of his hip, just inches from his fly. No need to listen to the rustling of silk as he hitches the skirts of her ball gown above her waist, nor the snap of elastic against skin as her French knickers come down. I will tell you that, once he's hefted her aloft, once he feels her legs squeezing either side of his hips, and her slippery wetness enveloping him, there is nothing he can do to hold on. Yes, of course, they should have used a rubber. But never in even his wildest fantasies had Ted foreseen being in need of one. As for Gloria, she of the charmed existence. Nothing for her could ever possibly go wrong.

Shooting stars in reverse, we streak up through the Maltese evening, leaving your grandparents to their fate. We pick up speed, a tremendous acceleration fuelled by intention alone. I have a train to rejoin. You – well, you have whatever you have to do. There is no need to watch this particular catastrophe unfold: the absence of menstruation, the shameful consultation, the pregnancy confirmed. Oh, the trembling fury of dear old Angie, her precious doll come back from Malta despoiled. Demanding that Archie do something to fix it, infuriated that there is nothing he seems able to do. The humiliation; they will have to move. Pack up, lock stock and barrel, take themselves to an entirely different neighbourhood – another town – where there is no one they know.

The only consolation? Gloria – disgraced, sullied Gloria – does at least remember the name of the man concerned. Oh, had Angie ever imagined herself finding solace in such a thing! Archie always was a pathetic specimen, entirely unequal to action, and that is now revealed in glorious Technicolor. Angie takes it upon herself. Insistent enquiries of the Admiralty track first Ted's ship, then Ted himself down. An interview in the presence of his commanding officer. There could be charges brought, Angie declares – he should be thoroughly ashamed, forcing himself on a defenceless young woman far away from her home. Infinitely better for all concerned would be a wedding, and if that is to be Ted's preferred course then he'd better look sharp about it.

The further we go, our twin tracks tracing the sky, the lighter it becomes, almost as though we are chasing and catching and refusing to allow the sun to dip below the horizon. White cliffs, the Kentish coast, on over London and the Home Counties. I can sense something in your flight, a heaviness, as though you are gaining mass. I hope you realise that was not the start of Mummy's life you witnessed. Your aunt was the first born. But as children these kinds of family details seem unimportant, don't they? If ever we're told them, they're quickly forgotten.

Not the start of Mummy's life, then, but the overtures to it, and eventually to you.

But it's not that. That's not what's troubling you. We're back in full daylight; I catch sight of my train fast approaching Didcot below. Gradually, you veer away, our paths diverging. I think I get it: you came this far on a leap of faith. But all I've shown you are a few squalid scenes, and an unseemly interest in a sex life of long ago. Nothing, it seems, that's anything to do with you.

I am doing the underpainting. Marking the canvas with the shapes and tones that will inform what will soon become visible. That is all.

We've time, if we're quick about it; Oxford isn't so very far. I scorch across your path, my slipstream sucking you along in my wake. Down to the golden limestone colleges, hurtling past spires that have probed the heavens for centuries. We screech round Carfax, cannon down St Aldate's, Old Tom sounding sonorously from his tower. Flash over Folly Bridge and arrive at a house on Chatsworth Road.

We peer through the bay window, our extra-corporeality leaving no out-breaths to fog the glass. There you are, two-and-a-half, cute as a cute thing in your OshKoshB'Gosh dungarees. You're sitting cross-legged on the carpeted floor of this Victorian terrace that is your home. It's a Sunday, I can tell you that, because the *Observer* is open on my lap over there on the sofa. My tortoiseshell glasses are pushed up on

41

my forehead. You're busy stacking plastic cups, and playing at hiding a yellow foam ball.

Noises from upstairs: your baby sister waking from her afternoon nap. Mummy hears them, too. She comes through from the kitchen, appearing in the doorway, and she starts to cross the room. You look up at her, your chubby face breaking out in a grin, and you lift your arms in that time-honoured gesture that says pick-me-up-and-give-me-a-carry. She pauses right in front of you, does Mummy, with her tumbling blonde curls, the face that you see as beyond beautiful. Except that her face just now is as a mask. She stares at you – your raised hands beseeching. How does her expression come across to you, a tiny child? Hostile? Withering? Then she turns and moves past, out of the doorway and into the hall, you sat there stranded on your bottom on the floor.

From my place on the sofa, over the top of my paper, I watch it all. Your head swivels to track her exit. Your arms gradually fall.

You can't possibly remember this, it is from a time before your memory begins. But it is scored into you, a foundational part of you, a wick running through your flame. A hidden baton conducting the orchestra of you.

Away we fly, sucked backwards as though by a vacuum, Grandpont receding beneath us. There'll be hell to pay if I don't rejoin myself before Didcot. That was it, your own start point, and for now all I have time to show. I'm worried for you, and try to gauge you in your flight. I recognise something in your energy, a repressed, high-amplitude vibration that is new. I have felt this in you before. Fury, though I doubt you understand it. A memory: you on the path up to the swings near that rented place on Drake Avenue. I'd brought you to see it, before I moved in, so you and your sister could choose your rooms. You were quivering with feeling, didn't know how to name it, could barely speak. When you finally managed it, all you could say were some puny words: It's not exactly a family home.

Suddenly, you swerve away, hitting warp speed, and vanish to a single point of light like a daytime star. I'm alone in the sky. Once upon a time that would have eaten at me, but now I can let you go. I'm heartened that you came, hopeful you will rejoin, but these are matters for you alone.

I course off in the opposite direction, and follow the tracks till I catch sight of my train. A shallow dive till I'm alongside my carriage. I edge forwards, examining each window. Eventually, I find myself: sightless eyes, wooden limbs. The iPhone in my hand is the perfect cover for my lack of engagement with the world around. I flip through the air vent, pull off a neat somersault, then I'm back inside myself, animated once again.

Them

THIS IS THE story of you, her, me, and them. You'll never meet them. But they are people you should know.

We're at the Half Moon. A figurative name if ever there was one, speaking of the watches of the night, of the eternal battle being waged between darkness and the light. They're evenly poised, those opposing forces, straining and vying to best each other, neither apparently managing to wrest the upper hand. The Half Moon, then, but the crucial question, the thing on which everything depends, is whether it will prove to be in wax or in wane.

Prof is leading the meeting. Prof – the nickname is meant to be ironic. It conjures up ideas of crazy white hair, pince-nez spectacles, eccentric intelligence. Nothing like Jet actually is. That's her real name: Jet. She's Swiss, or Swedish, or Dutch, I never remember which: ice blonde bob, Bombay Sapphire eyes, a cool measured voice that delivers depthless wisdom with a delightful lilt that somehow makes you feel you must definitely be one of the most special people she knows.

Jet, I love.

I love Rev, too. Tamsin. A Northerner like me, who exudes warmth and positivity. She was a nurse, once upon a time, back home near the Tyne. She showed me a picture of her wedding day at the end of a meeting one time: my god, what a beauty, her face the embodiment of a tenderness and innocent love for the world that near broke my heart to behold. Now she's a vicar. Not a vicar, in fact; a curate or something. But that kind of thing. She wears big beady necklaces, and has about twenty bangles around each wrist.

I think: how could anything like this have happened to people like them? Back in the day, before I knew such things were even possible, I used to see occasional items on the news: Superman waving from the Queen's balcony; Spiderman scaling Westminster Abbey. Purple banners unfurled. Like everyone, I used to think: must be something dodgy about them. British justice: fair, impartial, the envy of the world. Judges don't make mistakes, not over and over. If you happened to be in the room at the time, I would kill the telly with the remote control. I would hug you, hug your sister if she was there too, though neither of you would have known why. You didn't want to be seeing things like that. If the courts had decided those guys mustn't see their kids, well, there must be something very far wrong with them. Methinks they doth protest too much. #dodgydads, #dangerousdads. We all know how cruel men can be.

And it was only ever dads. You never saw Wonderwoman atop the dome of St Paul's.

But Prof. And Rev.

The Zambian you would believe, I'll grant you. He's across the table from me, hand wrapped round his pint, quiet as ever, brooding. Six foot four, built like the proverbial outhouse: bull neck, close-cropped hair, broad nose. His cheeks are ruddy with sun-damaged vessels, a legacy of his sub-Saharan childhood. Toby, his real name is. He runs a bottling plant out near Portishead. Thick Afrikaans accent, making him – inaccurately but inevitably – sound every inch the white supremacist. We know how they talk, don't we? We saw so many on the news, spouting their vile propaganda during the anti-apartheid years. The Zambian is every inch the dodgy dad – just to look at him you'd think he oughtn't be allowed anywhere near a child, his or anyone else's. Until you get to know him, that is.

Zambo I love, too.

The Half Moon is our regular haunt. Draught Wadworths, woodburners, nooks and crannies, antique tin-plate advertisements arrayed around the exposed brick walls: Golden Virginia, Fry's Chocolate, Empire Gin.

There's a crop of new members here this evening, three in one go, after some months of it being just the four of us. Prof is outlining the rules of the group, all the housekeeping stuff: how often we meet, what to do if someone hits a crisis between times, the importance of mutual respect and confidentiality. I check them out while Prof's speaking. Two blokes and a girl. She's some sort of care assistant, Cheryl is, and clearly finds much comfort in food. One of the guys, Roger – Rog – is a fireman, the other is a postie named Eric. I find myself wondering how on earth he does the job, what with his sawn-off arm and all.

They all appear dazed, hanging on to Prof's words like they're inflatable rings that might just keep them afloat. My heart goes out to them; I would like to seize each of them roughly and give them a fierce hug. I don't, of course, it would freak them out. But I know how they feel – I felt exactly the same, back at their stage, back when I was first caught in the maelstrom.

What do they think of me, I wonder? Leather jacket, grey hair shorn in a number one cut to disguise its sparseness. A day's worth of stubble on my jaw. I look like a #dodgydad, too. The trouble the others had, fixing on a new name for me.

They tried out Claude, Leo, Pablo, but couldn't find anything that seemed to fit – they didn't know too many painters, to be fair. For a while I thought I was going to be Vince, even though I have both my ears. Vince. I didn't like it; it sounded menacing, had a rodent-like quality – monosyllabically harsh compared with the sing-song Stevie I am used to. But the others seemed amused. In the end, though, they came round to my way of thinking. Rev it was who came up with the pun on plain old art. So Art, I became.

Prof, Rev, Zambo, and Art. Other members come and go, but we are the core.

Eric the postie is troubling me particularly. His hand is shaking every time he reaches for his beer. He can scarcely control it. Eric, get a grip, for Christ's sake. I can't stop staring at his other sleeve: half-empty, the redundant material of the lower part pinned up at the shoulder. Emphasising his elbow stump. He has a receding chin. He looks vulnerable, feeble. How the hell is he supposed to protect himself, let alone those he loves? I feel a rush of incredible anger: you just shouldn't do something like this to someone like Eric. I take a mental step back, do a quick bit of Prof-coaching. These are my feelings, I'm projecting them on to him. I'm not his rescuer; this is his journey. I can support Eric, help him. But his problems are his problems. And mine are mine alone.

Just as yours are yours, I break to remind myself. I can offer myself in help and support. But I must not intrude.

Zambo feels it, too, though, I can tell, the same impulses about Eric. Every now and then I catch his eyes straying to Eric's amputation. Like me, Zambo is living it: all the things Eric must struggle with – dressing and undressing himself, cutting up food, even going to the loo. Imagining the unkind comments, the sniggers he must run into from hurtful people. And now this new, brutal, psychological amputation. Zambo's fingers are tight round his glass. Leave it, I will him. Leave it, Zambo. It's a tough one. A bunch of empaths with a disabled person joining their group. There are bound to be what Prof terms transference issues.

Prof isn't exactly a professor, she's a psychologist, psychology lecturer, something like that. What she doesn't know about attachment trauma isn't worth knowing. I watch as she talks to the newbies, outlining the format of our meetings, the rolling programme of activities. Her neck is slender. Her peach coloured jumper is knitted from some sort of fluffy wool, a frizzy haze shimmering round her like an aura. The fact that she's been blighted by the same plague as the rest of us – with everything she knows, with all the theory at her fingertips – is both depressing and consoling. Depressing because for someone like her to have lost her kids shows just what we are up against. Consoling because I think, well, if superheroes can't prevail then what chance for mere mortals like the rest of us?

Prof has finished the introductory bits. She asks the newbies to give us a run-down of what's been happening to them. They look awkward, glancing at each other, seeing if someone else will dare to be first. In the end, it's Rog who volunteers, taking a big breath before he begins.

Rog is embroiled in battle. His lawyer managed to secure an order that his kids – a boy and a girl, eleven-year-old twins, non-identical obviously – should spend every other weekend with him. It was going along OK for a few months, but then suddenly there were tears and distraughtness in the car every time their mother came to drop them off. Most of the time his ex drives them right away again. He texts her, asks what the hell's going on? What can I do? she texts back. They don't want to see you, end of. She's not forcing the kids to go through something like that. He should try and start thinking about their feelings, too.

I recognise the pattern. I wonder if you do. How a little while after I moved to that rented place on Drake Avenue, you started to leave something important, some vital school book, back at Mummy's, so she'd pick you up straight away and you wouldn't end up staying. Leaving me and your sister alone together. Again and again. Or how you would just fail to show up in half terms and holidays when your uncle and aunt and cousins, or your grandma, came to stay.

Four times Rog has been back to court, he tells us, trying to have the order enforced. Rog is pugnacious, a man of action, that much is clear – how else can you be when you're sent in to tackle infernos every day of the week? I watch the spittle flecking his lips, the colour heightening his cheeks, as he fulminates against the injustice of it, the impotence he feels. The court won't do anything, beyond ordering more social work reports, which simply note the escalating disinclination of the children to have anything to do with him. #dodgydad. The months have ground on, become a year. He hardly ever sees his kids now, and when he does the meet-ups are fraught with upset and bad behaviour. I imagine the stress in his meetings with his solicitor, who is doubtless ruing the day Rog came a-knocking at his door. Rog is heading for a contact centre order next, I reckon, or maybe just phone calls. A staging post on the way to losing them for good.

Prof thanks him, then turns to Cheryl. She looks

momentarily mute, as though now the time has come to vo-calise her story, she has been struck completely dumb. That, too, I recognise. When she does speak, I have to sit forward to be able to hear. I wish some of the others in this pub would pipe down – boozy chatter, jokey tale-telling, the scroosh of the espresso machine from behind the bar. Cheryl has lost hers completely already: two boys, eight and ten, writing sur-prisingly articulate letters to the judge saying she's a horrible mother, how they've always been scared of her with her crazily veering moods, begging him to let them live exclusively with their dad and to stop Cheryl having anything more to do with them. #madmum. The social worker's report, confirming the distress that any contact from the mother causes. Well, faced with that, what is a poor judge to do? A prohibited steps order, Cheryl tells us, and I see her eyes welling up. No form of communication permitted with her kids at all. Not even texts allowed.

Fucking hell, I think, you poor woman. Is it worse for a mum? No, just a different pool of conclusions for everyone to jump into. Men are bastards, angry abusive drunkards. Women have depression, general patheticness, mental health gone wrong. As soon as an accusation is made, it's like a label's been applied. It's like a tattoo in blue capitals right across the forehead – it's all anyone sees.

Eric's situation is particularly vexing. He indicates his dismembered arm: because he's disabled, he can't be left in charge of a child – that's what his ex's lawyer persuaded the judge, anyhow. How can that possibly be, you think. Ah, she's clever, ex-Mrs Eric – or at least her solicitor is. He stressed to the judge the importance ex-Mrs Eric places on an ongoing father-son relationship, and in view of that she's offering to allow Eric to visit every other Sunday afternoon, for two hours at a stretch. Well, thank you, ma'am, how refreshing to see someone with their child's best interests so close to their heart. Eric stares into space as he describes it for us. How he sits in an armchair on one side of the room. How his ex and her mother flank his son on the sofa throughout. Eric brings a gift every time – a box of chocs, a comic or a magazine – handing it across with his one remaining arm, and tries to make conversation with his fourteen-year-old lad for as long as he can. No eye contact, grunting responses. Long periods of pained silence. The scowl-faced women on either side, arms crossed like bouncers. After two hours he gets up to go. No one else stands.

Can you imagine the humiliation? The messages it sends to the boy?

Eric's tremor has worsened as he talked. He tries to steady his hand by holding on to his glass. Immediately, his knee starts yammering like a pneumatic drill. His nostrils are flared, his eyes dilated. It's one thing to feel the effects. Quite another to be forced to sit and participate as the agony unfolds. Imagine: your child, the son you've loved and played with and laughed with and comforted; who's come to you for help or advice or a cuddle or just to chit-chat about every amazing thing they've learned that day. I think: I am so mad at these women I have never even met I could grab hold of their heads and smash their faces on the table, either side of my pint glass, if they were here right now. Lording their power and control over this one-armed man, destroying a boy's love for his dad as they go. That's how I feel. That's how it makes me feel. I know I wouldn't – I'm a good user of the road. But that's how this shit works, how it breeds and reproduces itself like a virus, a contagion. That's what this poison wants to induce me to do.

Prof is speaking again. Her voice has a seemly seriousness to it, an aural balm, promising a different sort of power. A waxing moon. She thanks the newbies for giving us an idea of their stories. We've all, she says, casting her eyes round the table, we've all been in – are in – similar situations. I nod. Rev smiles. Zambo is lost in his thoughts; I sense that he's wrestling with the same impulse to do something retributive to ex-Mrs Eric, too.

Over time, Prof promises, looking back to Cheryl, Rog, and Eric, you will build an understanding of what is going on, and what you can and can't do about it. She pauses for a moment, to give her words time to penetrate. What were they, did you think? Words of hope? Hardly. But at least not words of despair. The first words of not-despair these three casualties of war will have heard.

She says: let me show you something. She pulls her iPad from her case, moves her wine glass aside and props the tablet up so the newbies can see the screen. I've watched the clip countless times, we all have – Prof, Rev, Zambo and me. A woman called Caitlin, speaking at a rally in Washington DC. In 2007, for Christ's sake. How agonisingly long it takes for new understanding to catch on. Prof hits play on her YouTube app – this is her favourite testimony, she uses it every induction meeting. Caitlin's voice comes from the speaker, arriving across years and space to join us at the Half Moon. She's a brave lass; she's twenty-two, twenty-three, talking to hundreds, maybe thousands, of people. Standing behind a white podium, the mic on its stand in front of her. Her voice is wavering – nerves, emotion; there are tears wetting her cheeks.

I listen with the rest of them as she describes how, even before they separated, her father began building a picture of her mom as neglectful – always out at work, never any time for you kids. She doesn't really care about you. She doesn't really love you.

And seeding in their minds that he was sorely neglected, too. A poor-me man. And that he was the only one to truly love them, to be there for them. It went on for months, drip-dripping poison, gradually turning their minds, so that, when the divorce eventually came, they clung to him, drank up his protestations that they were his whole world, that he was so happy that they'd chosen to stay with him, how it meant more than anything, meant that his life had true meaning. And they didn't need their mom. She was never around, anyways. Always off galavanting with friends, coworkers – never a thought for the three of them back home. Caitlin's voice cracks as she confesses how she came to truly hate her mom. Cut her off completely. Ignored every card, text, email she ever sent.

There's a long pause while Caitlin recomposes herself. Behind her, the long banner tied to the railings, besloganed with the name of the organising body – Bringing Children and Families Back Together – ripples in the breeze. Further back, the White House stands impassively. An airplane inches across the sky overhead, its engines just audible. A horn from distant traffic.

Gathered again, Caitlin resumes her story: how, after years of rejecting her mom, she got to the stage of leaving her dad's home to go to college, and started to see the world through different eyes. Began to wonder. Eventually, after a year of indecision, she made contact again with the woman who'd given birth to her. Didn't dare say a word to her dad. So began an amazing but disturbing journey. She learned the other side

53

to the story: how her mom had been the only one willing to go out and win the bread, how her heart used to break at the sacrifices she had to make, how devastated she'd been as her precious children had slipped like quicksilver between her fingers when finally the marriage was done.

I look round the newbies – Cheryl, Rog, Eric – all of them staring transfixed at the screen. I wonder if they feel the same way I did, watching Caitlin for the first time. Imagining you, in your early twenties, maybe your thirties, perhaps your forties or beyond, coming to your own realisations. Seeing in Caitlin's distress your own remorse and grief. Aching for you.

Caitlin winds up to a wave of applause. Prof kills the iPad and sits back in her chair. It's just a taster, she says, of the battle that lies ahead, and what you're fighting for. She pauses. Around the table we are all thinking of our children. A memory: in the midst of your time of wavering, how one day, quite out of the blue, my phone went, and it was you. Excited by some great result in a physics test. That's fantastic, I told you, I'm really proud of you. That moment of authenticity, unguardedness, in which you'd been able to be once more the you I always knew – needing to share this triumph, and hear your daddy's congratulation. And another: we were going to the Peak District – you, your sister, and me – to join Uncle Gerry and his clan at a holiday home. How at the last minute Mummy arranged a trip of her own which squarely clashed, so I ended up going alone. I had to drop something round for you on my way. Your face, as you stood at the front gate while I put my seatbelt back on and started the engine – it kept crumpling, then you'd pull it back together, then it would crumple again; it was more than you could control. I waved cheerfully as I drove off, then pulled up half a mile away and sat howling like a wounded wolf.

Prof speaks again, interrupting everyone's thoughts. Caitlin, she says, Caitlin is just like your own children. Remember her – every time you get blocked, or ignored, or suffer a tirade of abuse. That's not your child or children – they're simply doing what your ex-partners are having them do. It doesn't matter what it looks like to anyone else; it doesn't matter how much hatred and scorn they appear to have for you. Inside each of them is another Caitlin. At some point, maybe in the far distant future, they're going to need to know you didn't walk away, just like Caitlin's mom refused to do.

The muscles in Rog's jaw visibly stand out when he clenches like that. Cheryl is close to tears. Eric's tremor is more pronounced than ever.

But enough for now, Prof says. She folds the iPad away, then shakes out her hair. First thing we need to do, she tells them, is give you new names.

That always catches newbies unawares; they're simply not expecting it. They glance at each other. It's all right, Prof says, it seems a little strange, but there are very good reasons for it. She doesn't elaborate; it's different for us all. For Prof, it's the assumption of a new identity, a psychological trope to endow courage and fortitude. For Rev it's more a biblical thing; apparently, God was forever re-naming those he chose — Abram became Abraham, Jacob became Israel, Simon became Peter the Rock. And so on. Zambo has a different take on it, more like going undercover, becoming a secret agent in a bush war. As for me, I think of it as giving a title to a piece of work, an encapsulation of all that the painting is for.

Prof looks round the table. So, she says, what does everyone think?

I can't get past Rog and Eric. I can't think of anything else: a fireman and a postman joining us simultaneously. They simply have to be Sam and Pat, no other names will do. But it would be beyond tactless. It would be verging on cruelty. We can't call them after children's TV characters.

Suddenly Rev is laughing. She raises a hand like a kid in class, bangles jingling down her forearm like a slinky. How about calling Roger Blaze? she says. Her Geordie accent somehow communicates the very essence of camaraderie. We're all pals together, and laughing at the madness and the pain is the best thing we can do. Blaze. Yep, that's brilliant. There are murmurings of approval from everyone. Rog himself looks very pleased. Blaze it is.

I wonder, Zambo says. All eyes look at him. I realise these are virtually the first words he's spoken tonight. I wonder, he says again, about Eric being known as Merc.

I'm wondering, too – wondering how on earth he got there. Wondering quite what a high-end limo has to do with anything. The others look bemused, too.

Mercury, Zambo says, as if disappointed that he has to explain. The winged messenger? Ancient Roman god of communication? He gives Eric a half-smile. That's what you do, Eric, isn't it? Deliver the mail?

That's the thing about Zambo. He looks like a thug. But underneath he's extremely well-read, and as cultivated as Radio 4.

Eric? Prof asks.

Well, OK, Eric says. If you think so.

Blaze and Merc sorted.

Cheryl's more tricky. A lull falls. People look at their drinks, at the table, anywhere but at Cheryl, whose expectant smile gradually fades the longer it goes on without anyone coming up with anything. It's awful. It's not that I actually have any ideas that I have to self-censor. It's just that her size dominates. She must be a twenty at least. Great rolls of flesh press against the cotton of her dress. I'm so afraid that I might suggest a name that has even the faintest fattist connotation that I can't think of anything at all. I glance swiftly round: Prof, Rev, Zambo - they're struggling with the same thing, too.

I wonder about, says Eric - Merc - at last. He looks a bit embarrassed, as though he shouldn't be coming up with anything at his first meeting.

We all nod encouragingly.

Well, I wonder about Angel, he says. He turns to Cheryl. You look like what I always imagined an angel to be.

It's perfect, in a Rubenesque way. There's generalised glass-raising, and grinning, and toasts to Angel. Who goes fetchingly pink and looks tremendously happy. Eric also appears chuffed, and for the first time I notice the tremor gone from his hand when he places his glass back on his beer mat. This is the power of kinship, camaraderie.

This group, I love.

There's so much shame swirling round when someone's stone-cold rejected by their child. You think: what must they be like as a person, as a parent, for the kid to have done that? It's obvious, isn't it - what other conclusion can you possibly draw? They must be a monster. A fucking monster. And right at the front of the queue of conclusion-drawers, the hapless mum or dad themselves. They're thinking, Christ, I must

57

have been really really awful – and I didn't even know it. That's what goes round and round your head, through the long wakeful hours. You try to fight against it, try to hang on to all the things you thought at the time were plain loving and good. But even as you cling desperately to the edge of the reality-cliff you thought you knew, the fact of your child's rejection, their sudden hatred for you, is like a macabre Moriarty, prising your fingers off the rock one by one by two. You are completely, utterly wrong, you must be. I felt it, the shame of it, the shame of being reprehensible, an outcast, the lowest of the low. What Prof, Rev, Zambo, gave me was, they gave me reality back. The reality that I am good enough as a parent – that being a good parent is precisely why I'm now in this hell. They saved my life. They helped stop the contagion in its tracks. They shored me up to become a transitional person. And that's what we hope to do for the newbies, for Blaze, Merc, and Angel too.

⁂

I hope you don't feel got at. This is not to make you feel guilty. That's one of my greatest fears, that the more you understand of what happened, the more you will be consumed by remorse. I can't bear the thought of you going through life limping and staggering under a burden like that. The sight of Caitlin's grief. None of this was your responsibility, even though it looked like something you yourself elected to do.

Listening to Angel, did you wonder about those well-honed letters from her boys, condemning her as an irretrievably unfit mother? Did it make you think of your own email to me? A perfunctory two lines, breaking off all contact, asking that I respect it. You finished with your name. No love. No

58

acknowledgement of all I have been to you, you to me. The thing about emails is they're timed precisely. This was sent just eight minutes after you'd have got back from school. Just days after the last lovely evening we spent together, excitedly discussing our long-dreamed-of trip to Italy – Florentine art, and the Siena Palio. You had just turned fourteen. You were good at English, as you are at pretty much everything. But: *so I ask that you respect it?* That's one hell of an adult turn of phrase.

You spent the whole of the next week off school ill. Amid the shock, the eviscerating pain, my mind stunned as though by a cudgel blow – amid all that, the thought of what you were going through. How you must be teetering, on the verge of falling apart. You didn't; you held it together. Got back to your books and your studies. But I knew.

Sometimes I tell myself: forget it, walk away, don't even think of trying to sort it out, you'll only load more crap on her shoulders. Let her go. But you're so bright. And there's the alt.narrative of your sister's life. You're likely, as you progress through adulthood – in your twenties, thirties, forties or beyond – to work it out. Like Caitlin, like Prof's countless other YouTube testifiers. It's a long life, in many ways. So many others have trodden this path before you. If you get there, if the pieces fall into place, how will you feel? Will you desperately need somehow to hear me saying: this wasn't your fault? You were not responsible? There was nothing else you could do?

It's later now, the fires are dying, the crowd has thinned, and the bar staff are cashing up the tills. Blaze, Merc, and Angel have left for their homes; only the core of us remain.

Rev, says Prof, you should mentor Angel. There's general assent: woman-to-woman makes perfect sense.

As for the others. Prof looks at Zambo, then at me, weighing things up. At length she says, Art, you take on Blaze. I nod in agreement, though in truth I'm a bit nonplussed. He's consumed by anger at the moment, is Blaze. It's natural, something I completely understand, but it will make him tricky to work with. When we're flooded with rage, it has to have somewhere to go. And if it can't go where it properly should, then often, like lightning, it seeks the nearest path to earth. I don't much relish the thought of acting as conducting rod, but I guess from time to time that's what I will have to do.

Zambo, Prof says, that leaves you for Merc. Zambo says a brief, Sure. I'm aware of a twinge of jealousy: Merc is the one I'm drawn to, the one who provokes my protective urge. But I accept Prof's decision – I guess what's true for me is also true for Zambo.

Would things have worked out the same, if Prof had made a different call? There are no re-runs in life; we'll never know. It haunted her later; she tormented herself with what-ifs. I gave her back some of her own advice. Prof, I said, it's not your responsibility. You did the best you could. What others choose to do is for them and them alone. She knew I was right, intellectually. But that didn't help all the shit feelings, which she carried back with her to Switzerland or Sweden or Holland, or wherever it was she ultimately returned to.

Were we complacent? Did we think, just because we'd found our ways to cope, that others would necessarily manage it? Maybe, but I don't think so. Sure, we'd had successes with other members, but Prof was always alive to the potential for the trauma to perpetuate itself, for the contagion to spread. That's what we were doing, trying to wax that moon. I said to her once, a casual remark, how alike we all were: her, me, Rev, and Zambo. We're a self-selecting population, she told me. We never get to see the ones who get sucked into the drama, they never track down our group. They're elsewhere even as we're meeting, cuffed in police cells, sectioned on psych wards, critical in hospital, or cold as tundra in the morgue.

Me

WHO AM I? Maybe you think you know. Maybe you have a settled opinion. If Prof's to be believed, most of your happy memories of me have been scrunched and squashed and boxed away like so many ill-fitting clothes in an attic trunk, never to be shown the light of day again. A few select garments remain: times when, like any good parent, I would tell you No when what you wanted - what you felt entitled to, in the raging egocentricity of childhood - was Yes. Times, sure, when I got things wrong - who doesn't make mistakes? Those choice few already unflattering outfits have been trimmed and re-hemmed by Mummy, their cut unrecognisably altered; the cloth has been embroidered with elaborate stitch-ups, embellished and transformed into something other. The end results have been draped on a voiceless tailor's dummy and pronounced: There! That is your father.

None of that is me.

I am Stevie Buchanan. Steven James Buchanan, to give me my full name. Steve to my Ma and Pa, unless I was in trouble over something. Born in the late Sixties in the old Heathfield Maternity Home out Broomborough way. Born on that strip of land surrounded on three sides by water: Mersey, Dee, and Irish Sea. Wirral. The Wirral, as, to everyone thereabouts, it is most often known.

We were well-enough-to-do, at least to begin with. Pa was a naval architect at Cammell Laird. I don't know the history, how it came about, but he married Ma late, was into his forties when my brother and I came along. The earliest memory I have is of doing a drawing with him – no idea how old I would have been. I loved the cool precision of his propelling pencils. We were doing a picture of the companion set that stood on the hearth beside the grate. It was all coal fires back then. I remember it so clearly: the elegant parallels of the dangling handles, then the way each implement branched out into its particular termination: poker, brush, tongs and shovel. Drawing was something to do to entertain me; something he was good at, something he could pass on.

I don't have too many other memories of him, in fact. We don't, really, do we? – remember much of our time as kids, growing up. I can picture us, him and me, going to the beach at West Kirby, and walking out to Hilbre Island at low tide. Clambering together over Thor's Stone, the red sandstone rough on my hands and bare knees. Goggle-eyed trips to Toy and Hobby in Birkenhead. But that's about all.

Don't die young, not if you can help it. I was ten, Gerry twelve, when Pa succumbed. Some kind of lymphoma, I now know. I guess he was ill for years – that strange pressure-cooked sense I have when I think back to my early life. Days at a time he would disappear. We weren't told he was in hospital. They kept it hidden from us. I don't know if he even knew he was dying. He never said goodbye. He just vanished from the home as he so often did, only this time he never returned.

Ma: Gerard, Steven, come here. I have some bad news to tell you.

Ma, crumpling, sobbing, as she tried to get the words out.

Me, instinctively putting my arms around her. Wanting,

with every ounce of my being, to make it better. Being utterly unable to.

Kids didn't go to funerals, not back then.

Ma, disappearing for a whole number of days, just like Pa had used to do. Aunty Maggie coming to look after us. How we were expected still to go to school, like nothing had happened. Fretful, unable to sleep, thumping on the floor to make it sound like I'd fallen out of bed, anything to get Aunty Maggie to come up and see me, so I knew someone was still there, so I knew I wasn't alone in the dark, so I knew there was someone who wouldn't just disappear.

Jumbled recollections after. Gerry going off the rails, pinching money from Ma's purse, thieving from the newsagents at the top of the road with some of the lads from school. A local bobby came round; I can still picture his helmet sitting there on top of the upright piano. Then he went away, Gerry, was sent off to boarding school. I guess she thought it would help him. I guess she didn't know what else to do.

Two down, two to go.

Ma, short of cash, needing money for the fees, some of Pa's old friends helping her out with a secretarial job at the Mersey Docks and Harbour Board. Across the river to Liverpool every day. Me going to the Rimmers' after school, having my tea there. The times I wouldn't take my coat off, keeping it on for hours, waiting for her to come fetch me when she got back home.

The things I did to their lad, Barry.

Ma, weeping by the fire of an evening, when she thought I'd gone to sleep. Me creeping down the stairs, scared that the treads would give me away, but for why I've no idea. Going in to give her a hug. Wrapping my ten-year-old arms across her heaving shoulders, trying to hold her together, trying to stop her falling apart.

Nothing I could do to make it better.

Ma, beset by migraine, moaning and retching, me in my flannel pyjamas hotching about on the upstairs landing listening to it all going on down there, scared witless that she, too, was going to die. Praying to God to please please take me instead of her.

Barry. Little runt of a lad, a few years younger than me. I'd hit him when no one else was around. Give him Chinese burns. Make him cry. Then I'd deny I'd done a thing when Mrs Rimmer came, furious, to see me. Going blue in my face with lies.

I was sent away to boarding school, too.

The sternness of the teachers, the leering snideness of the prefects, the bewildering lessons, not being able to take the first thing in. I remember being terrified of everything. So shy I would hardly speak. Looking back, I was on the verge of selective mutism. The trauma of it all. Gerry was there, a couple of years ahead of me, in the thick of a gang. I was an embarrassment. He didn't want to know.

I took refuge in the art room. Making pictures. Mr Mills, the only kindly teacher I knew. I remember one painting, of a market stall, loving the three-dimensional effect of the wet poster paints as I daubed glistening blobs of different colours to represent apples, oranges, potatoes. And that disappointment – crushing, out of all proportion – when I returned the following day to find the picture dried out, and all the fruit and veg flat and cracked.

I did shit at O-levels, no more than Cs in most of them, only Art was an A. They didn't want to let me through to sixth form but Ma pleaded with them. She had sobered by then into a strange kind of existence. Whole terms on her own, working at the Board, socialising with a motley collection of other shipwreck survivors come the weekends. She never met another man, though; there was no internet then. Half-terms and holidays, back we'd come – Gerard, her arrogant eldest, and me the dullard younger son. She did her best to love us, but by then we'd become semi-strangers – painful remnants of a life she'd once known.

I took Art at A-level, got another A. Scraped an E in English, and sank in History with a U. There was only ever one thing I was going to go on to do. None of the prestigious colleges would even look at me. But Hatfield Poly was less picky. I enrolled for a Fine Art BA.

Something about it, taking my own step, the first time in my life I hadn't been storm-tossed by events that I couldn't control. Leaving the Wirral, going somewhere no one knew me. That day moving in with my trunk packed with my possessions, meeting other freshers on the corridor, finding an instant rapport with a guy called Mark a few doors down from me. Also studying Fine Art. Him asking what my name was. Me telling him: Stevie.

Stevie. From that day on I became Stevie Buchanan. I found my voice. The lad who sounded like he was a Scouser, only he wasn't, he was from somewhere called the Wirral. A year doing life drawing, finding I was bloody good at it, me and Mark the best in our year. My confidence grew. I thrived on the criticism of my work, the kinds of commentary from tutors that laid other students low – I found no discouragement in it, only the drive to improve. At art school I reinvented myself. At art school I changed

66

unrecognisably. I started to become what I soon thought of as me.

Only I did and I didn't. I see that now. We do and we don't. We think we've left our pasts behind, but they are with us, permeating our souls, hidden, unseen. Puppet master hands, twitching our limbs, directing our choices. Only when we become conscious of them, only once the veil is pulled up and the workings revealed, can we begin to exorcise them. How is that self-consciousness to be achieved? Unless we know to go looking – and unless we are sufficiently brave – it will be life that has to try to teach us those lessons.

That's how it was for me.

Twenty-one. Two and a bit years already at university.

How is it, I wonder, for you?

TWO

Baby Changing

THE CONNECTION AT Didcot isn't due for a while. I stand on the platform, bags at my feet, getting my bearings. Under the rafters, next to the departures screen, there are signs for the Ladies and the Gents, and one for Parent With Baby-Changing Facilities. Beyond those, a café. I never got that coffee in Bath; I have a sudden craving. Between me and caffeine, though, there's a man in a bright red jacket, with a huge belly and a Brian Blessed beard, and some kind of uncontrollable waving going on. He's pacing about, muttering, and flapping both hands over and over like a fledgling trying to achieve flight. Tourette's, I wonder, or plain simple oddness. I exchange a secret smile with a young woman. Her long brown hair is tied back in a pony tail; she's wearing a woven cotton top, thigh-length, vertical stripes of varied blues, that makes me think of Peruvian panpipe buskers. She has a gentle feel. I think my presence reassures her. I guess I look capable – leather jacket and crew-cut – a comfort when there may be madness close by.

Much as she tugs my protective instincts, she's on her own. There's coffee to fetch, and other things I need to do. I send Peru girl an apologetic look, give red jacket man a wide berth, and take myself out of the autumn chill.

Steam rises from my polystyrene cup. The weak sunshine is warm behind the glass. I sit at my table, open the *Guardian* I've purchased, and adopt the pose of someone intent on the latest news.

Then I'm out. Slipped through the gap between door and frame, tickled by the brush of the draught excluder. A half dozen revolutions round red-jacket man, spiralling up like a will o' the wisp. As if to say: this is how to do it, this is how to fly. Then I'm up, near vertically, a missile launched from a silo.

Are you with me? I search the bleached horizons for any hint of you. Nothing. It disappoints, but it doesn't surprise, not after Chatsworth Road and what you saw. When pain rears up, pawing its metal-shod hooves like a startled stallion, the instinct is to turn and flee. How will you have coped? Will you have tried to rationalise it? OK, it was disturbing to sense Mummy's wintry rejection, but it was just one incident, wasn't it? Maybe she was tired. Stressed. Depressed even. It doesn't amount to much. It doesn't really matter, not in the great scheme of things. And it doesn't at all accord with the devoted Mummy you know. Perhaps a deeper suspicion: who do I think I am, pitching up after seven years of absence, muddying the waters with things you can't even remember, with things it may be better never to know. What is my intention? To poison you against Mummy? Please believe me, that is not what I'm about at all. These are pieces of a jigsaw that you will need if, at some stage in your life, you ever yearn to understand – like Caitlin, like the rest of Prof's YouTube testifiers – what it was that happened to you. That is all.

Have you soothed yourself with justifications, excuses, explanations? Maybe. But in the faint turbulence of the air through which I course, I think I can feel you wrestling with an unanswered question: What could I possibly have done, a two-and-a-half-year-old girl, to have caused her to be like that towards me? Can I sense your indecision? Are you somewhere out there, torn between the supposed bliss of ignorance and the coming to rejoin me to see what else I might show?

I rocket above the now-demolished power station, gaining effortless altitude from the thermals rising from the mass of concrete still scarring the site. Streaking through heat-shimmering air. I feel a desperate sadness, and a familiar fear for your future. How can you make sense of things – if ever you should want to – if you won't stick with me? I know it feels easier, safer, more comfortable, to remain where you are. But that would be to stay trapped in a prison of your mind's own making, never to taste fresh alpine air.

I do a couple of loop-the-loops, huge great arcs, pulling more than a little g, as if to tempt you with the thrill of flight, the liberation it can bring. I soar like an angel on a mission from God, overflying human pain and misery – an annunciation of a message of hope.

And, amazingly, it works. Somehow, against all the odds, you're suddenly there – far far away, snailing a faint white trail across the blue. Even though you're at this great distance, you are heading this way. You are definitely heading towards me. Come on, there's no time to waste. Even now my coffee's cooling, and there's only so long a middle-aged man can stay transfixed by one page of his paper, drink untouched, before someone becomes concerned that there might be something askew.

Counties flash past, Warwickshire, Leicestershire, Nottinghamshire; I'm an accelerated particle, propelled by the fields of unimaginably super magnets, blistering ever closer to the speed of light, that universal constant. We're heading for North Yorks once again, a different farm this time but not unlike that Derbyshire one of long ago. Every now and then I check on you, shadowing me like an escorting fighter. It's enough, more than enough. I'm full of inexpressible love for you.

There we are, quick now, down we dive. Cars parked out front, sheep hurdles sectioning the yard, a collie curled asleep near the front door. In through a flue, bursting out of the boiler, then floating, serene after the headlong rush, along the landing, down the stairwell, and into the capacious kitchen, the heart of this farmhouse that was Mummy's childhood home.

It's dark in here, the curtains drawn, a strange flickering light the only illumination. For a moment you're disorientated; you have no idea what you've come in to. There's a background hum, and a faint tickertape chunter. You're adjusting to the murkiness, you can make out four adults sat side by side on a large sagging sofa. Like an audience at a private view.

Who are they? It's difficult to tell, isn't it – that dazzling light behind them rendering everything else in shadow. But that there is Mummy, second in from the left, Ted and Gloria to one side of her. Me on the other. The rims of my tortoise-shell glasses glint in the gloom; reflections bounce off the lenses. She's grown-up, is Mummy, somewhere in the middle of her twenties; we're young and in love and on one of those dutiful parental visits that the newly romanced do. It'll be a couple of years yet before Ted and Gloria are finally cut right out.

Maybe you've never seen one before. You, whose generation lives by touch screens and browsers and Netflix downloads. That machine there, spewing its beam of light, is a projector, its seven-inch reels whirring, sprockets funnelling the Super 8 cine film past the light source in an incessant fluid flow.

There's no sound; this is a silent movie. There's no screen; we're watching the whitewashed wall, us four adults of yesteryear, on which dance insipidly coloured images of a time long before. We pause, disembodied you and me, take a moment to join the others in enjoying the show. We see a little lass running, laughing and running, straight into the arms of her daddy, welcoming him home. His delighted grin reveals splayed front teeth. Ears like bat wings. That's Ted, a younger Ted, scooping his daughter up and twirling her round. And, yes: bountiful blonde curls. That is Mummy as a five-year-old girl.

Don't concern yourself with the home movie, with why we're watching it, all four of us together, and with what effects it will bring. We'll come to that another time. That's not why we're here. Now, I want you to see something else, something that will help you come to terms with what you saw on Chatsworth Road.

There. I'm standing. I don't remember, maybe I needed the loo or something. I start to leave the kitchen, the others remaining seated in their row. Watch. Just as I step into the projector beam. Just then, Mummy says something, asks me a question. I stop. I turn to look at her. Squint into the light. Maybe she wanted me to fetch her a jumper or something, when I came back down.

It doesn't matter. This is the point of it. Look. See how the images land on me. Suddenly, I'm a projection screen. Flitting shapes and features dance across my shirt, my jeans. The edges of the movie spill past me, landing on the wall behind. My own face and body become indistinct, subsumed in the cinematography. The movements of those filmed memories are all you now perceive.

And see there. See how for that brief few seconds, young-father Ted – gazing directly at the cine camera that was capturing those moments twenty years before – maps exactly on to me. My eyes become his eyes. My mouth his mouth. My hair his hair alone. It's extraordinary, like a full-size holo-gram; it's like that cine-film daddy has been summoned back to three-dimensional life. It's like he's standing there in this very room.

That's it, we're out of here. Leave me to my errand, leave the four of us to continue with our private show. We'll come back to it, perhaps. It's so fascinating to see your mum as a child, isn't it, to see things you never before have known.

We're roaring back towards Didcot like two bats fleeing hell. You're closer to my trajectory on this return trip, puz-zlement and curiosity getting the better of you. I can sense you seeking explanations, trying to understand what I'm on about. What it is I intended by bringing you here.

Two-and-a-half-year-old you. Sat on the floor of that Chatsworth Road living room, your arms raised in carry-me supplication.

If we'd but had time.

If we'd had but time, I would have lingered us in that North Yorks farmhouse, taken you further back into the past. Shown you Ted and Gloria, their shotgun wedding over, setting up their unlooked-for family home. Gloria's pregnancy now far gone. Ted down at the market, stocking up the sheep and milking herds, spending money Angie and Archie have loaned. It used to strike me as curious, why Ted chose to go into farming – why he followed in his dead dad's footsteps – once his Navy discharge came through. I now know from Prof that it was inevitable. Our unconscious sucks us like a rip-tide; we create our worlds to replay past traumas, craving them this time to be happy ever after. But it never works out. Healing never travels by that route. We make the tragedies replay themselves, over and again, variations on the same discordant theme.

If we'd had but time, I would have shown you your infant-aunty's arrival, and how Gloria, hating the ignominy of this farmer's wife's life that was now hers, immersed herself in her baby living doll. Projector beam flickering. Your infant-aunty's face a screen on which Gloria cast the cine film of her own squandered childhood, in which she was the god-girl who could do no wrong.

She didn't want another. Hadn't she always been blissfully happy on her own? And as for that act, the thing by which another child would have to be made. Subliminal flashbacks: the bark of that white poplar against her shoulders, the snap of elastic as her French knickers came down. The force with which she'd hurled the future that had been carved out for her away into the far dark reaches of the night.

But Ted was persistent. You have to remember, this was back in the sixties. Back then, careers were for life, and farming was a great bet. By the time he was getting on, slowing down, finding it tougher, Ted should own the place. Outright. He'd have repaid Angie and Archie's grudging loan. A strapping lad would be at an age where he could be properly useful. And when retirement came, Ted would hand it on, the farm, son succeeding father as the sun succeeds the moon.

She wasn't a boy, Mummy, obviously. She lay neglected in her crib, day after day, her pitiful wailing unattended for hours, while Gloria spent all her time with her first-born, her very own living doll. Eventually, learning helplessness,

Mummy's voice fell silent; she became the baby who no longer cried. As she grew to become a toddler, a little girl, she could move about under her own steam. She would seek out her mother and sister, interrupt their *jeux à deux*. Gloria would hiss and curse her, exclude her from what was going on, that projector beam playing over her, spooling reels of resentment for all that had ruined the perfect childhood that Gloria had once known.

And what of your child-aunty, Gloria's golden girl? We're like sponges as children, absorbing everything that exudes from the adults in our worlds. We don't know any better. Any time your aunty was mean to her younger sister, she found tacit permission, even approval from Gloria. How good it felt to be the second pea in that pod, closeted in her mother's affection, the pair of them united in their love for each other, and their spite for the scrap who had dared to try to come between.

If we'd had but time to see the bleakness of your child-Mummy's days. What we did witness was just a glimpse of the transformation brought about when her daddy came home. Long days topped and tailed by milking, manhandling sheep between times, loading lambs on to market-bound trailers, spreading fertiliser, making silage from hay. He was tuckered out by the end of it. He didn't get much back from his first-born – she was so wrapped up in her mother. But the joy on his second-born's face when she caught sight of him coming through the farmhouse gate. She may not have been the boy he wanted – and nor was this arid marriage the thing he'd ever thought he'd find himself locked in – but this, this little girl so beside herself at his return, well, that was what gave him strength to carry on. In some ways she could give him more than he could ever have got from a son.

What show reels were playing in his own projector? He wasn't blind; he saw the rejection she lived under, child-Mummy, the pinched cheeks and lustreless eyes of the unwanted second child. Her face became his face, the boy abandoned by his mother after his dad blasted the back of his head off, sent to live with a succession of grudging relatives, none of whom wanted to know. Somehow in some way it felt like it must have been all his fault. He was defective, unworthy of love, a scabrous also-ran in the race his brother, Nigel, won. In gathering your child-mother, twirling her round in delight, giving her that island of specialness at the end of his every farming day, Ted was lifting his child-self aloft, and loving himself in the way he had always craved.

⁂

Didcot station appears in the far distance. We swoop towards it. There's a train approaching, heading up the line from the south. My connection to Oxford is about to arrive. I squeeze yet more speed, gravity assisting even though I have no mass. I am further fuelled when I notice you matching my upped tempo. Something is changing; tentative connections are forming between us. Am I imagining it, deluding myself? No, I can feel them, fragile bridges of gossamer. What I would give to hug you, hold you. For a moment I allow myself to picture it, to experience just an inkling of how it would feel to have the wounds in our souls self-heal. But I push the picture aside, cover that longed-for canvas with a drab beige drape. It is way too soon.

Twenty-one years ago you were born. There followed two years of indoctrination in your own god-girlhood. We were equally responsible, Mummy and I; you were drenched in love by us both. Story-books, endless games, your door-frame bouncer; cute little rattles that whistled when you put them in your mouth and blew. Towards each day's end you would grow fretful, tired, became almost impossible to entertain. You'd be slung in the sling, Tiggering along the road, galloping chases in the garden, anything to keep you happy and amused. Bouncing on laps – this is the way the ladies ride, trit-trot, trit-trot. Me, throwing and catching you. I would make up songs, different ones for each of your soft toys. Mummy would feed you, lull you, divert you. For two whole years you were never once plonked in front of the telly for a bit of respite. You were never once granted a moment without a parent in adoration of you.

We were always planning a second. And not too big a gap, if possible. Two years after your birth, your sister joined us, too.

You helped to change her nappy once, when she was just a few days old. She screamed, incessantly. You never tried again. Every moment of every day she was there, sucking attention, compromising the love you'd always known. Only during her sleep times was any semblance of your normality returned. Your speech was amazing for your age; everyone said so. You told us to send the baby back; you didn't like her, you didn't want her. You wanted it just to be you.

Dethronement. Every first child's experience, when a sibling is born. For you, exquisitely painful, given how far aloft on the pedestal we'd hoisted you.

I worked hard to compensate; when I wasn't out earning us

80

money, I took you for special trips, doing lots of one-to-one things. I encouraged you to vocalise your feelings about this squalling new arrival who had upended your world.

You roared back at her when she was crying in her high chair. Roared and roared, a continuous bellow, as if trying to drown her with sound. It didn't work. She didn't go.

Then once, when she was six months and the pair of you were sat facing each other in the bath, you pushed her, hard. Mummy, kneeling beside, lunged to save her from going under.

Two-and-a-half-year-old you. Sat on the floor of that Chatsworth Road living room, your arms raised in carry-me supplication. Mummy, approaching, stopping, looking down at you. Only it was not your face she saw – its chubby cheeks, flyaway blonde hair, little upturned nose. Whirring hum, tickertape chuntering, beam of light flickering. Your face was a projection screen for that of your child-aunty, Gloria's golden sidekick, joint perpetrator of endless misery, co-conspirator in your unwanted-second-child-mother's doom. Mummy's expression as you sat, arms raised, beseeching? That sense of wintry rejection – that should never have been applicable to you.

That was your start point, the beginning of years spent struggling, clawing, trying to regain your golden god-girlhood. Sometimes loving your sister, at other times being filled with searing antipathy. Nothing you did seemed good enough to restore what you had lost. And again and again you encountered the same incomprehensible block in the road back to Mummy that wouldn't allow you through. I still have the little journal you wrote; I found it among your stuff a year after I lost you, when I was packing up your room. Written age ten. Trying, so very hard, to work out in your child's mind how it was that your sister seemed to get everything right, and you to get everything wrong.

⚘

Red coat man's still pacing the platform, hands aflapping. Peru girl's taken herself elsewhere. The incoming train decelerates with a grinding of brakes. I'm still sat in that café, *Guardian*-gazing, coffee at best lukewarm.

I'm frantic with worry, I have to make this connection, but you're here alongside still, just one step removed. It's as though you know we're not done yet, that we've not reached a break-point, as though you can sense there's a page left to turn.

Back in that Chatsworth Road living room, I watch from the sofa, Mummy's departing back, your arms sinking slowly to your lap. Two-and-a-half-years old. It's as though you're sitting in a puddle of your own dissolving loveliness.

My heart goes out to you. I put my paper aside, go across to join you, hold my hands out to lift you up. Come on, sweetheart, I say, let's go for a walk.

Do you remember the Daddos? Two identical dollies, plain plastic features, dressed in white baby-gros, eyelids that closed when they laid flat, and bobbed open when upright again. Old Daddo, the original. New Daddo, the replacement bought when Old Daddo looked to have been lost in some swing park.

We take them and stroll hand in hand down Chatsworth Road. You come to somewhere about my mid-thigh. I always shorten my stride, go at your pace, your brave little legs ambling forwards. Reaching the junction where Whitehouse Road crosses, we sit at our favourite spot. Your dungareed bottom on the brickwork, and my jeans-clad one alongside.

And we wait for cars to come. A grey one. A yellow one. A silver one. A black one. Every time, the Daddos get excited, start hotching about on my lap, only to flop back down, disappointed, when the next car comes round the corner and its colour becomes known. But then. Burgundy! A burgundy car! The Daddos go crazy, dancing about on my knees, me squawking Burgundy! Burgundy! in my cod-ventriloquist's voice. You love it, every time, sometimes you can't breathe for laughing. The Daddos live for burgundy cars.

The things as parents we do.

That favourite haunt, our place for Daddo car-spotting, the low brickwork bounding the garden of number 164. We would sit there for ages, you, me, and the Daddos. Our watching-the-world-go-by wall.

I can't delay another moment. I snick through the door behind an entering customer, slam back into myself. Suddenly I'm gathering my paper, abandoning my coffee, grabbing my luggage, and leaving the warm café room.

Out on the platform I realise you've left me, but that feels right, it feels good. I board my connection and find the next seat in which I will draw still closer to you.

Station Approach

A LITTLE WAY outside Appleford, we cross the Thames. It's just a stripling compared with what it will be by the time it reaches London, when it will have drained whole swathes of southern England on its way to the estuaries and the sea. The waters here appear pastoral, pre-industrial; supportive of life. I think: what contamination they will gather on their journey, what effluent and waste and agricultural pollution will sully them, what depletion of the oxygen that allows things to breathe. Oh, there are efforts aplenty further downstream: decontamination, biodegradation, tighter regulation. The fanfare that greeted the re-establishment of living fish. But at what cost? What cost to clean up the mess that should never have been allowed to be.

The driver sounds his horn, a drawn-out two-tone blast. We shoot straight through Culham; there's no one on the platform to have heeded the warning. Culham. Where Peter Lyle lived. Me, a BA in Fine Art to my name, no desire to spend my days flogging other people's stuff in a gallery, wondering how to make enough to live on while I established myself in my own right. Yeah, sure. All the dreams I had. The shining shimmering copper that would eventually tarnish and dull, and become tainted by verdigris.

Peter, my supervisor. The hours in his studio learning to apply my art to my new vocation.

We halt at the next station, Radley, scene of summer

fireworks concerts, where we'd go with blankets and picnic and booze-soaked trifle. Mummy and me. In later years, before moving south-west, we'd take you, then you and your sister, along. Do you have any memory? You loved the whole eating outdoors thing, the chance to gorge on crisps and mini-sausages and squares of fudge brownie. You didn't care for the music, neither of you did – boringly classical. And you hated the pounding percussions of the exploding fireworks. The suddenness scared three- or four-year-old you. I would cover your ears with my palms. Reduce the noise to a tolerable level. Allow you to enjoy the spectacular blooms of colour in the darkening August sky in relative peace.

There's a sign on the Radley platform, advertising the village shop, all manner of goods and services to be had there, staffed, apparently, by friendly volunteers. A community enterprise. Not for profit. Fairly traded wherever practicable. All the things we know we want, and fail to support when tempted by the cheapness and convenience of mass market home delivery.

The nearer I get to Oxford, the more places are laced with memory. It wouldn't have taken a genius. It rattles me; I begin to doubt the wisdom of this enterprise. I think of you, somewhere in that city, knowing I am on my way. What are you thinking? What do you think, every time you get a message like that from me? Does it generate anxiety that, no matter how careful you are, I might contrive to bump into you? Do you change your plans, cancel going out, bunk off lectures, stay in your room in college or in a rented house – wherever it is you live nowadays – minimising the chance of an accidental encounter? Do you fear I may have discovered your address, wheedled it off the internet somehow, or tapped your sister for news?

If Prof's to be believed, and her myriad YouTube testifiers, that's only half your story. Internal conflict. Cognitive dissonance. Deep within you, in your sills and dykes and magma chambers, molten lava shifts and seethes. The pressure of inexpressible love. The craving for acceptance from one half of who you are. A memory: post-separation, back when you were faltering, during your time of wavering, before I fully lost you. You outside in the garden at Mummy's, me turning up unexpectedly, dropping something off for your sister. How you came for a hug. We hadn't seen each other in two weeks. We held each other for a moment, and it must have felt so good. Something in you gave: you called a delighted 'Da-ddy!', did a little jump up, and latched your legs around my waist, like a koala. Twelve, thirteen. On the cusp. Just like when you were younger, and you would leap up like that, hang on tight with your thighs, and let yourself fall backwards, dangling so your long blonde hair spooled on the ground. Looking at the world upside down. I always had hold of you. You never came to grief.

That's what I have clung to these seven years, every bit as tightly. That somewhere beneath the unbroken silence, the unacknowledgement, the cold rejection, there remains that other girl, the one allowed to show her love, the one with the need to be loved by her daddy.

An earthquake comes, buildings collapse, burying inhabitants under mountains of rubble, immovable concrete, lung-choking plaster dust. For days and weeks the rescue workers keep at it, digging and excavating, their hands and clothes filthy, their fingers scuffed and grazed, pausing and hushing every now and then to listen for the faintest sound, never losing hope for that moment when they might pull a survivor from some miraculous air pocket. We rejoice in any life saved – what great good news stories – but none more so than when the resurrection is of a child.

Have pennies finally started to drop? Is your apprehension giving way, little by little, to curiosity? Has the alt.narrative of your sister's life at last begun to speak? I don't know if I dare, but I allow myself the thought that even now you may be contemplating to rendezvous with me.

⚜

I skim through my *Guardian*, the train rattling on towards Oxford and you. I hardly ever read a paper nowadays; the news is invariably grim. In among the politics and foreign affairs, items leap out at me. An academic has killed herself by jumping off a balcony, in despair after her ex abducted their daughter abroad. #deadmum. A fourteen-year-old cancer victim has been cryogenically frozen – in its excitement with the ghoulish idea of her far-future resumed life, the paper hardly bothers to comment on the more disturbing fact that her dad hadn't been able to see her for years. The mum barred him from visiting even as she was dying. He was refused permission to view her body after death. #deadkid. This stuff is everywhere. You don't see it till you're aware of it. Once you're in the clan, it comes at you from all sides.

I hardly drank any coffee, but all the same. I leave my bags on my seat and sway along the aisle. At the end of the carriage, the door whooshes open like it's startled to see me. I find red jacket man there, down on his hands and knees outside the WC, sweeping random debris from the lino floor with a piece of tissue.

I step round him and shut myself inside. Relieve myself. I feel indescribably weary. I lower the loo seat, and rest myself down.

I sit back, and close my eyes.

The rush of air outside the slid-open window.

I'm gone, like untethered possessions sucked through a sudden breach in an aircraft cabin.

Out in the blue again, but something is wrong. I feel different. My progress is sluggish, I don't seem able to pick up speed. I lumber aloft like a laden Hercules.

I know where I have to go, and the thought of it daunts me. Drains me. I half hope for there to be no sign of you. That is paradoxical, I know it is, but you are not the only one to be riven by that with which we have to contend. I'm barely at tree-top level, no faster than a microlite, my train pulling away from me somewhere beneath.

Suddenly I'm set spinning, a vortex catching me and twirling me like a drill bit along its axis. You. Vigorous, energyful, buzzing around like a late summer wasp furious at the dying of the heat. My mood has been reticent, adrift of my moorings, and for a few moments I feel utterly incapable of responding to your presence, the power of your emotions. But then I think of Prof's YouTubers, how anger, pure molten anger, can be the first sign that an eruption is about to take place.

Somehow, I shake off my torpor and set off after you, already miles ahead. And that old sense of duty soon fuels me, and builds my momentum. This I have started and, for your sake, this I must complete. Ahead, you are flickering, like silk in a wind tunnel, and I fix my gaze on you and will myself more speed. Soon I am powering, approaching your slipstream, and soon I have caught you, keeping pace at your wing.

You are single-minded. Determined. You always have been. You always were capable of the most persuasive writing. Over the years: Publisher trifolds, rolled off the inkjet, arguing the case for a wolf-dog as a pet, or for keeping a captive leopard. Never mind the utter impracticality. The outlandishness of the idea. You were drawn to those fierce creatures. You would brook no argument as to their impossibility.

I learned that the thing to do was to go along with it. Set you to researching the implications, the regulations, the experiences of those who had done such things, till in the end you could see for yourself how, for a little girl, it simply couldn't be.

We're here again. Our journey seems to have passed in a few blinks. The North Yorks farmhouse that was Mummy's childhood home, though some years earlier than when we were here before. I hang, motionless, looking down on it, the rain-darkened tiles of its roof. Postponing the moment, now that the moment is here. Fields all around are dotted with livestock. The farm is small in its landscape, dwarfed by the moors rising from the folds in the earth near Cropton and Spaunton to the north.

I tuck into myself and drop like a stone. You follow suit. We tumble like sagebrush across the deserted yard – Gloria has the car in nearby Pickering, where her older daughter, your child-aunty, needs fitting out with new uniform for school in a month's time. The bitter symmetry.

In through an open window, the pair of us dusting ourselves down inside the parlour. The polished surfaces, pristine antimacassars, crystal decanters, silver-framed photos. This is a dress room, a space kept immaculate. Woe betide the child who makes the slightest mess in here.

From somewhere else in the house, a piano. The haunting notes pierce me, cause my heart to grow faint. A point-of-no-return. I have an overwhelming urge to leave. So many conflicting considerations: this is something no parent would want to expose their child to, and it is not even mine to show. But against all that, all those ethical conundrums, it is surely something you will have to know.

Decided, resolved, I float noiselessly towards the parlour door, you like my shadow. We follow the music, slipping silently through the downstairs hall to another reception towards the rear. And pause in the doorway. There, her back towards us, is your ten-year-old child-mother, seated on an upholstered stool at the Challen baby grand. Her hands move back and forth, fingers depressing patterns of keys. It's beautiful, a Beethoven piece: *Moonlight Sonata*, first movement, familiar to every grade 5 pianist there has ever been. You are enchanted. You never knew Mummy could play. And play so wonderfully as well.

You listen for a while, the dreamy arpeggios in the right hand – dah-dah-dah dah-dah-dah – the counterpoint descent of the bass in the left. Your child-mother's back, clothed in paisley print blouse, swaying sinuously – she's really immersed in it; she's mastering the piece. You feel such tenderness for her; at the same time, puzzlement – faint hurt, even – that there was never any music from her as you were growing up. Not even when you, too, were learning to play. That was always down to me, sitting with you, your sister, at that Yamaha keyboard, dredging up my rusty musical memories.

A profound chill passes right through you. Rapt in the

music, we didn't hear him approach. Ted came from behind and walked straight through us, filling the threshold as we are. He stands in front of us. There's a streak of engine oil at the nape of his neck, where he's been fending off midges. He's had a recent haircut. Blue overalls. We can see his breathing.

He, too, is listening to his younger daughter play. The daughter who loves him so demonstrably at the end of each farming day. He stays there an age. Is she aware of him, your child-mother? Or has she, like us, failed to hear?

Misgiving rises like a well stream. I want us to turn round, back out the parlour window, up and away into air that is clean. But despite my qualms, I glide, noiseless as a panning camera, over towards the antique dresser, and perch on the cast iron columns of the radiator beside. The metal is cold; this is summer. You have come over with me. We look on, an oblique view, as Ted approaches his daughter, that fluid music from the baby grand an unbearable soundtrack to the scene.

Dah-dah-dah dah-dah-dah.

He halts behind her. Places farm-calloused hands on her shoulders.

There's a pause in the sonata. Just a few missed beats. Your child-mother looks up at him and smiles from beneath her blonde curls. Her daddy's come to watch her. He grins back, his gapped teeth. Moonlight resumes, repeating its notes, the mournful minors resolving sometimes into hopeful majors, the purity of the high tone melody riding on the darkening swell beneath.

No. Enough. My faint heart falters, finally and fatally. I twist, turn, spinning like a cyclone, dragging you into my furious whirlwind, a storm-tossed leaf. Like a sudden squall we're out down the hall, hurtling pell-mell through that immaculate parlour, funnelling through the window and once more we are free. As we rise steadily heavenwards, I can feel your shock, your disbelief. What the hell am I playing at? Bringing you here, then fleeing the scene. What trust has been growing has been dashed to smithereens.

We're thundering south, your vapour trail dark as a storm cloud. There's a fearsome roar, such is our speed. You are walled-off, I can't reach you; I have to content myself with keeping alongside. You are unbridled confusion – all I can do is send thoughts across the divide: I'm sorry, please try to understand. They feel puny, ineffectual – shrivelling and vaporising as soon as they near your white-hot heat. Bravely, if not fearlessly, you have come on this journey with me, and now I have let you down. Those ethical conundrums: some stories are not mine to show. And after everything I have lived and learned, I am not even sure what kind of truth we might have seen.

A Chinook scythes low across the sky below us. The noise of its twin rotors startles a small herd of horses, which scatter at a canter. Their movements seem strangely slow, ponderous even, like loping giraffes, from this altitude. We streak along. How you loved everything equestrian as you grew. You could name every part of a horse, and all the items of tack, all by the age of three.

Your speed gradually slows; your vapour trail now a woodsmoke grey. As Oxford heaves into sight, nestled in its charming Thames Valley, you peel away, back to your room, your college, I cannot say. Everything has unraveled, even before it has been weaved. My soul feels leaden; it is all I can do to remain airborne. Perhaps this story I will never be able to tell. Perhaps I just have to let you go.

I'm back in myself. My train is stationary. Outside the window I hear voices, doors slamming, tannoyed announcements. Oxford.

I daren't flush, not in a station. I slide back the latch and emerge into the gangway. There is no one to question my sudden reappearance; the carriage has long since disgorged its occupants. Even red jacket man has gone – leaving a swept-tidy floor behind him. I wonder at his destination, what's drawn him on his journey.

I get back to my seat in the nick of time, and set about allaying the fears of the train manager, who is spooked by my abandoned bags. Forgotten items, or bombs about to explode. He is cross that I've caused him anxiety. He makes a great show of demanding my ticket before he will allow me to leave.

Them

I'M TRACKING THE clay, keeping my sights just ahead
of its path. When I've had a good couple of seconds anticipating its trajectory, I pull the trigger. The noise is no more
than the crack of a stick being snapped – I'm always amazed
at the ear defenders. How they sanitise the explosive violence
of the detonation. The stock kicks hard against my shoulder.
With the eye of faith, I can make out the shot spreading in
its pattern, a widening shoal of the faintest grey. It sails past
just behind the clay.

The natural instinct, when you come to fire, is to stop.

The trick is to keep the gun moving.

I swivel on my heels, tracking ahead again. Squeeze the
trigger a second time, overriding instinct this time, keeping
things fluid. Another crack. Another kick. This time the
pattern clips the back of the clay, sending a few fragments
splintering.

I lower the shotgun, break it, and eject the spent cartridges
together with wisps of smoke.

Blaze's turn. He squares his feet on the firing line and
raises his weapon in readiness. The worked walls of the old
stone quarry sweep around us like an amphitheatre. Over time,
weathering and vegetation have softened what will once have
been stark rock faces, jagged and fractured and scarred. It's
the perfect venue for shooting – no chance that misdirected
shot will do anything other than slam against solid stone. I

wonder about those Mendip miners of yesteryear, laboriously breaking the limestone and hauling it off to build dwellings and barns and drystone walls: could they have anticipated the use their workings would be put to at this far future time?

Off to our left, Lewis, owner of the gun club, fires the trap once more, slinging another pigeon up into the sky. It arcs purposefully across in front of us. Blaze is too hasty. Crack, crack. Both barrels in rapid succession. The clay flies on, unperturbed.

Keep your cool, Blaze, I tell him, once he's back from the line. There's no hurry.

He nods, glowering. I clap a hand on his shoulder, give him a quick shuggle. I want to tell him it will be all right, but I can't, because it isn't going to be. The best thing I can do is get him involved with the shooting, something to focus his mind on, other than the thing that's eating him.

We watch Zambo step up. He's almost casual - this is his thing. Lewis pulls again, Zambo sweeps the gun to his shoulder, and a single barrel load smashes the clay right in the centre. Pieces fly everywhere, a spectacular disintegration. The effortlessness has to be seen to be believed. Zambo grew up close to the border with Zimbabwe, Rhodesia as it was then, during the latter years of the independence war. You learned to shoot well.

I can't fucking believe it, Blaze says.

I know, I tell him.

How the fuck could she do such a thing?

I know, I know, I say.

Just a fortnight after his first meeting with us at the Half Moon, a knock at his door in the early evening. He answered, thinking it would be a charity collector or a Jehovah's Witness or something. Instead, a couple of coppers standing there. He even knew them from shout-outs, dealing with the aftermath of house fires together. Dave and Neil. They looked pained, embarrassed. Roger Appleby? Neil asked him. Don't be stupid guys, he told them, his pulse picking up tempo, wondering what the hell was going on. Roger Appleby, Neil said again, we've received an allegation. I'm arresting you on suspicion of historical rape. You don't have to say anything but anything you do say blah blah blah.

I imagine the hot shame he'd have felt, being led to the waiting Astra in front of the neighbours. The hand on the top of his head as they ducked him inside. At least they'd had the decency not to use cuffs, Dave and Neil. Inside his mind Blaze would have been screaming *It's not what it seems! I'm fucking innocent!* But he would have felt the cloying judgements already forming in the heads of the scandalised onlookers. No smoke, after all, is generated without fire.

DNA mouth swabs. Hours of questioning. Then home on bail with the condition not to go within a quarter of a mile of his former matrimonial home.

Crack. Shatter. I watch Zambo dispatch another clay pigeon with equal ease.

Blaze is finding it hard to make eye contact. I know what's going on: he thinks I must have my doubts about him, too. We're so conditioned, aren't we? We see a grey-black column pluming skywards and can't help but conclude that, at its root, some family home must be in flames. It's what they all depend upon, those who deploy smoke bombs. How to explain to Blaze that I know it's fake news? That we've seen the same patterns again and again with other war-torn parents down the years – we all of us have, Prof, Rev, Zambo and me.

Blaze is restless, shifting his shotgun from hand to hand. When he breaks it, he can't get the spent cases to come out; he has to fumble and shake to get them loose. It's as though every last thing is against him. His tension is infecting me; I feel jittery, edgy. I consciously breathe more slowly, trying to counter-infect him with calm.

And the fucking kids, he says.

I know, I say.

I knew what was coming, as soon as he told me about the rape allegation thing. So fucking predictable. How the next day a case worker from child protection was on the phone, wondering if she could interview him about allegations that had been made regarding his daughter and son.

I'd been wrong about Blaze heading for a contact centre order next. He and his kids have been plunged into all-out war.

Merc is next up. I didn't see how he was going to manage it, but he's turned up to the shoot with his prosthesis. It's fascinating, watching him in action – there's some kind of harness and cable set-up that means the claw-hand opens when he extends his arm, and closes tight when he moves it back again. I guess it's how he holds letters for sorting. Zambo spends a minute getting him to practise grasping the shotgun barrels in the pincer. Not exactly stable, but. Then he stays close by, explaining things to Merc, his arm sweeping left to right as he describes what the clay will do. Lewis pulls. The pigeon flies. Crack. The recoil causes Merc's gun to buck, rattling the metal of his claw. The clay flies on. Zambo shouts to Lewis. Another pull. This time, a few bits of shot from the edge of Merc's pattern wing the target. A chunk breaks off and falls to earth.

I turn back to Blaze. Listen, I say, resting my hand on his shoulder again, you've got to prepare yourself. It's going to be shit.

He's due in court in a few days' time, an emergency application by his ex's lawyer. The key is rapidity. They've got to get it before a judge PDQ. That way, the only thing the court will have had time to do is a basic agency check. And that will turn up an arrest for suspected historical rape, and a child protection enquiry. It won't look good. It won't look good at all. Smoke and fire, soot and flame. What's a poor judge to do? So that'll be Blaze out of his kids' lives for five, six months minimum, banned from any contact, direct or indirect, while the wheels of formal investigation grind on. Six months of undiluted influence on the children from his ex. Six months for her to complete her work of poisoning. By the time he sorts out the mess, his kids will be completely turned.

He doesn't like my explanation. I knew he wouldn't. But I'm just the messenger. He shrugs violently, displacing my hand from his shoulder.

Can't they see what's fucking going on? he shouts.

I know, I tell him. I know.

Fucking *hell!*

The thing is, they all do – they all do know what's going on. The unscrupulous lawyers, playing the game. The police, the social, the judges. The coppers who arrested me – alleged domestic violence; supposed emotional and psychological abuse – even told me: they explained they'd had exactly the same scenario countless times. Always in the context of a divorce or separation. When allegations of offences that were supposed to be years old were suddenly and urgently made. The discomfiture of the judge in my case – a bearded bloke, in his forties, quite inexperienced, so my lawyer said. He was acutely aware he was being manipulated. He was angry about it, had a go at both of us, Mummy and me, as though I'd had anything to do with putting him in that position. But that's the sick beauty of it. Make an allegation, no matter how transparently cooked-up or pathetic or bizarre, and everyone has to take it at face value. Everyone has to play the game. No one wants to be found to have failed to take something seriously, if later it does turn out to have been the stuff that actually happened.

I felt almost sorry for him, that judge, prohibiting me from any contact with your sister and you till a date months away, to allow time for enquiries to be done. Actually, feeling sorry for him came much later, after the utter shock had subsided, shock like I'd never before known – like a car bomb had detonated just yards from me, rendering me deaf with tinnitus and disorientated and sickeningly confused, debris smacking on my head and clattering on the ground all around. And after the anger had subsided, too – anger that he should so spinelessly roll over and fail me, your sister, and you. But once time had passed and the aftershocks had finally burned out, that's when I could see his side. That petulant tantrum, berating me along with Mummy, when it was her trumping up the crap – well, he didn't know how to handle it, other than to go along with what he was being forced to do. And that'll have felt shite. So he did the only thing he could do with his own anger, and lashed out with his tongue. If he'd had a bowl up there on his mahogany bench, I guess he'd have washed his hands, Pilate-like. What's a poor judge to do?

Feeling sorry for the fuckwit judge. It's an empath thing.

You, of course, would've been oblivious – kept in the dark

like an overwintering bulb. Not one word about the emergency proceedings, and who said what about whom. The ruling, though. I imagine you were told about that, weren't you?

Blaze has stalked off, gone to stand alone for a while. I turn back towards the firing line. I don't know why the girls hang back – they do the same on every shoot. Rev is taking up position. She's got a padded parka on, she looks like she might be going down town on a shopping expedition. But I've seen her in action before. She might be full of the love of God for her fellow man, but she has it in for clay pigeons. Crack, smash. Crack, shatter. She's almost as good as Zambo.

Angel is hopeless. She's so startled when the gun goes off that she drops it on the ground. Zambo rushes forward, making sure it's safe, then wipes the mud off the stock.

I walk over to where Blaze is standing. His shoulders have dropped. I halt a pace or so behind him. I know it's hard, I say, but the thing is, Blaze, you've got to keep your cool.

He turns and looks at me as though I'm speaking Mandarin or something.

It's the classic sting. You get fitted up for the worst kind of crimes a person can commit, then when the professionals come flooding in, making their enquiries, turning over stones, what do they find? One charming parent, tearful in places when describing the horrific ordeals they and their children have endured, their kids flocking adoringly around them. Then the other one – the one who's supposed to be the violent rapist, the oppressive abuser; the one the kids are supposed to be too scared of to ever see again – that one is foaming and fulminating, writhing under the injustice of it all. And they come across to the professionals as exactly what they're being made out to be: uncontrollably angry, spewing counter-allegations of perjury and lies. Honestly. Which one would you believe?

I try to get this across to Blaze.

What's the fucking point? he asks. I'm fucked either way.

He's bright, is Blaze. He can see it in a way that took me a lot longer to get. Or maybe it's because he's had a head start on me. It was ages till I first turned to Google, which in turn sent me to Facebook, where after a few posts on a public group I got a DM from someone called Laurence, offering to add me to a secret forum he knew. Getting put in touch with others of my clan who live nearby. Prof, Rev, and Zambo. I dealt with everything Blaze is going through on my own. Blaze has already watched Caitlin at that rally, and had Prof to start to give him the measure of what's going on. How in several months' time, once his name has eventually been cleared, it'll all be over bar the shouting. How the social workers will present their report to the judge, detailing the children's 'wishes and feelings'. How just like before, old judgey will find he has no choice. Who would send kids back to a parent they say they fear and hate, a parent they profess to have absolutely no desire ever to see again?

The miracle, really, was how your sister managed to resist it. How she held on to the reality of her daddy through all she was being subjected to. I think it was Jacqueline Wilson. She loved her stuff, your sister did, read every single one of her books between the ages of about eight and twelve. Do you remember them? *Hetty Feather*, *Tracy Beaker*, *The Suitcase Kid*? You were never into them; you preferred dragon tales and fantasies. Through reading, your sister had already encountered just about every conceivable permutation of family breakdown. Through imagination and empathy, she'd had a chance to test out in her mind how each might make her feel. I remember her - just ten, she was - standing in the kitchen at that rented place on Drake Avenue, not long after I'd moved in, once she could see that I had a place not far from the old house, and that she was going to get to spend half her time there. She confided in me then: her greatest fear had been that she would lose one or other of her parents. Now she could see that everything was going to be all right.

I guess she held on tight to that, all through the months when I was banned from seeing her. I guess she used it as a shield to fend off the disturbing things that were going on. I guess Jacqueline Wilson saw her through.

You, though. It wasn't because you were into dragon fantasies. It was you. Two-and-a-half-year-old you, your supplicating arms falling despondently by your side. Ten-year-old you scribing away in your little notebook, trying to work out why it was that Mummy always seemed to favour your sister. It was you Mummy seemed to have power over. It was you it seemed she was able to use. Does that sound like I'm blaming you? I am sorry, if so. Believe me, I'm not. Anything but, as I hope to show.

I don't tell any of this to Blaze. He doesn't need to hear it. Maybe one of his kids will prove resilient like your sister; perhaps both of them will. Stranger things have happened. But, in reality, he's right. He's fucked whichever way. So few children withstand this shit, not when it reaches all-out war. Prof, Rev, Zambo can testify to that. Two completely conflicting beliefs about one parent - one formed of experience, the other propounded again and again in all sorts of different ways by one of the two people in the world they most love and most implicitly trust. They don't have the critical thinking to sort it out. Cognitive dissonance. Intolerable internal conflict. The contradictory beliefs simply cannot coexist, cannot be held simultaneously in the one young mind. One belief has to prevail, the other has to be suppressed, boxed away, abused. Splitting. A fracture occurs. A child is forced to choose.

I look at Blaze, his solid jaw, his slightly frizzy hair with just that hint of red in it. The courage in those fire-fighting eyes of pale blue. Maybe it would be a comfort to him – to know it's the fragile one, the inconstant one, the parent that looks like falling apart, that's the parent they choose. The one they perceive as strong, reliable, unshakable – that's the one they figure, in their desperate unconscious quandary, that they will simply have to lose. That's the one who won't disintegrate, that's the one they secretly hope will still be there for them, when the raging storm finally passes – as they think, in their innocence, it must surely someday do.

I shake my head. I'm getting ahead of myself. There'll be time enough to explain all that to Blaze further down the track. For now, for all his anger and gloom and bitter sense of fate, somewhere inside him lingers the hope that this mess might just come good. The time to get him to see it's because he's the only true parent – the time for that is once he's lost them for good.

Prof's just finished her turn. Both barrels discharged without troubling a clay. I watch her coming away from the firing line, more English than the English in her green Barbour. She's her own worst enemy, Prof is. She overthinks the process every time. Shooting is a matter of instinct – there's no room for calculating, for trying to work it out with maths and algebra and triangulation. A few simple rules, then let your gut take over. Blam blam. But her cool rationality, her grasp of psychological theory, that's been the saviour of us all – Rev, Zambo and me, and loads of other members over the past few years who have since moved on. Prof, I love – all the more so for her utter incompetence with a gun.

Come on, Blaze, I tell him. Our turn again. We start forward, side by side, a newbie and his mentor, back to the front line. I slide a couple of fresh cartridges home as we go, loving the snug precision with which they fit into the lightly oiled breech. Lewis tells us never to load till we're in position, but what does he know? I cast a glance at the rest of the group. Zambo's ribbing Prof about her blank score sheet. Rev looks lost in a moment of silent prayer, as she is wont to do. Angel and Merc are standing a little apart from the others, talking quietly together. Angel still looks shell-shocked, as though perplexed by all that's happening to her like it isn't quite real. As if disbelieving that she is here, in some Mendip gun club, trying to fire a shotgun to hit a spinning disc of clay, and wondering how comes she has gone from being the loving mother of two delightful boys to this outcast, surrounded by so many others of the living child-lost. But there is something else there, a new light in her eye. She's looking at Merc with it – a certain sort of attention that suddenly hits me. He's looking at her the same way, too.

You go first this time, Blaze, I say, as we get to the firing line. And remember, I tell him. Take it nice and slow.

❦

We debrief at the Half Moon, the newbies heading for home.

How's Blaze doing? Prof asks, once we've got our drinks and our regular table.

I shrug and say, Oh, you know.

Zambo has heard about the lawyer Blaze is up against. Some woman called Violet something-or-other. Her name conjures up prim properness, but Zambo tells us she's known as Violent on the circuit. He figures she's yet another trauma victim, projecting her own stuff on to the cases in which she's involved. Hell-bent on destroying the other halves, avenging her own childhood wounds. I think: is there no end to it, this juggernaut of pain and destruction? But I don't voice it out loud. I know what the others will say – if there's any hope, it lies with us and those of our clan.

How about Angel? Prof asks Rev.

Rev raises her eyebrows. Surprisingly, keeping her chin up, she says. Not great, of course, but on the whole I'm quite amazed.

Ah, but she's found a chink of hope, hasn't she? I say. The other three look at me, quizzical puppies.

Merc, I tell them. Haven't you seen the way they look at each other?

Rev laughs, and tucks her hair behind her ear, bangles clinking. You're kidding!

Prof's brow creases. I do hope not, she says. It's way too early. They've got to sort themselves out first, before they can take someone else on.

Zambo shakes his head. Lighten up, Prof, he says. Good luck to them, if they can find a little happiness.

Prof huffs.

Merc could do with something good right now, Zambo says. He's about at rock bottom.

He tells us about the previous weekend, when Merc's son Mark was playing footie for the first time for his school. Merc went to watch the game, as dads are wont to do. Soon as he got there he saw his ex and her mother, so he kept to the edge of the parental crowd. Mark's team won, three nil, and he scored the first. Come the final whistle, Merc went to congratulate him. Before Mark even made it off the pitch, his mum and gran shot from the touch line and escorted him straight past Merc like they were prison guards. He still called out something: well done, Mark, you played really well – great goal! And the boy completely blanked him. As though he didn't exist.

We all fall silent after that, thinking our own thoughts. A memory: fetching your sister from school one time, after I'd lost you. Her having forgotten some book or PE kit or something, so we went round to Mummy's on our way home to mine. Me sitting in the car while she popped inside. At that moment, the bus pitching up, and you getting off, bag slung over your shoulder. You. You saw my Renault and the next instant you darted behind the side of the shop over the road. I sat for a while, trying to figure out what to do. How long you'd wait for. Whether I should get out and go over. Then a door banging, and turning to see if it was your sister, but it was Mummy, who jumped straight in her car and raced out of the drive, whipping the twenty yards to where you were hiding. You, dashing from cover, diving in the passenger side. The pair of you racing off like bank robbers. The power of the mobile phone.

Me

COLOUR SPEAKS FOR me, to me.

Cadmium deep red. Ineffably sober and serious, as few reds are, dignified and noble, too. The depth to it. Its vibration.

Manganese blue hue. Dufy's southern French seascapes. Hot, lazed beach days, condensation on a glass of chilled beer.

Milk white. Fear.

Cobalt turquoise light. Experimentation and optimism. Perhaps youth.

Flake white hue, underpainted with viridian. The morning mist hanging low over fields of grass, that has come overnight from the dew.

Winsor yellow deep; rose madder genuine. The light of a late autumn sunset I have only twice seen.

Do you pause sometimes, arrested by a particular hue? Does colour sometimes speak to you? Or are you too busy, never noticing, rushing from one lecture to the next, from the wards out to see a film, from the film to meet friends for a drink, hurriedly grabbing some food. I know nothing of your life now; the version I have of you is frozen in time – a different sort of cryogenic girl, seven years since your passing. You never were interested in make up, not up to when I last saw you. Fourteen. Your sister is, she who was attracted by the effect of cosmetics from an early age. She would save up her money, even as a little girl, then buy a blue nail varnish, or a luscious black eye liner, applying them more with enthusiasm than sophistication, but all the while experimenting, becoming more practised in the art. You, though; you were indifferent. You preferred to be as you were made. Has that changed over these past seven years? Or do you still like to be natural you?

Seven years. You are twenty-one. Twenty-one going on fourteen, to me. Somehow I have to let you go, fourteen-year-old you, though it is the hardest thing; though it feels like abandoning you. But I have to manage it, if I'm to be ready; if ever the moment comes to get to know adult you.

The memories keep snagging me back. The one time you tried a hair colour. Some friend of Mummy's – a woman she met well after I'd gone, some earth-mother type who had her wedding in a cornfield. I can't remember what her name was. She was around for a while, cropping up in your and your sister's chatter. Then, as so many do, she suddenly disappeared, never mentioned again. Some misconstrued remark displacing her from friend to enemy, my guess. Whatever her name was, she fancied herself as a salonista. Did you and your sister actually want her attentions, or were you caught up in Mummy's mood – cementing things with this latest rescuer in her life, presenting her children to the altar of this new-found, promising-much friendship? She deepened the brown of your sister's hair, and cut her fringe even though she'd been asked not to. Eight months your sister had to clip it up in an unwanted style, disguising the butchery, till at last it had grown back through. Time and again she washed, trying to get the stubborn dye out; in the end she had to mask it with something closer to her original shade. You. You had your mid-blonde deep bronzed. You disliked it. Disliked what had been done to you. I remember you, down by the Drake

Avenue rope swing, explaining how you wished you hadn't had it done. You were resigned, though – you made none of your sister's efforts at restoration. You seemed accepting that you just had to bear it, until it was no longer part of you.

You wanted hair chalk one Christmas, though – the last Christmas I saw you. Hair chalk in blue. No mere step or two from the natural. A great stride in a different direction, no faked naturalness for you. Streaks of French ultramarine like no hair has ever been. Something you decided. You controlled. Something of you.

Perhaps clothing. Perhaps that is where you find expression in colour. The first couple of birthdays and Christmases after I lost you, I would go round your favourite haunts, choosing garments to give to you. I knew the styles you liked, baggy sweats and hoodies. I chose colours that spoke to me, set them against each other, contrasting combinations that I hoped would tell of the thought I had given. I gave that up by your seventeenth. The Year 11 passing out ceremony I'd gone to that summer. Realising I no longer had any idea what size would fit you.

Writing that card the previous year. Trying to get it right, every single word I wrote. And that fatal distraction, from being so dog-tired from all the sleeplessness, and writing: Wishing you a very 16th birthday. Having to insert the word happy as an afterthought. The pictures I sometimes saw on your Facebook, on your public-facing page, after you had un-friended me. Standing with a semicircle of friends at your Year 11 prom, your hands clenched. The strain subtly etched on your face, your smile getting nowhere near your eyes. Am I doing my own projecting, seeing what I crave to see, reading the runes wrong? I don't think so. Cards. The cards you occasionally drew and sent to your grandma, whom you never now saw, which she copied and sent to me. I interpret people's art for a living, but it didn't take a genius. One showing a black silhouetted girl on a tree-swing, the branches bare of all foliage, a lake of dark water in the foreground. Another with a blue-sky-bound reindeer at Christmas, its body intricately realised in brown detail, surging upwards over the legend Break Free. A thank you card after one particular birthday: a dusky pink and purple bouquet, arranged in a mottled blue vase, one solitary stem lying fallen on the table beside.

Colour.

Picture me: in my mid-twenties, first placement on my art therapy course, uncertain still if this was something I could do. Attached to the elderly care unit where Mummy worked as an occupational therapist. One of the very first patients brought to me for a session. A mute man, he was, previously rendered speechless by a stroke, and afflicted now by an incurable cancer. Untidy stubble on his hemi-drooped face. Dried egg yoke at the corner of his mouth. It was Mummy who wheeled him down – the first time I'd laid eyes on her. She was wearing a replica England rugby shirt over jeans; no uniforms for those in that unit. Watching him swirling and blending different gouaches in a dense kaleidoscope – streaks of ultramarine, brilliant yellow, sap green, primary red – like palette-washing water swirling down a sink's plughole. How eventually all brightness darkened, all vibrancy was consumed. If he'd had speech he could have tried to put words to it, words like rage, confusion, grief at all that was being lost. But words would have been inadequate, hollow – wrung out of any but the most banal meaning by centuries of overuse. Like trying to encompass the experience of a storm by naming wave, white horse, gust, lashing rain. Those ribbons of colour and pattern and form, they expressed his whole, the raging in his soul.

That's when I knew this was something I could do. More than a job to keep me in funds while I developed my own career. Art therapy, an arena in which I could be of use.

Prof laughed, you know. We're all doing it, she told me, all us empaths, trying to heal the old wounds by care-taking in the here and now. If I'd been like you, with a talent for science, perhaps I'd have wound up a doctor. Art. The one thing I excelled at, and I managed to find a way to put it to healing use.

You were good across the board, mind, not just at science. Excellent at History, English, RP, all the subjects where there is no single answer. All the subjects where one has to account for different points of view. It fills me with hope for your future, that you will eventually overcome the black and white thinking of the splitting defence. But it was science that you chose to pursue. Medicine. Care-taking. The way in which you will put yourself to use, too.

I can hear you ask: Was that not what Mummy was doing? Care-taking, helping all those frail old people? On the surface, it looked the same. But there was, I think, an added dimension. The gratitude and admiration of the gravely ill, and their family and friends – that is a constantly replenishing supply. Don't get me wrong: all caring people get satisfaction from what they do. But for some it can become much more: a life-sustaining thing.

Would I have listened, if someone were to have warned young, naïve me: among the legions of carers there are some with very deep wounds indeed? Would I have known what that might mean? Would I have believed it would ever affect me? Those are questions for another life. Those are things I will never see.

⁂

My abstracts are studies in colour. How the same square of flame red, blocked in a sea of brilliant green, becomes another shade entirely when, across the canvas, it is reproduced surrounded by intense blue. Different undertones drawn out. We are changed by the background around us; only against white is our truest hue revealed. As for the observer: we rarely perceive things in isolation, unadulterated by the interference of adjacent pigments. Only rarely do we see truth.

Something else I play with. Two thick slathes of contrasting pigment, their edges opposed. Gouache is best; watercolours bleed too readily, acrylics and oils hardly at all. Gradually the wet colours seep into one another, the border between them becoming less and less distinct, their entwinement producing some entirely new pigment at the interface – an insipid green, a murky brown. What should be two individual colours merge, enmeshed in each other, the purity of their selves sullied.

What am I in this study in colour? The palate knife, shaping what the eye sees. The artist, composing, juxtaposing, creating effect. I cannot help but have agency. Perhaps you will reject what I paint, suspicious of my motives even for having started to daub this canvas. Or perhaps you will decide, regardless of my artistry, that my picture has authenticity. Conceivably, in weighing the actions of my own hand, you will start to discern the brush marks and blade strokes of other implements that have hitherto been hidden from you.

112

Those are questions for you alone, and maybe ones that will seem differently important to you at different stages of your life – your twenties, thirties, forties and beyond. All I can do is paint my own picture. The artist, creation done, retires to their studio, and leaves their work to make its own way in the world. The effect it has on any given observer is ungovernable and unique.

THREE

Triangular Life

A LONG FROM THE station there's a modernist edifice, towering walls of pale brick and glass intersecting at surprising angles, block chrome lettering declaring it to be the Saïd Business School. The Royal Oxford Hotel was once the imposing welcome for disembarked arrivals to this fabled city. Now it looks puny and insignificant, stranded between bifurcating traffic streams.

I walk on along the Botley Road. What was once an artists' materials shop is a pizza takeaway. Revivre secondhand clothing is now an outlet for the British Heart Foundation. So much is unfamiliar from when I lived here. So many years in the city. There must have been demolition, construction, closings and openings, improvements to the roadways going on all the time. But we don't notice, not really, not when it's happening around us gradually, incrementally, day by day. The starkness of the change you see, once you've been away.

In some ways I feel like a trespasser, an interloper. This is your city now. The things that jar my eye will be just-how-it-is for you. You'll have no idea of the layers of past buried under what you see - the faded-paint lettering and the rawlplug-filled holes pocking the stonework beneath each shiny new plastic shop frontage - the hopes and disappointments, the lives and the losses, the stories that the very brickwork could breathe.

How would it be to see you, were you to make this

rendezvous? Five whole years since I last laid eyes on you, and that from a distance during your Year 11 passing out ceremony. An unwanted presence. But I came, to clap along with the rest of the mums and dads as you received your certificates; and to laugh falsely, along with everyone else, at your head teacher's résumé of your year group's antics through the years of your GCSEs. It was almost difficult to recognise you: six inches taller since my previous sight of you; braces on your teeth. Sweet sixteen. Your uncertain air. Your adolescent gawkiness and nascent grown-up grace, coexisting. As I watched you climb on to that stage, I was struck by the forcible realisation: I knew as much about your life now as I did the lives of any of the other pupils there. My daughter. You.

Did you notice me, sat towards the back of the hall? I thought a few times that you looked my way. Prof says you most definitely would have. That my having come would have dripped a quantum of love into you. That – even when, back home, for Mummy's consumption, you probably made a show of scorning my temerity in having shown my face – somewhere else, in some walled-off secret place adjacent to your beating heart, you would have been unspeakably pleased. I have dared to believe Prof, with her shelves laden with the weight of knowledge, and all that her myriad YouTube testifiers have to say.

George Street. What used to be a cheap homeware emporium – where I used to buy sheets, curtains, kitchen gear – now reinvented as a swish eat-outerie. The old Lloyds bank an urban outfitter.

Who are you now? Medical student, starting your third year. Cycling about town. Late-night essay-writing. Pubs and clubs with the gang. What do you tell friends when you are swapping life stories? What do you say about your dad? Do you have a prepared narrative: the bullying, the betrayal, the wastrel he proved to be? Or do you do what Mummy did with Ted and Gloria: look upset, as though swallowing back something painful, and explain that I'm no longer around. No longer around. The simple truth, concealing so much. It's a brave soul who will trespass further. But if any ask what happened, do you shake your head just the once, say it was very messy and traumatic, and say can you leave it. Cancer, they'll conclude. Maybe a horrific accident. You'll be the girl with the dead dad. #deaddad. The girl whose dad can never then be allowed to be seen.

Je me rends. Rendez-vous?

Somehow, I can feel your presence distributed throughout this city, as though, from some far vantage, you are monitoring my progress. I don't know – is that a yearning? After our last pell-mell airborne dash of the train journey, my abject failure to follow through, I thought you would never again rejoin me in flight. Now though. I have a strong sense of you; a sense that, despite the setback, you are still hankering to learn more. It's warmer here than it is out west, the sun feels stronger. The Oxford Retreat is still there on Upper Fisher's Row. There's the patch of grass, sloping down to the canal bank, where in summer months drinkers take pints from the pub, and pretend they're in the country.

A brief diversion. No need for flight; we need merely step through the gate that leads down to the towpath. My feet land on turf. I stop, trying to sense if you are with me. Yes, I can feel you at my shoulder, suddenly with, if a little behind, me. I keep a tight lid on my emotions; neither relief nor elation would be helpful. Come and see us, me and Mummy, stretched out and facing each other near that draping willow. Tartan travel rug. A couple of wasps buzzing near our drinks. That's her, lying on her side, propped up on her left elbow, her hand disappearing into her mass of blonde curls. Her skin young and smooth. Her eyes of green. And me, propped up on my right elbow, mirroring her posture, as though a mismatching reflection. I'm in jeans and a grandad top; she's in jeans and a T. I'm so much younger than you could ever remember, mid-twenties or thereabouts, my wire-framed John Lennon's not yet replaced from art-student me. We're here on a date, not too long since I met her. We're still revealing those bits of ourselves that we want to be seen.

Cross the grass with me. Traffic noise fading behind us. Birdsong above. Till at last we are close enough to hear.

She's speaking, is Mummy. She's telling me about Ellen at work. I've met her a few times myself, Ellen; she seems nice enough. But now I'm hearing another side. How she's taken against Mummy, how she cuts her out of things, spreads lies and gossip about her behind her back, how she has recruited various of the other OTs against her. It's spiteful stuff, going on well below the radar, so nothing is provable, everything deniable. An absence of evidence. There is nothing your mother can take to management, nothing she's able to do to turn back the tide. She's so miserable, she used to adore the job, but this bullying by Ellen is making her think she's going to have to leave.

Her eyes are frequently downcast. Other times they meet mine, her expression bewildered.

What do you think, listening to her? Does your heart go out to her, yet one more instance of the cruelty the world has doled out? Maybe you don't think, maybe you simply feel. A familiar wrenching inside, an admixture of anger and pity and empathic grief.

What I am thinking? The me of then is thinking it sounds truly horrible. I've witnessed your mother's kindness and lovingness with the patients she brings to and from my art therapy room. She simply doesn't deserve to be treated this way. The me of then is experiencing powerful urges, the feeling that I should do something to help. And if I can't help, then at least I might make her feel better. Cheer her up. She looks so abject. Beleaguered. At the same time, I'm puzzled by Ellen's behaviour; I can see I've got a lot to learn. I'm beginning to see Ellen in a new light. Like Mummy, she also is a good-looking occupational therapist – though tall against Mummy's petite stature. Perhaps Mummy feels to her like a rival, a threat to her ruling of the roost at the unit. Perhaps that's why she has unleashed such a campaign. She's not my type, Ellen, but when I think about it, I can remember her flirting mildly with me. Packs and animals. The dominance of the alpha. The sorting of hierarchy.

Let's away, that's all I wanted to show you. The casting of a line. There's nothing more to see here. Perhaps you're fascinated, seeing your parents as young lovers at the very start of things. But I can't dwell, it's too raw. Let's get ourselves back to bustling George Street, for me to continue my journey through this city that was once my home.

As we leave this past moment behind, I cast a glance back to the me of then. Willow beneath willow. Young and naïve. Regarding Mummy so attentively, with such concern. If I could be heard, would the me of now speak? What would I say to myself? I shrug off the thought. It doesn't get me anywhere. Round and round in circles. Only by living and learning do we gain the wisdom we wish we'd had, so that we would never have had to have lived and learned.

The pavements are crowded, even though the height of the summer tourism is long gone. A troop of Chinese school kids marches past like a Roman phalanx, their face masks modern-day shields against invisible enemies. I have to stand in against a café window to give them room to pass. Behind me, a guy is incensed. He must be in a tearing hurry. Take up the whole pavement, he shouts, I mean, why not? I hope none of them has the English to comprehend.

Across the street, there's the neoclassical façade of the history faculty. Niche-dwelling statues. Signs stating it is not open to the public. Gold-leafed above the portico, the mottos of both university and city: *Dominus Illuminatio Mea; Fortis Est Veritas*. Rev would like the former, Prof the latter. Zambo could certainly translate: *The Lord is my light; The truth is strong.*

The last of the Chinese kids goes past. Pavement passable again, I cross the entrance to Gloucester Green. That shop Rowan, where once you bought that most exquisitely soft brown rabbit cuddly toy – that, too, now vends fast food. The things that stick in the mind. Those years with you as a young child, you and your sister, your sweet innocence and wonder at the world. Such times. This is the hard part, the brutally tough bit, the parenting that really counts. The digging in for you, with precious little to guide me as to what it is best to do and not to do. Thank God for Prof, Rev, Zambo, too.

I come out at the bottom of St Giles. Waterstones, groaning with the weight of a billion words clamouring for attention. Boswells, old-school department store, still going strong. The church of St Mary Magdalen castaway on its island, ranks of bikes like boats moored along its railings. Everywhere I look there are reminders and memories.

The Eagle and Child, where Mummy confided in me about the disturbing things that had happened during some twenty-somethings' summer trip to southern Spain.

Browns, where over a meal she told me some of the harrowing unhappiness of her childhood. The Lamb and Flag, where I was regaled with the betrayals of a former fiancé. Again and again, the world meting out cruel, bewildering blows.

I was crushed for her, all that she had endured. Full of tender admiration for how she had turned out, how she had wrested this perfect self despite all she had been through. She was determined to overcome it, she said, to live a life that was beautiful and good. I responded to her rallying cry. I would join forces with her, partner her in creating a love-filled life. I would be her trustworthy ally.

She told me once: I have never in my entire life been truly happy.

I can make you so, I thought. If you would let me.

She finished our relationship on two occasions during those first six months. Offered tearful explanations when I called round to ask why. It was nothing I'd done. I was perfectly lovely. Everything she'd so long dreamed of, in fact. But her past experiences had shattered any capacity for trust. How frightened she was of inevitable hurt. How scared she was to get involved with me.

You can trust me, I thought. I said: You can trust me.

Pull, push, pull, push, pull. I was like a fish, hook barbing the flesh of its mouth, being reeled in.

We're on Pen-y-ghent, walking to the summit, that same trip to Yorkshire, a few days after that cine film private show with Ted and Gloria. It's uncharacteristically warm, the mid-June sun beating down from a cloudless sky. A solitary man passes us on his way down, dressed only in walking boots and Y-fronts, the rest of his clothing stashed in his backpack, calling a cheery 'Fine day!' as we stand aside to let him by on the path.

Your mother's voice choking as she explains how that home movie has made her feel. How utterly heartbreaking it was to have watched her five-year-old innocence, and to think what eventually became of it. How she had never, not once, known true love.I thought: I can show you true love.

At another point on our ascent: how she still had her dead grandmother's old ring, and wanted to use the diamond in it, have it remounted in a modern platinum setting, if ever she were lucky enough to meet a decent man and get engaged.

I thought: you have, you have met a decent man.

Snow persisting up near the summit. Lying on our backs in it, turning the camera round and taking a pre-smartphone picture, long before the word selfie was coined.

At the peak. Deep inside myself, misgivings about the depths of her sorrow, what I might be getting myself into. But I had such faith in a story in which good prevails. And I had no doubt about my ability to author my part of that.

I knew what I had to do.

Proposal.

Accepted.

How I have rued – yet cannot, because of you, and your sister, rue – that day.

⁂

I'm lodging in a room at Somerville, found through a website that lets out vacant university accommodation to visitors to the city. I can't think they're too hard up, these Oxford institutions, but I guess every little helps. It occurred to me that this might be your own college. How I might just run into you at the lodge, or in the refectory. But as Rev would say: if it happens, it was meant to be.

The porter checks me in, gives me my keys and a map of the college, and points me in the right direction. Through the wisteria-lined front quad. Up the staircase to the Darbishire attic. The room is along an eaves corridor; I have to use a keycard to gain access from the stairwell. How these days we try to do everything to keep our young secure. Wall lights, sensing my movement, glow more brightly as I make my way. The room door has a memorial plaque on it, some former student who's made some cash and donated to the college for posterity. I turn the key and let myself in: basic, studenty single-bedded, but it's cheap and it's somewhere to stay.

I think: is this a way of being closer to you, booking myself into a place that must be like your own digs? Later on, when the sun is starting to set, and I'm still sat there on that watching-the-world-go-by wall, you never having shown, will I regret even thinking I should stay overnight? Waving from this distant shore. But what if? What if you came, what if you did make our rendezvous? I don't know how it would go. Would you be spitting with anger, furious at the myriad ways you feel I let you down? Or grieving and guilt-stricken, light bulbs having already switched on about what happened to you? Either way, I would need to absorb and acknowledge your emotions. I wouldn't want to be under a timetable, I wouldn't want to be constrained. I'd want to be able to offer whatever you needed – take you out for a meal, get repeated rounds of drinks in, talk together walking round and round Christ Church Meadow for as long as it might take.

⚘

I think I know when it might have started for you. When the line was cast over your own waters, plopping lightly on to the surface, floating its bait.

February. I'd finally accepted the marriage couldn't be saved. Should we have spent thousands upon thousands on therapy, attending weekly, in hope of a way forward? I tried to persuade her, and maybe it wouldn't have helped. I think it would have proved too painful, too overwhelming for Mummy. What if a therapist had begun to probe beneath the surface, to get to the reasons she repeatedly experienced the world as she did – when that started to happen, would she have pulled out? Before long we'd have been back where we started. Ticker tape chuntering, dust motes in the projector beam. Images of the past playing over me. Rings coming off her finger. That's how it played out anyway, with late-night, pages-long rants scrawled in an unraveling hand, detailing the traumas I'd wreaked on her, you, your sister. Threatening social services if I didn't get out this instant and leave. The morning she came into the room where I slept, and told me her brother-in-law and a mate of his were on their way down from Yorkshire, coming to throw me out. Of my home. In front of my kids. The truths she'd told them they'd completely believed.

February. We agreed a date on which to tell you and your sister. Before we got anywhere near that day, I found the card you'd made, displayed on the chest of drawers in the room where Mummy slept. Do you have any recollection? Your neat twelve-year-old writing, line after line telling her she is a wonderful Mummy, and that you, your sister, your aunty and uncle, this friend, that friend, the other friend, the cat, the dog, even various favourite soft toys ALL LOVE HER.

Uncle Tom Cobbly and all.

Everyone except me.

This is what I ask myself: did she come to find you, slump herself down on the bed in your room? Or was it more accidental: perhaps you happened across her when you got back from school. Tearful, inconsolable, wracked by shuddering sobs. Managing, somehow, to get out the awful news that your daddy no longer loves her.

I can picture you, your fingers twisting together, butterflies fluttering frantically, the heart thumping wildly in your chest. Mummy dissolving in front of you. My God, how that must have made you feel. What does a child do to try to make things better? What can a child do to soothe such grief? You go to the craft cupboard, your fingers still trembling, take scissors and colouring pens, and make a card – just like the cards that have brought such delight at birthdays and Christmases and other special days down the years of your life. WE ALL LOVE YOU! It's all you can possibly do.

How do you deal with your feelings towards your father, one of the two people in the world you love the most? The one who has visited such grief upon your mother? Ages and ages you spend in your room, lying on your back on your bed, tossing your netball in the air, patting it back up with your feet, catching it again. Hands, feet, hands. Hands, feet, hands. Repetitive action. Soothing you. Allowing you to concentrate, focus, on anything other than the intolerable war raging in your heart.

March. The weekend we'd planned to tell you and your sister about the divorce. Both of you were ill. Mummy, desperate to get it out in the open, pressing for the next weekend. It's Mothering Sunday, I say. No matter, she says. She wants to tell you the day before Mothering Sunday.

It's important to tell you together, present a united front over the matter of our disuniting. I suggest we talk immediately before, make sure we're both signed up to what will be said. She is tremulous at our meeting, comes across pathetically bewildered, says she doesn't know if she will be able to speak; asks if I will be the one to say what we have to say.

Ever the chivalrous. One more tug on the barbs, even as I'm tearing myself free. Only in retrospect did I see what I had allowed to happen, how I'd let myself become the mouthpiece.

The worst day of my life, giving you, your sister that news. The terror I have for you, terror of my own, too.

You come to find me in the kitchen a few days later. Your vulnerable twelve-year-old body sheathed in that floral print dress. Hands twisting together in front of you. Eyes imploring. Daddy, is there *any* hope?

A different memory: we're at Disneyland Paris, you, Mummy, your sister, and me. You're seven. All through the stay you've been eyeing that rollercoaster, Big Thunder Mountain, trying to summon the courage to ride it. It's way more scary than anything else in the park; way more scary than anything you've ever done, you who hates heights and steep slopes. And that's precisely why you so want to do it. But every day you baulk at it, and taste the flat ignominy of defeat. The last hour on the last day – that's it, you've got to try it. You can't contemplate returning home without conquering your fear. We race round, you and I, leaving your mother and sister to catch one last go on It's A Small World, which your sister so loves. And we find Big Thunder Mountain temporarily closed, some technical hitch that's got to be fixed. The clock ticks. Ten minutes, shut. Twenty minutes, still shut. Thirty minutes and it's re-opened. Massive queues have built up. We join, inching forwards through chicanes of barriers, hordes of thrill-seekers snaking back and forwards on themselves. The hands of my watch creep ever closer to the time we must leave. You're so desperate to do it. I cannot bear that you'll be crushed, disappointed. I pray to a god I don't know is even out there, still less is bothered with a young child's dream.

Daddy, is there *any* hope?

I look at you standing there. Entwined fingers; floral sheath. Feel the full impossibility of what we are facing. I don't want to give you false hope. But even now I myself am holding the gossamer thin thread that links me still to this family I helped create. Even now I believe she might just pull back. Two years, maybe three. That's what it might take for a therapist to help her sort out the stuff inside her head. I told her I would stick by her for the duration, not expect anything from the relationship, and when she was healed we could see. But she wouldn't entertain it. Even then, though, you standing there with your twisting fingers, your pretty print dress, I still hoped she might have a change of heart, see if she could finally deal with the traumas, gain control of the projector.

Almost certainly not, I tell you. But just maybe there is a chance.

You think it's down to me. You think it's in my gift.

We made it to Big Thunder Mountain, you and I. A couple

more minutes and we'd have had to have called it a day, but we reached the front of the line in the nick of time. You rode it. You actually rode it. You crested the peaks, plummeted down sheer tracks, getting flung side to side by switchback bends, soaked by a water spray; raced towards a bridge that looked certain to take your head off, the carriages dropping down in a last-minute dip that brought us safely underneath. You were so full of it when we exited. You had mastered your fear. Your Disneyland trip was complete.

᷀

I have a quick wash in my Somerville room, sluicing the grime of the journey from my face. My hands are big like spades, cupping the water. There are creases in my palms that a fortune-teller could read. I dry myself, get a couple of things from my holdall, then take my canvas roll bag and prepare to leave.

Crossing the main quad, a figure snags my attention on the other side. An academic, searching his pocket for the keycard to let himself into another staircase. Somehow he becomes aware of my gaze and looks back over his shoulder. Close-cropped hair, brown suede jacket over jeans, round-framed glasses, papers tucked under his arm. He meets my eye. It's a strange moment, over in an instant. It's as though I am looking at a different, younger me. Zambo reads a lot of cosmology – multiverses and parallel realities, quantum uncertainties, our lives branching an infinity of times with every decision point. I wonder if somewhere else, in some other version of this world, I have followed a different path, and am now a lecturer in fine art letting myself into my rooms in an alt.college just like this college appears to be.

I pass through the main gates, out on the street again, and my feet find their rhythm. I skirt round a smashed Dolmio jar, its sauce splattered like a red Rorschach blot on the pavement. Bells peal from a distant tower, announcing the impending hour mark. Two tolls. Sixty minutes till our rendezvous.

As I walk, I think about hooks and lines. Do you even know you were caught? The world is as the world is, and the world is normal for you. It took me years to see it, understand it for myself – even now I'm still sounding the full depths. What hope you?

Maybe this will help. Karpman triangle, courtesy of Prof; some call it the drama triangle. Or, as Rev would have it, that which Jesus could so presciently see. Let me draw it for you on the sketch pad of your imagination:

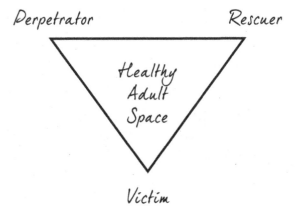

No sooner have I finished the diagram than I'm suddenly knocked out of myself, winded – like a gale-blown leaf. I tumble upwards, uncontrollably acrobatic. Half a dozen heads over heels and then somehow it stops. I hang motionless for a moment, trying to get my bearings. I catch sight of myself on the pavement below, a walking automaton, hands thrust in jacket pockets, feet landing rhythmically on the cracks between the paving slabs. It's one hell of a surprise: flight comes only when I am stationary. I'm still trying to work out what's gone on when I catch sight of you, a furious shimmering further along St Giles, your energy refracting and wildly scattering the light that passes through you.

You. Careering into me. Anger and frustration and grief and abandonment boiling and broiling in a seething brew. I set off in pursuit, swiftly overflying my plodding, earth-bound form. I wonder how long I've got; how long till my body reaches the end of St Giles and steps sightlessly into the traffic on Broad Street. Impossible to be sure, but I'll have to be quick.

You're surging ahead now, weaving between the spires that loom into your path – St John's, Balliol, All Souls, Oriel. I slalom through them on your tail, twisting and turning at break-neck speed. It looks for all the world as though you're fleeing and I am chasing – but I know differently. That stunning impact, enucleating me from myself; then your headlong rush above the city streets: hit me, hug me – you want to do both simultaneously. I soar over Christ Church and follow you along Speedwell Street. Not for the first time, I'm struck forcibly by how you'll have grown and changed. Adult you, stranger to me. Charting your own course – a reversal of roles – me, the parent, now trailing behind. Yet for all your independence, your sturdy self-confidence, in the matter of what happened to you, you have no map, no guide to the unfamiliar terrain.

Somewhere along Oxpens, the ice rink like a landed UFO

beneath, I finally draw alongside. We stay in formation for a moment, twin streaks in the autumn afternoon.

Then a sudden kick as though from my afterburners; I notch up an incredible acceleration. A glance behind; through the blistering air I can see you are with me, doggedly, determinedly.

We follow the train tracks back across Oxfordshire, Wiltshire, to Somerset beyond. We are Flying Scotsmen, our journey fast-forwarded at one hundred times speed. The irony is not lost: I'm retracing my day's travel. And it gives me no pleasure, having to retake the lead. But this, I think, will help you to see.

There, nestled in the valley, delineated by its twelve-foot security fence. Low flat-roofed buildings, sprawling staff car park, the swinging red barrier controlling exit and entry. This place you used to hear so much about, yet never before have seen.

We dive down, clear the barbed wire atop the fence like nerveless steeplechasers, and close on D block beyond the stand of beech trees. In through a window that's open but impassible to any but us, thick metal bars spanning the aperture from lintel to sill. Hovering now by a fluorescent strip light and you start to take in the scene - the cupboards, the trays full of materials — of my therapy room in the medium-secure unit. Is it strange at last to see where your father works? There's an easel in the centre of the space, faced by two chairs, me in one, an inmate - Billy - in the other. He's in his late teens, is Billy; we've worked together a few times already. His hair sticks up in random tufts, as though he's just got out of bed. My glasses are the oblong metal frames I wear now I am in my middle years.

You watch me open a wooden box of fifty acrylics. My voice: What colour is speaking to you, Billy?

Deep red-maroon. Caput mortuum. Some call it cardinal purple, on account of its popularity for depicting religious robes.

Billy starts to work the paint across the paper, a stiff three-quarter-inch brush, describing furrows like a ploughing competition. The tone is old blood and mourning. The texture is ridged like a frowning brow. Look at us: Billy and I are two adults in roles. He is a persistent young offender; I am an art therapist. We are in the middle of a Karpman triangle, occupying the healthy space right at the centre of its equilateral walls. Maybe, a little bit, we're off to the edges: victim Billy and rescuer me.

His hand begins to move more quickly, back and forth, applying more pressure, imparting greater depth to the crevices he's creating in the pigment. I tell him: your brush strokes are becoming more vigorous. What happens if we stay with that for a while?

He becomes absorbed in those side-to-side movements. They are mesmeric. Things are happening deep inside him, in the areas of himself that words cannot express. At the end of each run, his brush corners like a car in a handbrake-turn. Back on itself, accelerating again across the easel. Periodically, he loads more paint, giving himself more to work with. He doesn't seem to want to change the colour, even to blend it. The A2 sheet is a glistening rich russet but it's far from uniform, peaks and troughs scattering and absorbing light in infinite variegation.

Art is the royal road to the unconscious. Finding a language for things that can't be spoken. It's not just the image, it's the way it's produced. He starts jabbing at the painting, the bristles splaying, causing flowers, or starbursts, or explosions, to bloom.

Tell me how that feels, I say to him.

The jabs come harder, gouging pigment clean down to white paper, stark scars.

Tell me how that feels.

But he's gone too quickly. Sometimes colour, texture, creativity access deeply suppressed emotion with shocking rapidity. Suddenly Billy is stabbing at the paper, denting it, depressing it, shell craters in no man's land.

How does that feel, Billy, I ask, trying to keep him with me.

The latest stab, the brush heels-out, skidding sideways, ripping a hole.

Does that –

In that moment, I know he's gone. Something about my voice, my words; perhaps the dynamic of pedagogue and pupil. Something has displaced Billy from the space at the centre of the triangle. I'm on my own.

Billy, I say, trying to get through to him.

He throws the brush; it rebounds off the easel.

Billy, I say, trying to hold the centre ground.

Gripping the wooden frame he hurls it to one side, as though trying to cast it forever from his life. It crashes to the floor.

We're no longer two adults. Billy is a frightened, trauma- tised child. He has leapt to one corner of the triangle and is once again consumed by his victim role. And every tri- angle needs three angles; every victim needs a perpetrator, and craves a rescuer, too. I can feel the pull of it, the way his behaviour is sucking at me, like a giant eel from its underwater cave, trying to draw me on to one of those other two vertices. I resist, try to stay in the middle, try not to be pulled out on to the triangle with him.

I can see you're feeling very angry, Billy, I say. My voice is resonant. My words are unhurried. My accent is deepest I'm-your-pal-Stevie-from-the-Wirral.

But Billy now has to have it. He has to have drama. We have shifted a rock in his garden and all manner of squirming creatures have been revealed. He has to hit out, squash them and beat them, and stop the repulsiveness of their very being. But he can't. They're inside him. They're a part of him. All he can do is cast them out, project them on to some external thing. Then he'll have a target, something he can vent his rage upon. According to Rev, with her Biblical cast of mind, a scapegoat. And right now, for Billy, the scapegoat is me.

The easel, lying on its side on the floor. Billy glances round the room, his movements wild. I see his gaze fix on the fire extinguisher, brick red in its bracket on the wall.

Don't, Billy, I think. I think: It's not too late. Come back to the middle of the triangle with me.

Shall we finish the session there for today? I say.

But he's gone. Like a teetering tightrope walker he loses his balance. With a bound that knocks his chair backwards, he's over at the extinguisher, two hands on it. He rips it like a mauled ball, and hurls it towards me.

I've already left my chair, anticipating the action. He needs me in perpetrator role, someone to flail against, someone to hurt back. The red cylinder sails through the space where a second before I had been sitting, and clangs against the far wall, sending plaster flying.

And that's how it works. This is a fluid triangle. Billy moves between different roles, occupying them simultaneously. Did you clock it: how in acting out victim, in projecting his shit on me, Billy actually becomes a perpetrator, though he doesn't recognise it. I'm no victim, though - I can look after myself. I contemplate trying to restrain him, but I don't relish the thought of the enquiry. I do need a rescuer. I hit the red button by the entrance. Klaxons blare. The noise baffles Billy, buying me seconds to step smartly outside, push the door shut behind, and turn the barrel bolt to keep him contained.

They may be my rescuers, the two uniformed men who arrive in a twinkle, but to Billy they are fresh perpetrators to his victimhood. He's throwing all sorts around inside the room. At one point I hear splintering wood. They step in swiftly during a lull. Get Billy in a safe restraint. He bucks a few times, tries to stamp on their feet, but soon his fury is spent.

Security take him back to his room. A doctor will be called. He'll be drugged to calm him. He knows this, I know this. As he gets escorted along the corridor - facing backwards, heels dragging along the floor, each security guard with an arm clamped under one of his - he has new perpetrators. He gives me a pleading look, trying to remind me of all the trauma, all the shit he's suffered to be here in the first place. Trying to suck me on to the vertex I most readily get drawn to, that of rescuer. A word from me and these guards might be stood down. He is victim again, and this time he induces different feelings in me. But I'm having none of it - I'm resolute here in the centre - there have to be consequences to his acting out. I'm no longer an enabler, me.

A horn blast.

Suddenly I'm sucked, in a bewildering kaleidoscope of colours and impressions, down a wormhole.

And I'm back in myself, striding streets in the centre of Oxford. No time to register what's happened. The car pulls up short, ABS firing like a Gatling, its bumper finally halting just inches from my legs, which have seized in shock. I raise an apologetic hand to the driver. He gives me an exasperated look, his own hands flying up in a what-the-fuck gesture. I step back on to the pavement at the end of St Giles. He drives on past. I wait till it's clear and I can cross Broad Street in safety.

I feel rattled, shaken. And not just by the car. You're nowhere to be felt or seen. Are you still back there in that West Country medium-secure unit, outside that door in block D, surveying in wonder the damage that Billy in his maelstrom caused? Are you watching a former me ruefully righting his upended easel, trying to clamp the extinguisher back in its bracket, painstakingly gathering the tubes of paint that Billy flung to every corner of my therapy room, replacing them in their rainbow arrangement nestled in the slots of their wooden case? Will you know how to get back from there, now that I am no longer with you?

No doubt you will. You are no longer a child; you're perfectly capable of solo ethereal flight. But I wonder what you made of what you saw.

Triangular life. This, I believe, is how it is for Mummy. For years I played rescuer to her victim – and we stayed remarkably fixed in those roles for six, seven years, through a whole carousel of perpetrators whirlygigging round her never-ending drama: her family, her friends; my family, my friends. But if you're anywhere on that triangle, sooner or later those roles will shift, swap, mutate.

All she ever wanted was children. First you. I remember how pleased she was, proud even, to resume our sex life just weeks after your birth. She laughed about it, post-coitally, conspiratorially – what would the midwives say? Then, a couple of years later, your sister came along. Two of you. Family complete. All of a sudden, all that energy consumed in sustaining the trappings of a normal relationship was no longer necessary – I see that now, with the bitter benefit of hindsight. She seemed to let loose her grip, her muscles worn out with fatigue, and the lens cap fell to the ground, never again to be seen.

Ticker tape chuntering. Dust motes glistening. The projector, unbridled now, playing on me. Yet another perpetrator to validate her rescuer need.

If I expressed a different point of view: I was an oppressive bully. Trying to keep a handle on the family budget: I was subjecting her to rigid financial control. That time when you got a conduct mark for disobedience: I was siding with your hateful teacher for thinking that maybe she'd had a point. Things snowballed. Time-honoured endearments, mutually understood flirtations, the touches and caresses that once upon a time had meant only love and welcomed desire. All these now recast as the actions of a lecher, a pervert, a pest, unclean. My world was turned on its head, reality was upended and flipped on its arse.

And you. The fluidity of that triangle. The interchangeability of roles. I'd be helping you with your maths, the pair of us poring over your books on your bed where you always worked, me trying to dredge up the first thing about balancing equations, or geometric symmetry. Your door would burst open. She'd be standing at the threshold, staring. A normal moment – a dad and his daughter, square in the middle of the triangle, wrestling with algebra – felt instantly tainted. The very act of her observation, from the vantage of her rescuer vertex, would triangulate victim-you, and perpetrator-me.

⁂

Through the pedestrianised centre, past Carfax tower with its 99 steps and its views of the Oxford skyline. No planning permission will ever be granted for a building to be constructed above its height. Down St Aldate's, the town hall and city museum. Old Tom in his belfry at Christ Church.

So many things told through cards. How that Mothering Sunday – one day after we told you your parents were divorcing, one day after you learned your family would no longer be – out we went for lunch. Some tarted-up inn on the Mendips. Gastro pub. Roast beef. You ate hardly anything, you who so love your food. Your sister: question after question, trying to get a handle on how life was now going to be. Sometimes reassured, sometimes feeling aftershocks from the quake. Coming for hugs from me, from Mummy, anything to steady her feet.

You. Unable to speak. Withdrawn into yourself. Still in shock. Numbly unable to compute the reality. Broiling with anger and with grief; with shame and with disbelief.

Your daddy no longer loves me.

Your daddy.

Your.

Baited line landing on water.

WE ALL LOVE YOU!

Soft lips close around cold sharp steel.

A few days after, putting some things in your room, finding the Guess How Much I Love You card on your bedside table. Little Nutbrown Hare and his Mummy. Love you to the moon and back. Mummy's writing: how you had ruined her Mother's Day, but how she still loves you anyway.

Pull. Push. Pull again.

Barbs digging in through skin.

Them

THERE ARE THIRTEEN candles on the table, guttering in the draughts that play through this ancient building. Thirteen. Three for Prof's. Two each for Zambo's, Rev's, Angel's, and Blaze's. One for Merc's lad. And one for you. The flames flicker, twisting and jinking this way and that. It's as though they're desperate to break free, but find themselves tethered, like failed escapologists, to the wicks that run through their cores.

Zambo's session at the gun club is pure fun, but Rev's can cause problems. People react differently. Rev's thing is God, of course: Jesus, the Bible, that kind of thing. Some of the parents who've journeyed with us have been religious – quite a few, in fact; maybe it goes with the territory. Maybe when your life comes crashing down, that's when you turn to a god. We had a guy called Asif with us much of the previous year – I was mentoring him. He was a practising Muslim, and I figured he'd hate Rev's stuff, but he proved me completely wrong. He and Rev made all sorts of connections, finding loads in common between their respective faiths. Agnostics like me and Zambo, we generally roll with it, happy to pick up what wisdom we find wherever we can get it. It's the atheists who struggle. They tend to be every bit as fundamentalist as the most dyed-in-the-wool born-again, and the bedrock of their belief system is to reject all that Rev has to say. We've had a smattering who've stomped off part-way through her sessions. I'm wondering how Blaze and Merc and Angel are going to take it.

Rev is up front, closest to the altar dais, her eyes closed, her hands together. We're ranged in a loose circle, on plastic visitor chairs borrowed from the parish hall next door, the candle-bearing table a focal point in the middle. The lights in the body of the church are dimmed. The thirteen flames cast restless shadows of us on the stone pillars and walls. Unquiet spirits. Rev does her utmost to make things ecumenical – this is a meditation, not a prayer time. She asks us to focus our minds on our children, and to call upon whatever higher power we might rest faith in to bring them protection. She goes through, naming them, leaving a couple of minutes silence between each and every one.

Ethan . . .

Jeremy . . .

Emily . . .

Zac . . .

I close my eyes, imagining them in turn. I don't know their faces, not really. I've seen photos of some of them, but what they actually look like is beside the point. They're easy enough to conjure: once carefree children who have suffered the living bereavement of losing a parent. Whose love for their mum or dad has been curdled into hate. Whose primary attachments have been mashed and splintered like so much green wood. The confusion, the pain inside. The desperate need to survive, to find a way to cope with a world that was once happy and light, and is now turned dark and forbidding by the conflicts in which they've been embroiled. I picture them as though in snaps taken during the time before war: tousled boys, plaited girls, big eyes, cheeky smiles, flawless creaseless skin.

Sasha . . .

Maxwell . . .

Sam . . .

Jay . . .

The naming of them. A roll call of the living lost. Rev always does them in random order, but never puts her own first – everyone's children are equally important to her god. I sneak a peek at the others. Prof has her eyes closed, but not because she's a believer. Her higher power is academia; her faith is in the piles of papers and ranks of textbooks that line her study shelves. She believes that through understanding the psychology of what's being done to them, by tailoring her reactions and responses to be precisely the opposite of what her children's outward behaviour seems hell-bent on provoking, she can eventually save them. Attachment bonds preserved. Her faith is in cognitive development – that one day, when they finally gain independence from their father and critical thinking emerges, they'll gradually, haltingly come to understand what went on. And when they do, Prof's steadfast refusal ever to abandon them – despite their every protestation that that is what they want her to do – will become for them her most precious gift. It happens – as so many of her YouTube testifiers bear witness. Young adults who have achieved reunification, and whose love for their outcast parent burns unquenchably bright again. But it doesn't always happen, as we're only too well aware. Our secret Facebook forum is populated by thousands of parents going through the same all around the world, some of whose kids have never come back, not even after thirty years.

That's Prof's bimetallic hope-fear. That her kids will break free. That they won't.

That's my hope-fear for you, too.

Russian dolls, that's how Prof conceptualises her son and daughters. Outer layers, hard with brittle shellac, painted smiles like fixed masks. Hidden within, right at the centre, their authentic loving selves, shrunken and miniaturised – the children they once were; the loving, trusting people they could one day be. It's how she deals with every scornful text, every block on social media, every declaration of hatred: those are their defensive shells speaking, parroting their father's propaganda. Somehow, she manages to let it wash past. Every message she sends, every card or letter, she addresses not to their snarling exterior but to the wounded child buried deep beneath. The child who loves their mum. The child that has had to entomb their craving to be loved by her.

I think of you like that sometimes. Like a Russian doll. I cling to the hope that the real you – the you I raised and lived alongside and knew so well for fourteen long years – is trapped inside there, able to blossom back to life once free. But other times the impenetrability of your carapace seems never-ending – seven years without so much as a word – and it overwhelms me with despair. Two whole years away, into your third at university – how free, and for how long, do you need to be? Sometimes what hope I have seems impossibly puny against the all-too tangible prospect that this is how it ever more shall be.

Next to Prof, Zambo is staring at the far wall. I follow his line of sight; he's studying a depiction of Christ in his passion, half hidden in the gloomy shadows. The bloodied figure is buckling under the weight of his cross. Zambo's faith is in non-violence. He saw so much of it growing up – brutal beatings from his Rhodesian Army colonel father;

butchered white farmers and flayed black freedom fighters during the independence war. His determination is never to raise a finger against anyone. He's like a muscle-bound, six-foot-four Gandhi. The rage we all experience at times – the nerve-searing agony at being denied relationships with the most precious people in our worlds; at the damage and harm being done to those we are hard-wired to love and protect. The fury at the professionals – their failure to recognise what's going on right under their noses. Even more, their unwitting collusion – what's a poor judge to do? It's this rage that fuels the stories that make it to the papers – the assaults, the murders, the suicides. Zambo is so powerful he could kill with his hands. He could maim, inflict terrible counter-pain. His potency terrifies him, lest he let slip his control and prove to be the kind of creature he has never wanted to be.

Blasting clays is his release.

Christopher . . .

Taylor . . .

Kitty . . .

Mark . . .

Rev's Geordie accent is eerily haunting, delivered *sotto voce* like this. The naming of names. There's something tranquil about the acoustics in the church – the solid stone walls that have stood for centuries, the high vaulted ceiling. It strikes me: there's no echo. It's as though sound, once uttered, is absorbed softly by the very fabric of the building, like snowflakes landing on wet ground. It's as though Rev's words are actually going somewhere. As though they are being heard. Last on the list, she enunciates your name.

Your name.

You.

I hear it with surprising equanimity. In the early years, it would constrict my throat, lurch my gut, cause my vision to mist. How far I've come. Rev's bangles chink as she adjusts her position. Unbidden, I picture you, standing across the kitchen from me – you must have been ten, eleven – the pair of us passing your netball repeatedly back and forth, me detailing the current government's betrayals, my analysis of the likely outcome of the impending general election, telling you about the great British tradition founded by Screaming Lord Sutch. You, lapping up the grown-upness of a politics talk with your dad. Declaring that when you were old enough, you would definitely vote Monster Raving Loony. We did them a lot, those sessions of netball-throwing chat. A long phase; you loved it so much. No idea how it came about – it just evolved. I would lark around, doing funny throws: under one leg; another from behind my back. The metronome of ball-to-hand, ball-to-hand. Dad to daughter, daughter to dad. Back in Rev's church, I am lightly stroking my arm with my fingertips. My skin sensitivity feels heightened, sitting here listening to her incantations, and my touch traces tingling lines. When I swallow, it sounds loud and deliberate. I can smell faint traces of incense. There's a deep peace. I could be in heaven.

Stories. We have to have our stories. Prof's: the capacity for therapy to heal psychological and emotional wounds. Rev's: the victory of love over hate. Zambo's: peace over war. Mine? I don't know. I'm not quite sure. The power of art to create beauty out of the very worst?

Rev's silence stretches on, inviting contemplation. Merc is next to Zambo. Tears have slid on to his cheeks. Hearing his son Mark's name. I'm not perturbed – there's so much crying goes on in this group, and it's mostly in Rev's sessions.

Spiritual wounds. Letting it out will do him good. He'll have no idea what his own story might be yet – he's still in the shock of the blitzkrieg. Maybe that will be it. Something like the Blitz. The grim determination of a bombarded nation not to succumb. Heroic Spitfire and Hurricane pilots, paltry in number, defying what should have been insuperable odds.

Angel is on Merc's other side. I watch as she puts out a hand and rests it on his good arm. He glances, gives her a weak smile, and shakes his head once, as if to say what-am-I-like? She gives him a quiet smile back. Another story beginning to unfold: love in the midst of trauma.

Rev is speaking again, she hopes no one will be offended, but she would like to say the central prayer of her faith. There are nods, and grunts of permission; no one demurs. She begins. Our Father, who art in heaven, hallowed be thy name. Thy kingdom come, thy will be done, on earth as it is in heaven.

The opening lines roll over me. Her voice has an affecting sincerity. I can almost reach out and touch her belief. She's so sure that her god has this, that in the fullness of his time he will bring resolution. I wish I had her faith. Forgive us our trespasses, as we forgive those who trespass against us. And lead us not into temptation but deliver us from evil. Amen.

I can't ever forgive what she's done!

It's Blaze speaking. Shouting, actually. He's sat next to me but my attention has been on the other side of the circle. Suddenly I'm tuned into him and I can feel his agitation. Now I'm aware of it, I realise I must have been sensing it earlier, while Rev was praying, but unconsciously I tuned it out. I turn to look at him; he's staring at Rev, his hands braced on his knees.

What she's done? It's unforgivable!

There's an embarrassed silence, some people looking at Blaze, others looking at their laps. But he has to be allowed space to speak. His court appearance went as I knew it would. Prohibited steps order banning any contact with his children, pending the outcome of a Cafcass report that will take months to complete. When finally it comes in, I can predict the contents: it will note that no evidence has been discovered to support the allegations made against him. An absence of evidence. And it will also note, with portentous emphasis, that his children's expressed wishes and feelings are to have nothing more to do with their dad. The damage will have been done.

I know, Blaze, Rev says, her voice cutting across the curdled air. It seems impossible just now. Forgiveness is long and difficult. But if we don't let go of what's been done, then bitterness will consume us.

Blaze gives a snort.

We owe it to our children, Rev says, to be whole, happy parents when they do eventually come.

And where's all your praying got you, then? Blaze's tone has an unpleasant edge. It hasn't brought your kids back, has it? Your god's not done you any favours, has he?

I flinch on Rev's behalf. Her daughter and son, eighteen and sixteen, still blocking her, still returning unopened the cards and presents at Christmas, and birthdays, and exam times. The school won't communicate with her any longer, either; says the children don't want them to.

No, she says to Blaze, her voice measured, He hasn't brought them back yet. But He gives me strength to carry on. And He gives me wisdom as to what to do.

Respond to rejection with acceptance. Hatred, with love. Blows, with the other cheek. Her favourite bible story has become the prodigal son. How she yearns for that sweet soul-healing, the day she gets to welcome them home.

I can't believe you people! Blaze is on his feet now, gesticulating. All sat here, just accepting what's happened. What's *wrong* with you? You should be out there, banging on doors, leaving no stone unturned, doing everything you can to save your kids. Not sitting around bleating about forgiveness and stuff, and lighting poxy candles. For fuck's sake!

I look to Prof to take a lead, Zambo even, but they're just sitting there, as if weighing his words. The atmosphere, so calm and contemplative, now fizzes and froths, like a massive rock's been slammed into a pond. I'm his mentor. I feel some responsibility.

The thing is, Blaze, I tell him, we've all been exactly where you are, and there's nothing you can do. I know you won't want to hear that, but it's true. No one recognises what's happening to our children – none of the people who should – they simply don't believe such things can happen, it's not in their worldview. Their whole system is geared around kids' wishes and feelings – and none of them has the first idea how easily those can be corrupted and skewed.

Me, standing on that night-time landing, flannel pyjamas, listening to Ma downstairs retching and vomiting and moaning with yet another sickening migraine. Fearing she was going to die, just like Pa had died. *Pleading* with God to take me instead. Those were my sincerest wishes and feelings. I desperately wanted to die, because that way she would live. There's no rationality in a young mind when it comes to attachment figures. Nothing but magical thinking.

I've had it! Blaze yanks his jacket off the back of his chair. My lawyer, he says, turning to look at us again, my lawyer says there have been cases, cases where judges have seen through this kind of shit!

Sure. Finally, Zambo speaks – he takes a keen interest in legal affairs. There's Parker in the High Court, and Macur at the Court of Appeal. But they're in London, and they're at the cutting edge of things. Out here in the sticks, in the family courts, they're decades behind. Art's right: you haven't got a hope in hell.

Blaze pushes roughly past me. I listen to his footsteps as he leaves. Oddly, they do echo. I think about going after him, but it would only aggravate things. He needs time to cool down, at the very least. Maybe that is the path he'll have to follow. Maybe only by dashing himself against the blinkered legal system will he finally accept the reality. I don't think he's ready for what we do.

To be honest, it's a relief that he's gone. The turbulence in the air seems to subside a little. I won't give up on him, not unless he wants me to. But it's a journey he's on, and he'll have to spend as long on each stage as it takes. I do get it. Every now and then, even after I'd come to understand it all pretty well, I used to get times when I'd worry I wasn't doing the right thing. Fantasies of finding enlightened judges, Cafcass people, lawyers; the gnawing feeling that I was letting you down by not keeping at it relentlessly. But the reality would soon reassert itself: so many others on the forum, up and down this country, elsewhere in the world, all finding the same accursed thing. Zambo says it's like Aids. How, to begin with, doctors just kept dealing with the weird illnesses that they could see in front of them – the Kaposi's, the pneumocystis,

151

the whole-body thrush. It took a long while for some bright spark to say: hang on a minute. More years to work out what was underlying it. Still longer for that knowledge to disseminate around the globe. The trauma for you of ongoing court battles, repeated interviews with social workers, everyone prodding and probing you, trying to work out what was really going on. And you trying to study, equip yourself for your future. It wouldn't have been the right thing to have done.

Rev has a portable CD player beside her chair. She reaches down and presses play. Choral voices, male monks, chants from somewhere called Taizé. Some semblance of peace is restored. Behind her, on the wall beyond the altar, Jesus hangs on his cross, looking on. I stare at him awhile. Rib cage straining, sinews taut like ropes in his nailed-on arms. Son of God, or preternaturally enlightened man – either way, he was ahead of his time. Born into a world where power alone talked. Where the law itself prescribed vengeance – eyes for eyes, teeth for teeth. Murders, even, for murders. Could I do what he did? Find understanding and forgiveness for people who'd scourged the flesh off my back, spat on and mocked me, driven lengths of iron through my limbs and hoisted me aloft to suffocate under my own weight? I really don't think so. Prof says he was the original psychotherapist, his talk of god's grace a metaphor for the compassion and self-compassion we all so desperately need. Zambo says he wasn't a lone voice. He can rattle off a whole load of Ancient Greek myths that told the same story – that the only way to end cycles of violence is for someone somewhere to find it in them to forgive. To wax that moon. Either way, he was one mighty figure, that Jesus. I give him a silent nod of respect. He stares back, unblinkingly.

Rev's Taizé chant comes to an end. She winds up by

getting us to write the names of our missing children on Post-it notes, which she then invites us to burn in the candles' flames. Not to cremate, you understand. To send you, in the smoke, somewhere better, somewhere else. Finally some verses from the Old Testament: Do not fear, for I am with you; do not be dismayed, for I am your God. I will strengthen you and help you; I will hold you with my righteous right hand.

I find I know it well enough by now to say along with Rev in my head, replacing the word God with Dad. Like a solemn promise.

We wish Angel and Merc a good evening, and I go with them to the heavy wooden doors at the far end of the nave. I linger for a moment, watching their retreating backs as they cross the dark car park. They get into Angel's white Focus, and drive off together. Blaze's MX5 is nowhere to be seen: he's driven off into the night. I shut the door and turn the key.

Well, that was fun, Rev says when I rejoin the others, who are stacking the visitors' chairs and sorting the table out.

Don't be too hard on him, I say. I think: I wonder where Blaze is right now? Whether he's roaring his sports car along narrow lanes, the powerful engine giving voice to his rage, his frustration, the dazzling headlights greening night-black hedges to either side. He's in the pits just now. I remember nights like that, unable to sleep, my mind turning-turning, going out driving for the sake of driving, accelerating hard through some village or other and wondering what it would be like not to turn the wheel at the bend up ahead, ploughing into the high stone wall instead. A way to end the pain and grief.

It's the anger, Art, Prof tells me. He needs to find some constructive outlet. Is there anything you can do?

Boxing would be good, I think, or a martial art, but I'm

not into either of those. I think about the wood for the stove in my sitting room, how a session splitting logs with an axe leaves me spent and tiredly relaxed. I don't know, I tell Prof, I'll have a think. I'm sure I can sort something out.

How about Merc, Prof asks Zambo. How's he?

Zambo is holding a stack of chairs, about to take them through to the parish room. Oh, he's struggling, he says, he's had some nasty texts of late. Zambo rests his load down and tells us what's been happening for Merc. How his son has started replying to messages with declarations of hatred. That's one thing I'm thankful for. Most of our clan get vilification and insults – Prof, Rev and Zambo have all been on the receiving end of tirades from their children at one time or another. There was the low-grade disrespect during your time of wavering, back when you were still managing to come occasionally to Drake Avenue – calling me rigid, accusing me of ranting at you, putting the phone down on me when I called you up – but not much more than a normal teenager might do. After I lost you, all I ever got was impenetrable silence. I know you denigrated me to others – I gleaned that from teachers, and from your sister; and Mummy delighted in telling me how much you hated me in her occasional scraps of correspondence. Prof reckons your lack of direct derision is a good sign – that while you've split me off, you haven't buried me as deeply as many kids do. She says it's like you're just the other side of the wall, listening.

Merc, though. It must be soul-destroying, the first time your child starts savaging you.

Prof's ahead of the game. It'll be tough, she tells Zambo, next time he's due to visit – it could be quite a critical moment. I picture Merc, latest gift in his one good hand, sitting in that armchair while Mark hurls abuse at him, the smug women either side not bothering to disguise their delight. Perhaps you could accompany him when he goes, Prof suggests to Zambo, at least sit in the car outside?

Zambo nods and says it's a good idea. He picks up the chairs again and heads through the connecting door to the hall.

And Angel? Prof asks Rev.

Surprisingly buoyant, Rev says, her hands full of extinguished candles. She's got a birthday coming up, but she seems to be doing remarkably well in spite of that.

Prof shakes her head. That worries me, too, she says. It's almost like she's in denial.

I laugh. I don't think it's denial she's in, I say. And I tell them about Angel and Merc having come in the one car.

Prof's not happy, but neither Rev nor I share her concern. It's like two shipwreck survivors, Prof tries to explain, they're adrift in high seas and they should be hanging on to floating debris, not each other. If one goes down, they'll both drown.

Who's drowned, Zambo asks, coming back into the church.

No one, Prof tells him. Not yet. And I hope no one's going to.

FOUR

Horse whisperer

I HEAD DOWN from Carfax, St Aldate's church down there on the right somewhere, some uptempo praise song escaping its doors, reaching up the street like a promise of salvation. Rev, with her love of God, her belief in Jesus and all that he had to teach. I pass the huge oak doors into Christ Church, the ranks of people waiting for buses at the stops there. I feel unable to reach you. Was it too much, what we saw on our last flight: Billy, triangular life; Mummy, you, me? Have you retreated somewhere into the maze of Oxford's streets, never again to be seen? I will myself airborne, craving the intoxicating freedom of the sky, wishing we could once again be coruscating through that crisp clear blue. But all I feel is heavy, earth-bound; my feet are made of clay.

Forty-five minutes to go. There is still so much I want to show. As I walk, I try to summon you from out of the fabric of this city. But all I can sense is your absence. It is as though you have utterly withdrawn, back to your digs, back to your lectures. Back to the life you have now, closed off and walled off and letting no one too far in, least of all me. What was it that resonated? What set your Tacoma Narrows Bridge buckling, the ground under your feet pitching and yawing? The *Your daddy no longer loves me?* The WE ALL LOVE YOU! card? The guilt-induction of that ruined Mother's Day? A glimpse of the triangular life, and an inkling of the way you became triangulated, too?

I think I know what's going on; I think I know why you have become unreachable again. Splitting, that's what Prof calls it. According to her, it would have been the only way you could defend your juvenile psyche from the intolerable conflicts that were ripping it asunder. The only way you could survive the cauldron that your childhood became. Black and white thinking. Mummy all good. Daddy all bad. Is any of this ringing true? Mummy, hoisted aloft on to that plinth, worshipped as the poor victim struggling against all odds to make it through. Me, boxed up, nailed shut, buried in a pit under a thick layer of concrete poured glutinously from the mixer and soon set firm, the site of the interment marked by a wooden cross bearing the one-word legend Bastard. So I needn't ever be thought of again – except to hawk spit in my general direction.

Now though. Have those hard-driven nails started to work loose? Has your bridge been set resonating; is that concrete cracking? If so, as the ground begins to quake, the statue of Mummy, up there on its pedestal, its plaque inscribed with a simple Poor Me, will be beginning to tilt, threatening to topple. Even now, perhaps, you've rushed over to it; you have clasped it in your arms and are steadying its great weight, desperate to prevent what you have for so long felt it was your responsibility to prevent: Mummy's shattering, Mummy's disintegration. Am I right? Then how about this. At one and the same time, in a feat most circus acrobats would give a lot of money to be able to pull off, you must somehow be managing to stamp down hard on the upheaving concrete, trying to keep my grave from bursting open, endeavouring to prevent my ghoulish exhumation.

I'm so sorry, I know it's hard. Believe me, I mean no harm.

What I say is said out of love, a dad to his precious daughter, however painful it may be to hear. It seems to me that there is pain at the very core of your being – no matter which version of truth you espouse – and that can never now be avoided. But it is far better that the pain you feel arises from that which actually happened. That way you can one day set yourself free.

Have I overstepped the mark? Who am I to tell you how to be free? Seven years – chapters and chapters of your life that have been a closed book to me. I've so little idea what story has been written there. Nor is it for me to know what twists and turns you might author in future volumes. All I want is to give you material you might otherwise never see. It's for you to decide whether to incorporate it into your narrative, or whether instead to scrunch it and ball it and discard it in the wastepaper bin.

I'm suddenly aware of a young woman right in front of me, coming up St Aldate's the other way. We stop abruptly and do that thing, each of us stepping aside to let the other pass, both going the same way simultaneously. To the right. To the left. I give a little laugh, remain where I'm standing, and sweep a theatrical arm to usher her through. She gives me a grateful smile, beguiling in its generosity.

Something about the encounter, its good nature and simple humanity. I find myself floating up from my body, up past Old Tom in his tower, sneaking an aerial peek of Christ Church's bowling green quads. Airborne once more, I keep a renewed optimism in check: despite a careful scan of the sky, you aren't with me. It's pointless going solo, a joyride devoid of meaning. I cruise like a Zeppelin above the parkland of Christ Church's fabled meadow, mirroring the routes of the gravelled paths that meander beside the tributaries to the Thames, hoping against hope that you will appear. Below me, rare-breed cattle dot the fields, mouths bent to the ground, intent on cropping the grass. Still you are nowhere to be seen. Eventually, becalmed, I turn in a gentle arc, start heading back towards St Aldate's and my arm-ushering body, there to resume my terrestrial progress. This, I decide, must have been a self-indulgent lift off, a wistful yearning for something that will not be.

But then I make you out, I'm sure of it. No more than the faintest of condensations in the pale blue way out to the east of the city. You, too, are moving slowly, creeping across the sky, as if weighed down by all you have seen. Not a hint of the lightning-bolt fizz and zing of our recent encounters. But you are here, you are here. I feel a tidal surge of love wash through me: how impossible it must be for you to leave the ground, what with how unstable it has become. Yet you have done that exact thing.

My mood lifts a little, bubbles of optimism rising despite the gravity of where we have been. I reverse my arc and start towards you, aiming to intersect your path. As I approach, you hold your course – not a hint of veering away. I join you in a loose formation, keeping a respectful distance, mindful of your soberness despite the brightness of the day.

What is your mood? I try to sense it. Resignation? Depression? Or resolution to continue this journey that we have started? You answer by your actions, sticking a hundred yards from my wing, gradually gathering momentum as I start to pick up speed. Certain that you're here for the duration, I accelerate still further, sure now of what it is you ought next to see. North over Oxfordshire, across the border with Gloucestershire – somewhere about there we breach the sound barrier, our sonic booms startling the sibilant air, one after the other in quick succession.

I'm searching forwards, probing the undulating hills, seeking out our destination, when suddenly I see movement. There, below us, beetling along the ribbon of road: my old car, that clapped out Peugeot of your childhood. Amazing. I swoop like a sparrowhawk after its prey. It's a hot day, back then, unseasonably so – the car windows are wound down; I've never owned anything with air con. I fly alongside, gauging my moment, then barrel roll myself inside.

A sudden end to the buffeting. I look across to see you slooping similarly through the gap between glass and frame of my driver's door. We slip noiselessly into the back. It could do with a good valet, this vehicle: discarded crisp packets, dried up mud marks in the footwells, sketch pads and car park tickets and newspapers littering the rear seat.

Pay no heed to the debris, our weightlessness will not damage anything. Sit with me. No need to fasten your safety belt – you cannot be harmed, even were a crash to occur. You settle yourself behind the driver's seat, the back of my younger head all of me that you can see. I do likewise on the passenger side, behind eleven-year-old you. Your long blonde hair tied back in a pony tail. Dressed in your favourite jeans and Fat Face hoodie. You're excited – you're out for the day with your daddy. This is your birthday treat we're going to. The road noise is thrumming, you find it hard to make out what we're saying, child-you and me, as we chatter our way along. The details don't matter – all I'll say is, you're full of news from your first term at senior school.

We thread up the big trunk road that takes us further into Gloucestershire. On past rolling Cotswold hills, though wisteria-fringed villages. I don't have a sat nav, not back in those days: you've got the map open on your lap and are helping me to find our way. A couple of wrong turns but it doesn't matter, we should still have time. Eventually, down an unpromising B road, we see signs for Hartpury College.

It's an amazing place. Who would have thought there could be such a thing, nestling in the countryside between Cheltenham and Monmouth and Wales beyond? A huge campus, multiple sports fields, enormous barns, rows of stabling ranged round sizeable yards. Here people come to study animal husbandry, outdoor pursuits, equine management. You're bowled over by it, child-you; you start wondering aloud if this might be the sort of place you would eventually come to. Your head full of dreams about a career in the equestrian world.

Today, though. Today we're here on a jolly. Today we've come to see a special show.

Our tickets admit us to a stadium the size of Olympia. Follow us as we go past the programme sellers, up the scaffolded staircase, arriving at the top to find a view of a vast sawdusted arena. The buzz from a couple of thousand people eager to be entertained rises to meet our ears. Stay close as we make our way down to our seats – I'm checking our ticket stubs to identify the right place. Ephemeral you and I perch ourselves cheekily on the laps of a couple from Worcestershire who happen to be occupying the row behind child-you and me. It's OK, don't worry about them; we weigh precisely nothing, and we're entirely transparent. We won't do anything to spoil their view.

Look at you there, made-up young girl that you are, a bit too small for the seat you're occupying. Eleven years old.

I've bought us a big pack of Minstrels. You're munching on them while taking in the sights: the brightly coloured poles arranged like a showjumping course, the areas of fencing and the swathes of blue plastic laid out in the ring below.

Then it's time. Some man's voice comes booming from the PA. Ladies and gentlemen! Girls and boys! Announcing what a great pleasure it is to welcome to the UK none other than the legendary Monty Roberts. Known to millions as the Horse Whisperer.

You've read his book cover to cover. You've even tried out some of his methods on ponies you get to borrow. If it were possible, you would want to be him.

He looks curiously diminutive from this vantage. Must be about seventy. Boots and chaps. Stetson on his head. Waving to the crowd, acknowledging the applause. Striding the arena, his voice broadcasting from a headset microphone. The first horse, he tells us, the first horse tonight is called Charlie. Charlie's come all the way from Northumberland, his owners desperate to see if Monty can do anything to conquer his dread of water.

Dutifully, Charlie is led around by his mistress in a real-time Before photo. Whenever they approach any of the wide sheets of blue tarpaulin, Charlie shies and scitters and digs his hooves in. The power of the animal; his owner cannot move him, no amount of cajoling can hold sway. No way is Charlie putting a hoof anywhere near something that even resembles a stream or a big puddle. Again and again he does it, till the entire audience is convinced of the strength of his phobia, and how impossible it must be ever to ride him in open country.

Then Monty goes to work. He takes Charlie into a

fenced-off circle in the centre of the sawdust ring, and sets him to trotting round and round the perimeter. He has a whip, Monty – standing in the middle of that circle, his body swivelling to track Charlie's progress – but it goes nowhere near the young gelding. He gives the occasional crack on the floor, though, any time Charlie starts to come in towards him. Running commentary: Notice the posture of Charlie's head and neck – they're upright, proud. Charlie is thinking he's dominant; Charlie is thinking it's his herd. But every time he veers closer to Monty, he's sent away with a whipcrack and a sharp cry and an arm flail. Trotting on he goes, back close to the fencing, round and round the miniature ring.

Horses, Monty tells us, fear nothing more than being separated from the herd. Survival depends on numbers, the protection only a group brings. What I'm doing at the moment is casting Charlie out, he says. I'm abandoning him. He's starting to get really worried – there are bound to be wolves and bears and untold other monsters out there, all eager for a horse-meat meal.

In Charlie comes again, head held high, mane rippling. Crack! Yah! Out to the perimeter once again.

What I'm looking for, Monty tells us, his voice filling the spellbound space, is a change in his body language. Watch for him dipping his head. That's how he'll tell me he's decided to submit. That's how he'll tell me he's got too scared.

On trots poor Charlie. Look at yourself. You're rapt in the moment. Even the Minstrels are forgotten.

Crack! Yah! Out he goes again.

Then, just as predicted, a change. Charlie ducks his head down, neck as graceful as a swan's. Once, twice. As soon as he sees it, Monty hides the whip behind his back, and his voice starts to croon unintelligible things, his tone one of welcome, of drawing in. Charlie turns, slows to a walk, approaches this strange human, head bowed, and stands there while Monty strokes his neck and his muzzle, the two of them bonded in the centre of that ring.

As soon as you see it, Monty tells us, as soon as you see the submission, you welcome the horse into the herd. It's instant reinforcement. He's now accepted you as the leader. It's what I call Joining Up.

Look at us. We're giggling, you and I, as Monty now leads Charlie up to stretch after stretch of blue plastic, and the horse meekly crosses each one. It is amazing. The absolute turn-around. The way Monty has completely changed Charlie's be-haviour. Applause strikes up; the audience is delighted. Just to demonstrate how completely Charlie now trusts him, Monty finishes with a flourish, taking the unperturbed animal along the entire length of one of the pretend rivers, Charlie at his shoulder the whole way. What an After photo. It's extraordi-nary, how rapidly this reluctant paddler has been won over. It's as though he's now eating out of the palm of Monty's hand. He is completely unaware of the power of his muscles, the sheer mass of his body, of how he could knock this puny human flying should he choose to. It's as though he is under Monty's spell.

Come, let's away, let's lift ourselves as feathers from the laps of the delighted Midlanders in the seats behind our erstwhile selves. It's astounding stuff – we could stay longer; perhaps you would like to. Perhaps you would like to relive the other amazing sights we saw that day. Another mare, Nancy, scared rigid by the sight of a horsebox, utterly refusing to go inside the enclosed space, in which she would be trapped, cornered, vulnerable. Then seeing her being led up and down the ramp, in and out, going at a trot such was her new-found eagerness to oblige once Monty had done his joining up on her. Or that young colt, Thunder, pathetically spooked by plastic bags, transformed in just a few short minutes into the epitome of unperturbed cool when confronted by their rustling strangeness.

The power of that short-arsed Californian magician – no wonder he's achieved such international fame. Most people training horses do so through fear. They know they have to be dominant, so they assert themselves with pain and punishment. But fear breeds fear, which merely stokes the phobias. How much more powerful is Monty's method. He has studied the nuances of horse psychology and behaviour. His dominance is wrought through joining up – through love and acceptance – underscored by the terrible threat of being cast out from the herd; of being abandoned, alone. He uses this awful power for good, of course, helping his equine charges to overcome their irrational fears and to grow. In that, it is akin to good parenting. But none of us is in any doubt that, were he to be so inclined, he could get these joined-up horses to do things that were damaging and harmful. That if he were so minded, Monty could just as easily cast malevolent spells.

Back we fly, returning to the Oxford of now. As we retrace our path, approaching once again the idyllic Thames Valley, I try to read you, arrowing alongside. Your mood feels reflective, contemplative, almost as though you are no longer here, though your vapour trail tells otherwise. You feel calm to me; still – despite your air speed. How much memory do you have of these moments, these childhood experiences? Did you remember even the first thing about that day? We don't tend to, not looking back from an adult age. Sporadic childhood recollections, random events, glimpsed as though through lulls in a heat haze. How different for me as a parent; these things are burned into my brain. And perhaps I have held on to them more tightly than most, flotation points to cling to as I have been progressively erased.

We part company over Boars Hill, our trails diverging as they ever must do. My heart feels heavy – for some reason, this feels like the last flight I may ever do with you. It's your placidity, I decide – it's as though the wind has abruptly dropped, and the Tocoma Narrows Bridge is untroubled once more. Back at Christ Church, I put in a final flourish for my own sake, rocketing upwards like a Eurofighter, clearing the college, then diving vertically. Straight back into myself again.

∗∗∗

My ushering arm falls to my side. The young woman – to the left, to the right – has long since passed. I start to walk, on past the police station, inside which play out myriad dramas of all our clashing truths. More Zambo's and my territory than Prof's or Rev's. I head nearer our rendezvous, contemplating the horse whispering that was done on you.

Once I'd moved into that rented place on Drake Avenue, your initial fury thawed. Your sister let you have the better bedroom, even though she won the toss. It had been made by joining together two smaller rooms; you planned to put a backless wardrobe across the narrow part in the middle, to create your own Narnia. You went with me to Tesco and helped choose all the kit I would need to start again – kettle with cool blue light when boiling, four-slot toaster, cooking utensils. You loved the idea of a Breville. Back at the house, unpacking our spoils, you stood in the kitchen-diner and said how much you liked it: it reminded you of a Center Parcs villa, with its sliding glass doors and long horizontal windows looking out over the combe.

Then you wouldn't come for weeks at a time. Or if you came you would have forgotten some schoolbook or some bit of games kit, anything that meant Mummy would have to come and collect you. Me and your sister left alone. Your grandma came from Merseyside on a visit. You didn't show.

You were being met with such grief. Impossible dilemmas, in which you were forced to choose. That Peak District trip with Gerry and his gang: your face crumpling, shoring up, crumpling again. The one time you managed to come for Christmas you arrived with eyes reddened, your face tear-streaked, utterly rattled by Mummy's disintegration when you parted in the car. Days when you came after school and no sooner had you made it up to your room than she'd be on Skype, tying you up for ages telling you – what? How much she missed you? How desolate she felt when you weren't around?It seemed that now I was no longer rescuing her, no longer tipping pint after pint of love into the heart of her, she had to find a new supply. You.

Making your bed once. Finding the note under your pillow. Her handwriting. Telling you how a mother and daughter are made from the same whole, how they are two parts that nothing can ever separate.

How did it make you feel? Wrenched apart, I suspect. How often I would find you, lying on your back on your bed, netball flicking. Hands, feet, hands. Hands, feet, hands. And – I imagine this; and I understand it, if so – amidst all the turmoil, a feeling of being special. Two-and-a-half-year-old you, sat on the floor of that Chatsworth Road sitting room, in your OshKoshB'Gosh dungarees, tracking her exit as she abandoned you in favour of your sister, your arms slowly falling from their carry-me supplication. That attachment trauma, running like a fault line through the core of your being. The pages of that tiny notebook, filled with neat rounded fountain pen writing. Trying to work out what you were experiencing. How your sister seemed to get everything right, and you to get everything wrong.

Now this. It seemed to me that Mummy would disintegrate each time you left her to come to mine. Were you in genuine fear as to what she might do while you were gone? How were things when you returned? Perhaps no words were actually spoken, but cool withdrawal would have been equally eloquent at voicing the pain you had caused. And all those times you chose instead to stay away from me. I'd hear from your sister the things you'd been up to: shopping trips, canoe expeditions, visits to the indoor climbing wall. Was this what Prof calls love bombing – the showering of gifts and affection every time it was Mummy that you chose? If so, it must have felt like the rediscovery of your god-girlhood. Of course you would have felt special. Golden in fact. Of course it would have felt good.

It strikes me you were like Charlie, Nancy, Thunder. Cast out. Accepted. Cast out. Adored. Push pull. Push pull. Push pull.

How did it happen for me? Differently than it did for you, but seeing something of my own Achilles heels may help. That very thought. Rwanda, reports of the genocide there, being chilled to read how the Hutus, faced with such overwhelming numbers of Tutsis to kill, would machete-slice their Achilles tendons, rendering them unable to walk let alone run away, so they could be finished off at leisure. Hobbling them at a stroke. Rendering them at their mercy. Mercy. Mercy me.

To begin with, the perpetrators were people in her own life. Ted, Gloria, her sister; various boyfriends and friends before my time. Then there was Ellen at work, of course, the beginnings of my being reeled on to the triangle. A couple of neighbours near our Grandpont home. The first one I witnessed up-close, though, was her oldest friend from college, Katy with the double-barrelled surname. I met her a few times, her and her dentist husband up in Leyburn, on our trips round Yorkshire. She struck me as a nice lass. Then, when Mummy was three-months pregnant with you, an excited girly phone call, telling Katy the news. I still don't know exactly what was said: some remark from Katy about how Mummy must let her help choose names for you. The kind of innocent, pally thing anyone might say. Not for nothing are they called triggers. That tiny movement, barely perceptible; the power of the resultant explosion. The cold-blooded fury, once the receiver had been put down. Fulminating. How Katy had always been domineering, controlling; how she'd never allowed Mummy to run her own life. Tickertape chuntering, dust motes dancing. Katy: unwitting screen for a past-times show reel. She was cut off without a backwards glance. There were a couple of hurt, puzzled letters from Katy over the next few months, which went straight in the bin. An unreturned message on the answerphone. Then she never heard from Katy again.

I didn't know their history, didn't really know Katy from Adam. Nor did I know Ellen. Nor the neighbours. Each instance in isolation seemed plausible enough. But then it started to happen with people I knew.

Julie, an old friend of mine from Wirral days, come for an R&R weekend after her partner's tragic early death. She called Mummy a bitch to her face, when I wasn't around. She had the hots for me; Mummy was in the way of her ambition to have me for her own, now she was single again.

My ma, your grandma, hot-footing it down from the Mersey to meet you after you were born. When I was out: Ma telling Mummy she wasn't looking after me properly, wasn't cooking me proper food. And Ma trying to prise you off her, take you in your pram round the park, because she didn't think Mummy was fit to be a parent.

Visiting Uncle Gerry and Aunty Gaby when your sister was just getting good at walking. Me and Ger out for a lunch-time pint, so we didn't see Gaby laughing when cousin Tom kept pushing your toddler sister to the ground. Gaby telling Mummy to get over it, it's just what kids do.

Going to Lancashire to stay with Mark, my oldest pal from art school, and Sal and their kids, up in their Clitheroe home. How he made a flagrant pass at Mummy while we were out walking, the two families together. How dare he! She couldn't bear the thought of his creepy lechery. She couldn't bear to ever see him again.

I knew these people inside out, Julie, Ma, Gaby, Mark. I tried to get her to see reason, tried to broker understanding of what was the truth – the stuff that had actually happened. But I was taking their side over hers, always believing my family and friends, when she knew, she knew, she knew. Where was my loyalty; where was the support she needed; where was the support she was due? Stone cold fury. Implacable withdrawal.

And the doubts creep in. Mothers-in-law can be tricksy, can't they? My ma wasn't perfect. Who knew what could've got said when I wasn't in the room. And, way back as a teenager, I'd carried a torch for Julie; maybe some of the old stuff had somehow seeped through. Gaby - well, we none of us like to admit when our own child is up to no good. Mark, though. I just couldn't see it. The kind of guy you'd trust with your life. I'd been on a residential with him one time, sixteen artists and a couple of tutors cloistered in an old farmhouse for a week. There'd been a girl there, a foxy sculptor from Brighton, came on really strong to him. Said he could have her and no one need ever know. He told her no thanks, he wouldn't do that to Sal.

Perpetrators to her victim. I was to play the rescuer role. And if I wouldn't play it, then there was only one other vertex available on that triangle for me. Perpetrator, too. Only she could be the victim.

She never vocalised ultimatums. It seems that is not her style. Everything must be deniable, everything re-interpretable. But as I tried to maintain those friendships, those family relationships, all there was, was this incredible emotional bombardment. How could I even think of doing that to her? Did she mean nothing to me? She hated it, felt undermined and devalued that I would even contemplate having anything to do with them, after what they had done to her. Grief, grief, grief. So in the end, I did my own cutting off, the only way I could find to lessen the pressure, dampen the tension. The only way it seemed possible to get through. No more visits from grandma, no more of us going to stay on the Wirral - just meet-ups for a couple of hours at a time at galleries and museums in Birmingham, Manchester, so at least she could still get to see your sister and you. Gerry and Gaby and their brood, not seen from one year to the next, the occasional strained lunch at our place should they happen to be passing through. Mark, my old best mate, reduced to sporadic phone calls. Julie left completely alone to get on with her grief.

Why the fuck didn't I get out? Round and round my head it goes. It gets me nowhere. Condensing it, telling it like this, it seems so bloody obvious. In real-time, though, it happened so slowly, so incrementally. And by the time the patterns finally became clear, and I saw the doubts for what they truly were, I was well and truly trapped.

Because by then there was your sister.

Because by then there was you.

※

At the bottom of St Aldate's, I cross Folly Bridge. The Head of the River, scene of many a summer drink, is on my left, behind it the gates to Christ Church Meadow, favourite haunt for an evening stroll. As I go, I reach out with my mind, try to find you wherever you might be. An unanswering silence. The Thames stretches away down a long straight, boathouses lining the banks like trepidatious bathers, where the eights and the fours and the double- and single-scullers all ply their watery trade.

One year this river froze completely over. This was before you were born, or even conceived. Mummy came out with her camera. Two amazing photographs. Bottom-up rowing boats, overwintering on the bank, shot from above from this bridge. Their contoured hulls of varied colours – reds, blues, turquoises – all frosted by a light dusting of snow. In another, a line of mallards, waddling across the solid river, each seeming to be balanced on an inverted version of itself, the ice so clear green as to resemble becalmed water, those ducks like faith-filled disciples.

I said she should enter the pictures for a photographic competition. They were both good enough to win. Neither did. But she was happy back then. Back then she would hold me, tell me how I had transformed her world, how unimaginably good things had proved to be. It swelled me with feeling, made me proud of what we were accomplishing, crafting a life of love after the bitterness of all she told me of her past. It seemed to make the cutting off of family and friends a price I just had to pay. I poured love into the heart of her. For a good few years I was able to fill it near enough to the brim.

But the craving for drama is insatiable. Again and again that victim role needs playing out. Fresh perpetrators must come in an eternal stream. Rescue, rescue, she has to have rescue. The rescue that never came for her, back when she had genuine need.

Two Achilles heels, one for each leg. You and your sister. The prospect of losing you. The fear of shattering your world. The need to stay in it, to give you the family you deserved. And my own tickertape chuntering, dust motes dancing. The need to rescue myself from the loss of my own family as I grew.

As for you, once your own family had shattered. Somehow, despite all the joining up I sensed Mummy doing, the relentless push-pull, you seemed to be making it through. That conversation we had in the car, late in the summer holidays during my first year at Drake Avenue. Me explaining the importance of relationships with both your parents, with your wider family, and how relationships need time invested to keep them strong. It was some kind of turning point. Back at school, starting your next year, you proudly showed me the colour code you'd devised so you knew which books to bring when you came to stay. You moved your rabbit down. A pet for the new place. Lady. A massive Belgian giant cross. No one else had wanted her from the shop. You felt sorry for her, bought her for your own, so she would know love and what it meant to belong. We trained her together. Sustained scars on our forearms from habituating her to being handled. Put that harness on her and took her walking round the estate like a puppy on a lead. You became known as the girl with the huge bunny. You quietly enjoyed the local fame.

Still there was pressure. The endless Skype calls, the flurrying texts. For the half an hour before she was due to collect you, you would be hotching about, words tumbling over themselves. Every time the same. Like an alarm clock had gone off inside your head, warning you of the grief that was shortly to come. But you were managing it. You were finding your way through.

For those few months – that September, October, November – it was like I had managed it, too. Broken free to rebuild my life, yet kept the family that was so precious to me. We established rhythms: you and your sister coming every other weekend, every Monday and Tuesday. Dropping you at school, picking you up after, hearing about your days. Cooking for you. Playing board games. Going to the swings. Every week a new DVD in the post from LoveFilm. We decorated my new fridge with words compiled from magnetic letters that had come free with multipacks of Innocent Smoothies. Daddy; your name; your sister's name. I constructed your wardrobe from a pine kit I bought off the internet, it fitted near exactly across the waist of your room. I left the hardboard back off, so you could step from your sleeping area, brush through your hanging clothes, and emerge into the secret study beyond with its bookshelf and its desk and its chest of drawers. We brought Lady indoors, took her with us to Narnia; laughed as she loped around, nose waffling. The rest of the time, when you weren't around, I was working at the unit, and doing my own art in the little reception room I'd turned into a studio. For those few months, life felt good.

But it seems it was intolerable for Mummy. It seems she had to have a supply, had to have someone pouring love into the very heart of her, each and every day. When you were away, did if feel as if her very existence was dissolving? Looking on, it was as if she had sensed your vulnerability; as though she had done everything she possibly could do to have you to herself alone. But it hadn't sufficed. You were becoming more and more like your sister, able to love both your parents at the same time.

Looking back on those few short months, I see us as Twenties' flappers, dancing merrily, twirling our pearl strings, the tassels on our dresses flicking as we go about our moves. The Great War is behind us, we live now in peacetime, we're throwing ourselves into a life that is good. We think of ourselves as the post-war generation. But our smiles are too broad, our Charlestons too fey; we have no idea how history will soon re-label us. We party under a shadow we're not even aware of, that will all too soon render our brief gaiety unbearably doomed.

Them

REV'S WORK IS jubilant, there's no other word. Huge sweeps of helio yellow genuine light, blending into cadmium red orange, all arcing over a cerulean blue sub tinged with dark streaks of phthalo blue. If you're after an interpretation: a choral dawn over a glistering sea. It isn't just the colours - vivid, vibrant - it's the brushwork. Bristles loaded, her arm moves swiftly left to right, left to right, her bangles chinking, as though brooming out canker and cobwebs, leaving gleaming trails of fresh bright paint in her wake. Curtains drawn crisply back, sunlight bursting into a room.

I watch her for a time, both rejoicing in her ebullience and feeling strangely subdued by it. Hers has been the news we've all long craved, and I hadn't anticipated it affecting me the way it has. Just the week before, a text, out of the blue, from her son - sixteen-year-old Sam - after years of silence interspersed with caustic abuse. It said nothing: a simple Hi Mum. And it said everything. Something had shifted, the ground had buckled, the love she'd been indefatigably dripping in was, at last, bearing fruit. How we all dream of this moment with our own. How many YouTube testimonies we have listened to, and wondered when - if - our lost children could possibly do it, too. And now Rev. Sam. It had truly happened.

Events had bewildered. He'd come round that evening straight from school, lots of hugs and tears and I'm-sorrys and please-don't-say-a-words. They were up till midnight, unwrapping newspaper shrouds from around the things of his that she'd carefully stowed once he'd been gone a year. Sharing innumerable do-you-remember-whens? as treasured mementos were unearthed. Like an amazing Christmas. She couldn't believe the speed at which his rejection had cracked and sheared away and fallen to the ground – even though we know this is what so often happens. The authentic child suddenly released.

The thought, for me, of it happening for you. Daring to hope.

At intervals: texts buzzing into Sam's phone like bullets. His father, threatening all-sorts if he didn't come home. Rev's phone vibrating, too, threatening worse. Control. It's all about control. These parents, the gaping wounds inside them, petrified that their child should love any one but them – the harm to them which that would do.

I'm standing behind seated Rev, looking down on her auburn waves, the patch of pale scalp glimpsed at her crown. Her Indian cotton top. The slender shoulders beneath. Shoulders that have borne much. Now facing many new challenges: the precariousness of her son's balance in the aftermath of his daring leap. Whether he will manage to stay upright, or fall back again. What impact the sudden shift might have on her still-lost daughter. How Rev must, to begin with, shield Sam from his father's aggressive desperation – yet, in time, help him to come to understand, and to build a new, different relationship with his dad, if such a thing can be possible. It is never about winning children back. It's about helping to liberate them so they can truly be themselves.

I turn away from Rev, and move towards the next easel. Angel. She'd declared herself devoid of inspiration, so I gave her one of my exercises. She chose an oil pastel, Sennelier Prussian blue, and has been walking it in a continuous line around every inch of the A2, creating intricate patterns like the world's most convoluted maze. At no point, I notice, do her lines cross over themselves – inside Angel is a fearful child, hemmed in by anticipated punishment for breaking rules. A shit time she's had since our last session. Her younger son's birthday, the first since she'd been banned from making any contact. She sent him a card, and a small present, some sort of transformer toy that he's into. Her ex must have been cock-a-hoop; he went straight to the police. She's been served with contempt papers – back to court next week, no idea what the judge will do: a fine, a suspended sentence, but it could even be prison. Rev said her distress was so great that she bit herself hard and long and didn't even stop once she'd drawn blood. I can see the livid arc of teeth marks on her podgy hand as she draws. Imagine that: locked up for showing your child love. For fuck's sake, as Blaze would say.

I look around at the others, working at their easels: Prof, Zambo, Blaze, Merc. They're all immersed, focused eyes or furrowed foreheads as they're absorbed by the projects they've set themselves. By day this space is populated by young men with attachment traumas so damaging, so profound, that they've spiralled right down, their lives mired in the murky sediment at the bottom of the pond. No prospect of getting anywhere near the surface again – if they ever were there in the first place – let alone breaking through and breathing alpine air. My therapy room. What do I really achieve here, though? Small gains, some times. Courtesy of the unit's sympathetic director, and with appropriate security clearances, every couple of months this space becomes the evening venue for my session with our group. Art. Royal road to the unconscious. A place for us parents stranded in the no-man's land of attachment trauma war.

You don't have to have any ability; there's no difference between those who can draw and those who can't. Representation is just one small facet. Colour, texture, juxtaposition, contrast, form, media, white space. Anything can express mood. Even so, Zambo's charcoal sketch is impressively true to life: a huge mane-ruffed male lion, standing atop a rocky outcrop, one paw raised as though about to take a next step, his head inclined gently in regard of the cubs just managing to scrabble to the crest of the rise behind. By contrast, Blaze's piece is abstract, tonal, surprising: overlapping squares of burnt umber, ochre, sienna. After the messiness of Rev's session, I'd expected leaping flames; roaring fire, not embers. But even as I contemplate, I think I understand.

Rev's news – its sweet bitterness has affected us all. The gladness I feel for her makes hope for you both nearer, and at the same time more distant, impossible. Something about someone else breaking the finishing tape when you yourself have indefinite laps still to go. It must be the same for the others. Rev's ex has controlled their children with an admixture of fear and reward – tumultuous anger if they ever even mention their mum; showers of gifts and treats and laissez-faire when they abide by his rules. I wonder how much easier it is for kids caught in that kind of bind to break free – terrorised as they must be by overt rage. Looking on, I'd say Mummy ensnared you in a different kind of mesh, woven from fibres of obligation and guilt. Obligation to worship her; guilt at anything she perceived as betrayal. Fear, too, but – it seems to me, at least – the fear you felt and feel is not about uncontrollable anger. It is fear of her utter disintegration were she to detect any hint of abandonment from you. That's an altogether more diaphanous net – difficult to discern, even more difficult to untangle – adherent and suffocating as spider's silk, drawing ever tighter around your flailing limbs, the more you struggle to be free.

A glance at the wall clock: near enough the two hours gone. We were late starting, Rev bubbling over with her news, so there's been less time for creation. Time. The stuff Zambo tells me, reporting his reading adventures in popular cosmology. How time, which we think of as constant, slows in the region of a gravitational mass. How a twin living up a mountain ages faster than their sea-level sibling. What is time? Our fourth dimension. It seems to pass ever more quickly as we age. We move through it, our lives branching endlessly with every decision and circumstance. Steps that can't be retraced. Maybe myriad other existences unfold in alternative universes – perhaps there is a life in which I lecture in fine art at an Oxford college, where I meet someone else, have different children, or no children at all. A life in which there is no you. Would I want that, a world with so much less heartache? Part of me sings 'My Sweet Lord'. If I'd been given a vision, a clear sight of what the future held for a younger me, would I have swerved away, left Mummy lying on that tartan picnic rug over the road from the Oxford Retreat, wished her the very best of luck with bullying Ellen and the rest of the repetitive victimisation she would experience, grindingly and predictably, until and unless she sorts out the stuff inside her head that makes it all true? No, for your sister. No, for you. But what about for me?

I move on to Prof's easel. Her work I usually find difficult to read. Always pencil. Sometimes just masses of messy scribbles, as though never satisfied with what it was she'd been trying to achieve. It surprises me in some ways, given the orderliness of her mind – though that might be the point. The choice of monochrome fits, though – the antithesis of the drama that has consumed her and her children's lives. Her ex-husband, another attachment trauma victim – the mirror image of the screwed-up father who was emotionally unavailable to Prof when she was a girl. Christ, how the patterns repeat. This evening, Prof's piece is recognisable: a solitary wind turbine. She's tried to give an impression of movement to the blades. Harnessing the wind. I wonder how she's feeling about Rev. Joy, of course. But whether a part of her resents or despairs. Whether in a corner of her heart she wonders why she wasn't the first of us to make a breakthrough. She's the oldest of us by a few years. Her kids are young adults now – the older two, anyway – just like you. Does she fear her ex's indoctrination will prove too powerful, that her love will never overcome? It's a fear I all too often share. She clings to her inside-out knowledge of developmental psychology – that even though we deem people adults at eighteen, the average age to attain fully fledged critical thinking is more like twenty-five. I lay a hand on her shoulder, and give her a smile when she glances up. She's been such an encouragement to each of us at so many times. My own mentor when I joined. I wonder how far down the sands have drained in her personal hourglass. Sometimes, she must need encouragement, too.

I don't talk much during my sessions. I set things up, demonstrate the media available, make hints or suggestions, urge an absence of self-consciousness, then let everyone get on with it. If they ask something, or want to discuss their work, so be it. There can be value in interpretation. It's as though a piece of art becomes an external embodiment, an objective vessel into which emotions are poured and can be talked about at arm's length. But most often simply the process of creation returns the greatest rewards. Some kind of language other than words with which to articulate, process, and release.

Merc I visit last of all. I've been aware of his stillness, how little he has been drawing. If I'm honest, I've been avoiding his easel, apprehensive at what I might find. What he's going through. Last time he visited his son, Mark, the lad just screamed at him: You're an embarrassment! I hate you! I hate having a cripple for a dad! You're a fucking cripple! You're no dad to me at all!

Zambo has been meeting with him between times, enacting our crisis response. Merc's been off work for a couple of weeks now, his sleep shot to kingdom come, his nerves all over the place. I'm sympathetic, I know how it feels, but I'm not sure sick leave is the wisest course. In my darkest months, when the hounds of hell were gnashing at me, fangs trying to gouge my flesh, it was this space here, and the rituals of working with colleagues and my chaotic charges, that kept me sane. Structure. Purpose. Maybe delivering the post doesn't give Merc that. Maybe it's too solitary, too mundane. Even so, I worry about him having so much time on his hands, time to brood on what's being done. He needs location, not dislocation. He needs occupation for his mind.

He gives me a wan smile as I approach, then turns to look once again at his A2. You only need one hand to make art. Even if you're entirely limbless, a brush clenched between teeth will do. A child's stick figure drawing. Round face with banana grin. Sticky out ears and tufty hair. Sausage body. Line-drawn limbs ending in splayed out feet and hand. Two legs, one arm. A boy's-eye view of a cripple.

⁂

The unit is too far from the Half Moon to go for a post-session drink, but the others hang back for a debrief once the newbies have gone. Blaze in his MX5. Cheryl dropping Merc home in her Focus.

It's fucking amazing, I say to Rev.

She grins and looks happier than a person can possibly be.

Where is he tonight? I ask.

Back at mine, she says. Her voice is shot through with exuberance. Playing on his DS and messaging his mates. It's wonderful to see him so free. Back at his dad's he had to be doing chores, or doing things with his dad the whole time, just to make his dad feel important and needed. He had to beg for time to do homework. She shakes her head and gives another grin. She's still getting to grips with the snippets of what his life has been like these past few years.

I have a twinge of misgiving: it must be so tempting, once a child returns, to spoil them, to make them feel *this* is the place to be. Christ knows, I'd find that hard to resist myself. But that would just be playing the same game. It's a tightrope. But; for the chance to walk it.

Prof either reads my mind, or else she has the same thought. She gives Rev a little pep talk about maintaining healthy parenting, enforcing sensible bedtimes and boundaries and meals and shit. Rev's nodding and laughing, like she knows all this, and knows she should be doing it, and swears she will but just now she's so over the fucking moon to have him back that she's just going to roll with it for a precious few days.

I'm kind of worried about Merc, Zambo says. Not to detract from your news, Rev – he holds out a placating hand – it's truly great. But he's troubling me.

Merc's been to the doctor's, Zambo tells us. Flurried consultation, no real connection – left with a sick note, a prescription for antidepressants, and a few tablets of something to help him sleep.

Has he got family, old friends, around? Rev asks. People to be with?

Zambo shakes his head.

What about counselling? Prof asks.

Zambo exhales, short and hard. He doesn't need to speak. We all know how hit and miss that is. I think back to the therapist I tried, shortly after the first anniversary of your disappearance – it's true what they say about how grief resurges. Roland, his name was. I'd gone beyond anger, tearfulness, bargaining; I was dead inside, finding it hard to get up in the mornings, impossible to eat. Unable to muster interest in my own art, let alone the outpourings from my troubled charges in this room. Finally, I went for help. Found Roland on the BACP website. Older, wiser, loads of post-nominals. But so few people understand, even those supposedly qualified. They bring their own interpretations, shoehorn your experience through the holes in the shape-sorter of their own beliefs. Things that look like something else. If you don't know something can happen, you can't even consider it. I remember him, asking me what I thought the future held for you and me. I told him: I wasn't even sure I'd ever see you again. I can picture him, smiling superciliously, smug in his professionalism, reframing your rejection as normal adolescent rebellion, and indicating that he thought the most *fruitful line* for us to work on was my tendency to catastrophise and fear the worst.

I'm going to keep seeing him, Zambo says, but I could use some help.

I could chip in, I volunteer. We've done this before, me and Zambo, shoring up a dad in despair, keeping their head above water until the torrents begin to subside. #drowning-dads. I'd felt that empathic connection with Merc, right from the word go. The rescuer in me would find reward. I picture myself, inviting him round to my small studio in the outhouse behind my home, doing some extra work with him, helping him put flesh, muscle, on his stick-thin cripple-man. Maybe even growing it a new limb.

Did you go with him? Prof asks. That last visit to his son?

Zambo shakes his head. I didn't need to, he says. He said someone else was going to come.

We part with hugs and shoulder slaps, Prof, Rev, Zambo, and me. The core. I lift Rev clean off the floor, so powerful are the feelings that wash through me when I bear-grip her. Prof's session next, in a few short weeks. I wonder what fresh news Rev might bring us then: her daughter back, too, perhaps; her son growing fast in his liberation.

Last to leave, I go round tidying up the therapy room, unclipping A2s from the easels. People are free to take what they draw, but you'd be surprised how often they don't. It's as though the stuff, once out of their hearts, is best left behind. Prof's pencil windmill. Zambo's lion and cub. I pause, admiring it again. A memory: taking you and your sister to *The Lion King*, the stage show of the film you both so loved. Amazing animal costumes, soul-stirring music. The young cub, Simba, being led astray by the evil uncle. The father, Mufasa, always with his son even after he was dead.

I move on, gathering Merc's stick-figure cripple. Blaze's sombre squares. Angel's infernal maze. I feel faint uneasiness. It's been a weird session. I try to put my finger on the cause of my disquiet. It's the debrief, I decide. Normally we discuss all the newbies, Prof taking us through them methodically, one by one. I remember us discussing Merc, how I'm to help Zambo support him. But we didn't mention Blaze or Angel at all. What's true for me must be true for the others: I was so preoccupied with Rev's breakthrough. It's thrown us out of kilter, distracted our focus. It felt inappropriate to dwell on bad stuff when Rev's news has been so good. And it's sent each of us off into brooding about our own lost children. We didn't do what we were supposed to do.

I go to Rev's easel last of all, thinking how cheering it will be to see her joyous seascape one last time. The A2 pad has a blank sheet uppermost. Rev, alone, has taken her artwork home.

I douse the lights and lock my therapy room. I think of you, what you might be doing at that moment. It's late, near enough half-ten. Perhaps you're out at some pub with your mates. Maybe with a boyfriend. Or a girlfriend. I just don't know. Possibly you're tucked up in bed, reading. Or messaging on a group chat, or polishing off some forgotten essay, your room softly lit by a pool of bedside light. Do you think of your dad, alone in those moments? Who is the dad that comes to your mind? Which version of me?

I drop the keys off at security, wish Jake a good night,

and walk through puddles to where my car is parked. All the years our group has been meeting, all the fervent imaginings of reunification, of soul-healing. And now Rev and her son. The dreams can come true.

I blip the lock, and climb in. The dreams can come true.

Me

I DID ART with dying grown-ups, with bald kids with cancer, with Down's Syndrome people living in a supported home. Last placement in my training: adult mental health. Based at the old Littlemore – you might see it if you're on attachment out that way, it's just across from the Warneford. Not that you'd realise it was once a hospital. Once sold off, the developers gave it a fancy facelift and renamed it St George's Park, a way of making things palatable to those purchasing luxury apartments in a former lunatic asylum. No idea why St George; it must be the dragon-slaying thing.

I have this one guy. Barry. I don't know much about him, not when he first pitches up looking bewildered and wrung-out, other than that he's coming in a last-ditch attempt to relieve hideous insomnia. PTSD isn't an accepted concept back then – sure, it's been described several years before in the States, but it takes an interminable time for new understandings to catch on; an eternity till people round the world know such things can actually happen. No one in Oxford has the first idea. All anyone knows about Barry is that whenever he falls to sleep, he wakes soon after, screaming and sweat-soaked from intrusive nightmares. The psychs have tried all manner of drugs, the shrinks have done their talking stuff. Nothing has helped. The terrors are so traumatic Barry can't vocalise them. It's got so bad he doesn't dare drop off anymore – he keeps himself going with constant coffee, Coke, fags, and Pro Plus caffeine. His mind is scrambled. He can no longer manage independent life. Barry has let go his grip, and withdrawn from the world. Barry is going insane.

The first two sessions with him, a few days apart, are painful. He sits there, staring at the easel and the blank A2 for an hour and a half, won't even choose a pastel or a pencil or a stick of charcoal. He's got a fine tremor; it makes the smoke trail up from his cigarettes in wavy lines. His hair is lank. He stinks of BO. I sit like the proverbial citrus fruit. I don't do talking, not unless clients want to. Twice, I discover how long it takes for ninety minutes to tick past.

The third session is more of the same, right up to the last moment. Just as I'm scraping my chair back and getting to my feet, he reaches out and grabs a Caran d'Ache - bismuth green - and draws a Star of David.

That happens a lot. The really powerful thing happens right at the end.

I sit back down, staring at the six-pointed star, my mind in overdrive. It feels like a breakthrough, and I'm so inexperienced I want to know what it means. I remember from his file that he used to be in the army, and suddenly I'm thinking concentration camps, and skin-covered skeletons staggering towards their liberators, and rooms stacked with skulls and bones. But he's too young, he can't have been more than a lad when the war was on. And he's solid Berkshire, not a scrap of Jewish in him.

It's so tempting, to prolong the session, try to tease more out of him, but I remember Peter Lyle's golden rule: never go on. Something occurs in the final minute, that's when it's meant to happen. And never express your own take on an image - that can scupper the whole thing.

So I stand once more. And Barry gets up and leaves.

Next session, a few days later, he walks in and announces he had the first night's sleep in years. He's scrubbed up, too, and has had a shave. I'm blown away, and perplexed too, with no understanding of what's gone on.

We have another half-dozen meetings. Bit by bit, as he daubs seemingly random colours and shapes, always choosing those Neocolor crayons, he tells his story. It's as though in occupying his hands, his mind is at last able to visit memory. He takes himself back decades – things often take years and years to surface – to when he was an NCO, and his troop was camped out in some isolated spot on exercise in Germany. The kind of night that brass monkeys elect to stay indoors. The lot of them staving off the sub-zero temperatures by gathering round a massive campfire. How his senior officer got roaring drunk, and they got into a barney about something he can no longer recall, and somehow in the mêlée Barry gets pushed into the fire and suddenly his uniform's ablaze from top to toe and there's people shouting and trying to pull his burning clothes off him and rolling him on the ground like a flaming carpet. Searing, excruciating, nerve-screeching pain. Eighteen months in a burns unit, multiple operations. You wouldn't know it to look at him: the skin of his face is unharmed. But at one point he draws up his sleeves and shows me his arms: the glassy gnarled scar tissue where once there was supple flesh, hairless and purple and grim.

I let him talk, and I listen. And I watch his movements, frenetic at times, at other times funereal. He works in primary colours, as though back in infants and learning everything again. And all the while, nagging away at me, I'm thinking: why the six-pointed star? The way that unlocked everything.

I never find out, not directly, because I don't think even Barry knows. And it doesn't matter – the transformation is miraculous. Slowly but surely, Barry unfolds into a human being again, his sleeping evermore sound. His consultant seeks me out to express his amazement. At one point, though, I think I see it. Barry has a fleeting memory – his whole body alight, all hell breaking loose around him, and him craning his neck and holding his head up for all he is worth, which somehow keeps it out of the flames. The rest of him is scarred to kingdom come, but he can hide that under clothes. His scalp and his face – that which we show to the world – were saved. What he fixed his eyes on, when he was keeping his head so desperately aloft, was the star-speckled crystal night sky.

End of training, you and your sister four and two. I'd sold a few pieces of my own work, and had one commission – three abstracts based on the curled forms and ginger tones of some North Oxford don's beloved cats – but they'd made nothing more than minor contributions to the family income. A job was needed. I didn't want to leave Oxford, it felt like home, and maybe there would have been something for me there. But Mummy wanted out. It got too difficult for her to stay. There was Clare, another mum down at the far end of Chatsworth Road, once a friend, now turned foe. Ditto someone called Jo. The bitter recitations of their betrayals and bullying. Triangular living. And Mummy's carefully crafted story about her parents being 'no longer around' – told to all who ever asked, to shut out awkward questions as to why you had no grandparents involved. An old acquaintance of hers from Yorkshire came to live a few streets away, the daughter of some friends of Ted and Gloria's. Mummy living in dread of her artful autobiography being exposed.

The triumph with Barry. I'd decided on mental health. The job advertised at the West Country medium secure unit. Working with lads in their late teens, with the most troubled of souls. Attachment trauma writ large. On a predictable conveyor belt: born into abusive, neglectful, dysfunctional families; then to more of the same in children's homes; graduation to young offender institutions then on to prison, with only Broadmoor left to go. There aren't too many jobs going in art therapy, yet I was the only applicant. The four of us upped sticks and moved westwards.

Stevie Buchanan. So far from the Wirral. So far from being Steve, and now with a family of my own. Two precious children. And a marriage that was fast tumbling down. Mummy, no longer any incentive it seemed to keep the cap clamped over the lens of her projector – she had her kids now, all she'd ever wanted to own. I became her latest perpetrator, victimising her in everything I did. I couldn't figure out what was happening, trying to be a dad, getting to grips with my new career, living away from the familiar, with a wife who month by month became someone I'd never known. I knew nothing of Karpman and his triangle then. I had no idea how I'd become the person I seemed to have become.

We staggered on through your first years at school, yours and your sister's, living a weird existence. Me trying to persuade Mummy to get help, her telling me the marriage was done. I should have upped and left. But my Achilles heels. And the terror I felt for you both – the thought of your family disintegrating – was also terror of my own.

An article one weekend, in the *Guardian* magazine. Mummy shoving it across at me: 'That's what you can do'. Some middle-ranking actress and her husband, living separate lives, conducting new relationships, but still living under the same roof for the sake of their kids. It wasn't what I wanted, not for myself, not for you two. I carried on sticking it out. I see now that what self-respect I had was dwarfed by my fear of losing my family. Contempt unleashed. Derision at the way I would sit on the sofa, curled up with a book. Disdain for my art, and how little it brought in. Disparagement of the clapped-out Peugeot that was all we could afford. Humiliation at dinners with other couples, parents of your friends from school, Mummy vocally deriding sex as a filthy thing. The averted eyes of the others, them wondering what on earth must be going on. Her screaming at me: Why don't you just go off and fuck other women! And then to truly scramble my thinking: those bizarre interludes, lasting months at a time, in which some random thing would cause me to be switched in my triangular roles – back from perpetrator to be rescuer again. Mummy scouring the internet for the best hotels to go for a weekend-a-deux, booking us a room with a Jacuzzi in the en suite. Dancing beguilingly in front of the mirror. Writing a card to me saying I was the most supportive partner she could ever have hoped for, and re-proposing marriage. Then just weeks later, finding her late-night stream of consciousness, the writing scrawled and unravelling: If I'm ever to escape depression, I have to be rid of him.

Back to bitter cold hostility again.

I should have upped sticks and left. But my Achilles heels. And that childhood terror of my own.

We have a sense of ourselves, an internal image, formed from our attachment figures when we are young. As we go through life, it gets reflected back to us by the people we relate to, as though we get constantly to see ourselves in the looking glass. But what if we have stumbled into a grotesque fairground; what if we're trapped in a bizarre hall of mirrors, every reflection giving an ever-changing but always distorted view of ourselves? Squat and ugly. Menacing elongated head. Hugely swollen praying mantis eyes. Bit by bit our sense of our true self becomes corrupted, malign. We no longer know who we truly are.

Ma, Mark, Gerry, Julie – people who've known me for years on end, people who could have been correctives, mirroring back the Stevie they had always known. Gone. Cut off. I'd allowed myself to become isolated. Fatally. Distorted images were all I was shown. Achieving that isolation is key – it consolidates power and control. That's why, I believe, Mummy isolated you from me, from your extended family. That way, it seems to me, you were hers to shape alone.

My art took on strange new directions, disturbing abstracts, dark dark tones. Utterly unappealing for anyone to hang in their home. Year after year I failed to sell. I couldn't even find a local gallery to agree to an exhibition.

Cash ever shorter. Mummy cutting her hours, embattled by fresh workplace bullying, by vindictive colleagues who meant her harm. Triangles, triangles. Then quitting her job altogether, saying she couldn't go on. Every penny needing watching. Every penny soon gone.

An email from an old contact, a chance to tutor a residential, like – once upon a happier time – Mark and I had done. I took a week's leave, set off for a rambling farmhouse in Devon, sixteen aspiring artists to mentor. One, a beguiling life painter from London. Mercy. Kenyan skin taut over angular cheekbones. Sitting together in tutorial, discussing the nude self-portrait she was working on. Her lifting one leg up, resting her foot on the seat of her chair, her skirt sliding midway down her thigh, running her hands contemplatively up and down her calf. Me feeling so utterly alone. Why don't you just go off and fuck other women? That wasn't what I wanted. What I wanted was to be loved and known.

Gaslighting, that's what Prof calls it – the capacity to twist and re-remember reality to fit whatever is needed for the victim role. I had cheated on her. I was having an affair. Point-blank denial of all she had said and done. All that stuff, separate lives under the one roof, go fuck other women: a truly double-edged sword. It seemed that while I was emasculated, subservient, she could perfect her victimhood with the thought of what she'd had to give me carte blanche to do. I don't believe she ever thought I would, though – I think she'd sensed my Achilles heels. The fury when I escaped her control. The blows from the other side of that strop-sharpened blade. The poor betrayed wife. The devoted partner cruelly undone. The eternal victim.

And once I had gone, scapegoat expelled from the family home? For those few short months of interwar, she appeared to be basking in victory. She had rescued her victim within. Damsel in distress turned St George. But it couldn't last. Just as cutting off Ted and Gloria, and Ellen, and Katy with the double-barrelled name, and Clare, and Jo, and Ma, and Gerry and Gaby, and your Aunty, and Julie, and Mark were never enough. It seems that, until and unless she sorts out the stuff in her head that makes it all true, the cycle has to repeat, endlessly. Over and over again.

You. Tickertape chuntering. A projection screen for her inner distress. A fresh victim in need of rescue.

More than that. It seems to me she has to have supply

– of constant adulation, of never-ending admiration for the poor-me who has somehow made good. Those days and weekends when you were with me, over at Drake Avenue: were they interminable lengths of time without you as the mirror in which she could look? Without an adoring reflection to gaze upon, without that image of herself as perfect victim surmounting all that the world could do, was there nothing to see but that which truly lies within?

Tell me if I'm wrong, but this is how things played out, isn't it? Some of it I know; some I've surmised; still others I've pieced together from scraps of your sister's conversation.

She began sleeping in your bed with you.

She would fall apart every time you came to leave.

Blizzards of texts and Skypes, checking you were all right whenever you were with me.

Taking you into her confidence, those secret chats about things only you were privileged to know.

Referring to me as Steven – Daddy no more.

Arranging things that happened to clash with whatever I might plan, meaning you had to choose. Daring you to abandon her.

Drenching you with sympathy whenever I told you No.

Hugging you supportively when you disrespected me on the phone.

Uttering words that meant you had to see me, when every ounce of her being screamed at you: I can't stand for you to go!

Leaning on you so heavily that your young frame, sheathed in its pretty print dress, was buckling and crumpling like a tin can beneath a juggernaut's wheel.

It seemed to me that she had to have you.

Then despite it all, against such huge odds, you started to win through. Our chat about the importance of relationships with both your parents. You moved your rabbit down. Colour coded your books for school. More and more like your sister, able to love me as well as her. Able to dance the Charleston in those months of interwar.

I think it terrified her.

It must have felt like she was losing control.

It must have felt that she had no choice. That she had to do whatever it would take to have you for herself alone.

FIVE

Outbreak of War

ACROSS THE RIVER there's the extraordinary castellated house standing on its own small island, the Thames flowing past on either side. 1 Folly Bridge. Brown brick, white-rendered statue niches. There was an art dealer lived here in my day, he ran a gallery from the downstairs. It was called One. Now it's a riverside café, white metal tables on its terrace, the chairs tipped forward in mourning of the summer just passed. I can't remember his name, the gallery owner. It's on the tip of my tongue. A flamboyant character, gay as anything. He took some of my work, used to invite me in for long chats over coffee. I don't think he rated my art, I think he just wanted to see if I was a potential conquest. He sold a few pieces, though, enough to make a difference to what I was earning training in art therapy. Enough to encourage me.

What the hell was his name? Something unusual, like Vaughan, or Rupe - but it was neither of those. He was South African, originally. Smoker. With a heavy gold voice. A Svengali character to aspiring artists in the city back then. I'm frustrated that I can't recollect what he was called.

Other memories flow all too easily. Along the towpath there's a great long hedge where we used to come, you and I, to see the 'tiny birds' as you called them in your toddlerhood. We'd crumble up bread crusts, then crouch at a distance, patiently waiting for them to feel all was safe, my legs sometimes going to sleep with the restricted blood supply. Then down they'd come, out from their privet sanctuary, first the few boldest, soon joined by a couple of dozen more. Sparrows. Pecking up the crumbs, tussling over the bigger bits. You loved to watch them. We hated it if a passer-by came; with a flurry of wings the tiny birds would be gone. It would take another long age before they reappeared.

Off the towpath, on to the top of Chatsworth Road. How they flooded it one winter, a few inches of water sluiced over the pavements. You and your sister splashing through it in wellies, wondrous at how your world had suddenly changed. How it showed in exquisite detail the subtle relief of the roadways: in one place homeowners had the pumps out, stemming the rising tide in their cellars, while twenty yards away the tarmac rose gently and broke the surface like a whale's back, and the houses remained dry. It was all managed. The river authority first filled the floodplains to the east of the Abingdon Road then, when they were at capacity, they allowed a controlled amount of water to wash out over Grandpont. The next winter, when the river again rose to overflowing, it was Kidlington that took the hit. Hard choices. Spreading the pain.

On past 42, the Victorian terraced house that was your earliest childhood home. I pause for a moment and contemplate its cream roughcast render. The side alley where you used to help me sawing wood for jobs around the place. The hypericum hedging is overgrown. I picture us, extra-corporeal you and me, peering through that bay window, watching you sustain your first attachment wound. I peer up through the front right-hand window, trying to see if the stars might still be on the ceiling of what was your nursery. Unlikely, after so long, but for some reason I wish it were true. It is impossible to tell, though, not in the daylight. If I were to come back later, if the curtains were to remain undrawn, then maybe they might still be doing their glow-in-the-dark thing.

Who are you now? I'm trying to reach you again, but feeling nothing but cold silence in reply. Twenty-one. Studying medicine, but still so young. At what age will you discover the sides to a story; understand that truths are refracted through prisms and lenses that have been fired in past furnaces, and if the blast was white-hot then the distortion can be severe? It took me till well into my thirties; into my forties for the full extent to hit home. I may be dead by the time you get there – already I've lost contemporaries. The span of our lives is for none of us to know.

The envelope arrived ten days before Christmas, thumping through the Drake Avenue letterbox one morning when I was home alone. The franking mark of Mummy's solicitors. Wodges of A4 paper, copious court forms. Words leaping out at me. Emergency hearing, scheduled for a date just days away. Photocopies of your mother's affidavit: how I had beaten her, tortured her emotionally and psychologically; how I had emotionally and psychologically abused you and your sister, too. Application for a prohibited steps order, banning me from contact direct or indirect, excluding me from a half-mile radius of your home and school. Faxes sent from her lawyer to your head teacher: there were grave concerns about me; if I came to school to collect you then the police should be called.

Five days to prepare, and in the run-up to Christmas. Not a barrister to be had in the whole of the south-west of England. My solicitor – a well-meaning man used simply to batting about sums of money – saying he'd do his best for me, but he was no advocate. Getting me to pen my own affidavit:

how Mummy's perceptions were benighted, causing her to see abuse everywhere where there is none. The concern I have over your care-taking behaviour, how I can see you developing a burden of responsibility for keeping Mummy's distressing emotions contained.

Four days before. Two policemen at my door, arresting me on suspicion of domestic violence. Courteous. But anything I say may be used in evidence against me. They seem rueful about what they're doing; they let me send Gerry a distress text before taking me to their car. Hand on top of my head as I was getting in. Five minutes down the road, heading for Yeovil and the nearest custody suite, their radio suddenly crackling to life. The CID man telling them to de-arrest me and take me home. Them telling me he'd interviewed Mummy, and decided it was a crock of shit. Dropping me off at Drake Avenue, coming in to check I was OK. Telling me how they see this time and again, most recently a week ago, always in the context of divorce or separation.

Three days before. Two social workers turning up to interview me about the ways I was supposed to have bullied and intimidated you down the years. Another crock of shit. Nothing I'm hearing, the social worker declared, clicking the lid emphatically back on her pen, is anything other than a normal-range parent might sometimes have to do.

Crocks of shit, but their purpose was achieved, the damage was done. In court a few days later, the bearded judge acutely discomfited, having a go at Mummy and me, trying to tear each other apart. That's how he saw it, the fuckwit. Shouted my solicitor down from saying anything. Too much power in such inadequate hands. Saying he had nothing to go on given the short notice of the hearing, nothing except the initial enquiries of relevant agencies, which had revealed investigations into me by both police and social services. As a precautionary measure, until detailed reports were obtained, I was banned from contact with you or your sister. He was sure I would understand.

Afterwards, my solicitor didn't know what to say. Apart from sorry. A loving dad barred from seeing his children, on nothing more than one woman's word and a bunch of preconceptions. #dodgydad. #dangerousdad. We all know how cruel men can be.

Until you've been in it, seen so-called justice at first hand, you wouldn't believe it possible. But we know differently, me and my clan. People think it's all he-said-she-said. No one wants to believe there could be such aggressive all-out war.

Months it had taken for you to gain your confidence, to fit reliably into your other family home. Then another earthquake, and every tentatively reconstructed building came crashing back down. How did she play it with you? Oh my darling, how awful, the judge says you're not to see Steven after all, that it would be dangerous for you to be around him. Did she pour out sympathy? I'm so sorry, darling, what a terrible shock. But what can I say? Steven's brought it on himself, all the things he's done. The judge has decided he's a very bad man. And the judge must know best. He is a judge, after all.

Five months to clear my name. Five months in which – is this how it was? – she could tell you her truths without any counter-experience of my love. Five whole months when, at the deepest level of your being, it felt like I had abandoned you. I can picture you, out on mother-daughter horse-rides, side by side, your sister – never the equestrian – elsewhere, Mummy murmuring confidences for your ears alone. How your sister's too young to take this in; only you are old enough, mature enough, to understand. They will be your special secrets, yours and hers. How good it is to have you to confide in. The thing is, darling, the police actually arrested Steven. You know what that means, don't you? And the social workers have been round. You don't think they would stop him seeing you unless they were really concerned, do you? They must think he's incredibly bad.

What do you do when something like that happens? I felt I was falling, spinning into a bottomless void, hair dishevelled, clothes being ripped off me by the force of the wind, plunging down and down wishing it would somehow stop, anyhow stop, but knowing if it did it would be because I had slammed into the ground. Driving my car, thinking how would it be if I simply failed to turn, and ploughed straight into that wall. A moment of violent rending, then nothing. Thinking of your great-grandfather, those generations before, wedging himself in his chair, his lips and teeth wide round that shotgun barrel, stock jammed against the edge of the desk to prevent recoil. Feeling the cold smoothness of the trigger under his thumb.

Google. You go to Google and try to find answers. And in this day and age it doesn't take long to find people exactly like you. Secret Facebook groups, closed discussion forums. Thousands and thousands of members, up and down the country – internationally too. #dodgydads. #mankymums. Support groups in the UK, the US, Australia. Every now and then the mods have a shout-out: where do the newbies live? And you're put in touch with others of your clan who live near you, the clan you hadn't known even existed. Prof, and Rev, and Zambo, too.

The Chatsworth Arms, where I used to go drinking with my neighbour Gil after we'd played squash, is now a coffee shop and bijou B&B. A little further along there's the intersection with Whitehouse Road. But this much at least is unchanged. The wall bounding the garden of number 164. Half a dozen courses of bricks. Height just perfect for a small child to sit on. Our watching-the-world-go-by wall.

Two thirty. I'd planned to be here well before. Yes sir, your bus will definitely be running. You will definitely get your train.

Bollocks to that. What time I have, will have to do.

I sit myself down, the bricks cold through the denim of my jeans. Nothing on my phone, nothing from you. There never has been, not in seven years. Why did I think it would be any different now?

What you have been through. On the surface, it looks straightforward: child rejects parent, parent must really suck. #fuckupparent. Simple.

Only it's so complex. You're battered day after day with a narrative that doesn't square with your experience. Some things are reinterpretable. So the ordinary boundaries of regular parenting – the rules and the expectations, the things you must and must not do – become oppression and bullying. All kids rail against their parents. What a mind-fuck, though, when one of their parents joins in with them against the other one. Other stuff – all the love, and goodness, and care, and compassion – that can't be made to fit. And the picture that's being painted is the one you must live up to - Crack! Yah! – if you are to be joined up with the herd. So you box it away, all the psyche-rending contradictions, hammer three inch nails in to seal up the lid, dig a deep hole in your heart and bury it, tipping from your mother's mix of stone, sharp sand, and cement a load of glutinous concrete that will keep the contents from ripping your soul in two. Then you can live. Then you can survive. But the you that survives is not you.

How do I know this? The times I've felt my faith waver, beaten and ground down by your implacable silence. Those times they would shore me up, Prof, Rev, Zambo too. Watching YouTube videos of adult survivors, confessing the hatred they'd felt towards their #fuckupparent, yet at one and the same time how they'd clung – in the quiet solitude of their room – to the cards, messages, and presents that had somehow got through. Hostages in their own homes. How the thing they now valued above absolutely anything is that their other parent never gave up on them.

Art, you can't give up. You mustn't. She needs you. It doesn't look like it, but she does.

Prof, telling me that all these alienated kids are out there on social media, checking up on the parent they can't love, wanting to know they're strong and all right. Wanting to know that they don't have to be responsible for their emotional welfare, too.

Facebook. Prof advising me to change my settings to public. I couldn't be sure at first. Occasional memes I'd posted would turn up on your public-facing page – that could have been coincidence; these things go round everywhere. But then Ma tripped and fell and fractured her wrist. I put a message up about it. Within half an hour your Grandma had an email from you, hoping she got well soon.

You're out there, watching.

Dad-dy! A little jump up. Arms round my shoulders, legs round my waist. The innocent girl I know is inside you. Who needs to be allowed to love, and be loved by, her daddy, too.

I take my canvas roll bag, extract my easel, erect it on the pavement in front of me. From time to time, cars come round the corner and pass by. None is burgundy – that colour is no longer even glancingly fashionable. I unfurl the A2 and clip the paper on the board. I've brought pastels and putty rubbers with me, in a seasoned wooden case that has seen much battering over the years. Pastels: capable of rendering the most evocative sketches. Possible, through pressure, to create some semblance of texture, too. As the hands of my watch draw closer to the hour, I begin to draw as I am waiting for you.

Them

MERC'S HOUSE IS on an estate in Radstock, fifteen minutes' drive from my village home. It's a 1970s semi built of brick and uPVC, with an overhanging roof that forms a porch, which keeps me dry while I wait. The front door is double-glazed with swirly frosted glass, into which, the other couple of times I've visited, Merc's pixelated form has coalesced as he's come down the hallway to let me in. Though I ring again, and ring a third time, nothing moves.

His adapted Astra is parked on the drive. Its headlights and radiator grille look like a face; its expression strikes me as forlorn.

I've got his landline on my phone. I can hear it trilling from somewhere deep inside the house. I give it twenty, thirty rings then hang up.

I call Zambo. Do you know what Merc's up to, I ask. I'm off today, I said I'd drop round, but he's not at home.

Zambo doesn't know. He doesn't think he's gone back to work, not the way he's been. I have to agree.

I don't have Angel's number, but Rev does. I write it on the back of my hand as she reads the digits out. I can picture them, Angel and Merc, off on some walk together, or round at her place drinking tea. It rings for a long time and I imagine the conversation: Do you want to get that? No, leave it, they'll leave a message if it's important. But eventually Angel answers.

Hello, Angel, I say, it's Art. From the support group? Sorry to trouble you. Have you got Merc with you?

She hasn't. She says she'll come over. I say I don't think that's necessary but she's gone, hung up on me.

The back garden's reached by way of a wooden gate. I have to get my hand over the top to slide back the bolt, but then I'm in. Weedy flower beds, cracked concrete pathway, mildewed TP trampoline. I have a sudden vision: Mark, Merc's son, bouncing joyfully. It's gone almost as soon as it's come.

The rain is steady, insistent. It's cold on my shaven scalp. There's a sliding patio door at the back of the house, locked from the inside when I tug it. I bang on the glass. Hello? Merc? It's Art!

Silence.

Through the double glazing I see the lounge, running the length of the house, a plate and mug on the floor by the sofa. Huge TV in the corner, screen blank. This was the family home. His ex decamped without warning to her mother's, taking their boy with her, controlling all access with fierce hostility. What would it be like to be living here still, surrounded by reminders? The Arsenal duvet on his bed, cold and unrucked night after night. The jumble of outgrown trainers in the cupboard beneath the stairs. The cot and the baby toys stored up in the loft, intended to be passed to Mark when he had children of his own.

Like living in a mausoleum.

No one in at the semi next door. The neighbour on the other side - a fat old dear with ankles the size of elephant legs - is out of puff by the time she answers my knock. Just for a minute I can't remember Merc's real name. Eric! No, she doesn't know anyone called Eric. No, she doesn't even know who lives there. There's bitterness in her voice. They keep themselves to themselves. They've never done a thing for me.

Zambo again, on the mobile. He's way over in Portishead, supervising the affixing of labels to a billion bottles of continental beer. There's nothing he can do. I'm on my own. He thinks I should call in a welfare check. I knew he'd say that. It's in the crisis protocol Prof drew up for the running of the group.

Prof's phone goes to voicemail.

Merc could just be out shopping. Or at a doctor's appointment. Or having his prosthesis serviced or something.

I hate to be dramatic, but I punch in 999.

Rev rings me back a few minutes later. Any joy? she wants to know. I'm waiting for the police, I tell her, can you come over? Oh God, she would, really, at any other time, but Sam's having a rough ride at the moment and she's got to stay with him.

The officer who attends is half my age. His radio keeps interrupting as I run the whole scenario through. No, I'm just a friend. No, he doesn't have too many other friends, and I've spoken to those that I know. No, I don't know who his next of kin are. No, they're separated – that's the whole problem – I don't think he'd want her to be called. He does the same stuff as me – ringing the bell, trying the back garden, asking the neighbour – all with the same result. Every now and then, the despatcher squawks from the receiver clipped to his lapel: nothing from his employers, nothing from the hospital, nothing from police or fire or social, nothing from any agency at all. Then his inspector barks out, giving him the go ahead.

He has some kind of battering ram in the boot of his Astra. A couple of feet of thick dense rubber, with handles near either end. Before he sets to, he radios for the boarder-uppers to be summoned to secure the property when he's done. Takes a fucking age for them to come usually, he tells me, sounding pretty grim.

He starts at the door, the ram thudding next to where the lock is. The whole frame jolts visibly, but nothing gives. Again and again. He grunts with each blow, like John McEnroe. Wood might splinter, cheap latches might pull off their screws, but Merc's door is made of sterner stuff. It's letting nothing through. I wonder if Merc will suddenly appear, in his PJs, still befuddled from the doctor's sleeping pills, demanding to know what the hell's going on. I wonder if the copper will have to smash the glass, reach a ginger hand round the shards, and release the lock from the inside. But then the next crashing thud does the trick. With a metallic clang, the door swings wildly in, smashing against the hallway wall.

I don't suppose I should have followed him, but he didn't say not to.

A few steps inside, leaving wet shoe prints on the post scattered on the carpet. There's an absolute hush after the violence of the entry. The kitchen at the end of the passage, washing-up piled next to the sink. And there's a view of the stairwell, rising to the top of the landing. Both bobby and I look up. The open loft hatch in the ceiling. The thick beige rope suspended from a distant rafter. Merc. Dangling. Completely still. Purple face. His black postman's boots. The trouser ends pulled up mid-calf by the traction. The pale skin of his shins.

Round and round my head, staring at his lifeless amputation: he's not even got his prosthesis on. How the fuck did he manage the knots, with his one fucking hand and all.

Then the copper's shoving me out of the house like he's

suddenly brick scared and he realises I shouldn't be there. And he's talking tersely into his radio even as I back-pedal out into the porch. And I bash straight into someone coming at a pace the other way. And I turn to find an alabaster Angel, her eyes wide in disbelief.

⁂

I'm looking to Prof for guidance, hoping she'll be the one to steady the ship that's pitching and yawing all of a sudden in the violent storm. Drinks in front of us, the bonhomie of the Half Moon going on around us, utterly incongruous for this emergency meet. Rev couldn't make it: her daughter, following hard on her son's lead, has been in touch, is round there with them now. At any other time, how that news would have caused our hearts to soar. Prof – uber-rational Prof who, if she experiences emotion at all, always has it firmly labelled and indexed and studied with objective dispassion – is visibly rattled. She meets my eye but can't hold my gaze. Zambo, brooding into his pint, berating himself silently. Everything's gone wrong. Everything's fracturing, fraying, going to hell beneath my feet.

There's nothing we could have done, I tell them. I think of the unit, the suicide watches, the 24/7 observation of inmates judged at high risk. And that's the problem. You can't spot the ones who will truly do it. The ones who make the loud noises, the cries for help, the ones who articulate their distress, they're probably the ones not to worry so much about. It's the quiet ones, nursing their self-hatred, the utter pointlessness of it all, the total entrapment they feel, fixed on the only solution they can see. They slip under the radar – they can even appear suddenly upbeat, as though things look all right for a change. Three of them managed to do away with themselves last year alone. One of them, that boy, Billy. Cardinal purple. Caput mortuum. Rest in peace.

I had no idea he was feeling so low, Zambo says, staring at the head imperceptibly shrinking on the surface of his beer. I thought it was OK. He'd been to his doctor, hadn't he?

I think of his GP, shaking his or her head, saying: I thought it was OK. He'd joined some support group he'd found on the internet, hadn't he?

No one knows how desolate it is, how it rends the very substance of your soul. No one except the myriad others of this benighted clan. Us. We whose children have also died to us, even though they still live. Me, who lost you.

Prof doesn't seem able to speak. I want her to say: think of all the people we have helped these past few years. We can't know how many might otherwise have gone under. I want her to put it into context. I want her to say that, dealing with what we're dealing with, every now and then something is bound to go awry. But she doesn't. I wish Rev were here. She isn't. In the end, it's me who speaks. And though they're true, my words sound as hollowed out as dried-up gourds.

Blaze joins us. Sorry I'm late, he says. He puts his pint on the table, and pulls up a seat. What a fucking nightmare, he says, shrugging his jacket off his firefighter's shoulders. Isn't it?

Poor Merc, I say. I feel like shit.

And I do. And then I feel anger, rising like a tornado inside me. The boy, Mark. #deaddad. His ex, telling him: Well, you were right about your good-for-nothing-cripple of a father. He's really gone and done it this time. He's only gone and killed himself! How on earth could he possibly think of doing that to you? There'll be no money now, no more maintenance, what on earth are we supposed to live on? So selfish of him – so typical of him – I'm so mad at him I could weep.

And the boy. Mark. The broiling emotions. Ever seared on his brain: the memory of screaming at his father, I hate you, you're an embarrassment, you're a fucking cripple! What the fuck is he supposed to do with that? The attachment trauma, grief compounding grief, resounding down the years of the boy's life, breeding and self-replicating. Chewing up Mark's soul, spitting it out, moving on to people he might partner, children he might father, ravenously consuming everyone in its path.

I'm lost in my thoughts, numbed by that vision of blackness. I don't know how long it takes. I've lost track of things. But at some point, Prof lets out a groan.

Angel, she says. Where is she?

Oh fuck. The time. It's slipped past us, it's turned an acceptable window of lateness into a probable no-show, and none of us have noticed. Angel.

We all think the same thing.

It's me who ends up driving. The four of us, tense in my old Renault, wipers going, the sodium-vapour street lights casting their mournful orange glow. As we're going, the thoughts tumble like bombs from a Lancaster. Angel. Her beloved boys turned hateful of her. Banned even from sending them cards on their birthdays. Faced with a fine, maybe even prison, for doing that exact same thing. Self-esteem already in her boots, now this utter desolation. Then finding that glimmer of hope, that fragment of love in Merc the winged messenger. The coy glances. Having them returned. Those few tentative steps towards building something new, something that might be a semblance of good. But so precarious, so feeble in the face of the onslaught. Maybe enough of a raft for Angel to cling to. But not for Merc. She was nowhere near enough to stop him from going under. She turned out to be no good. And Rev should have been supporting her. Ordinarily Rev would have wrapped herself round her size twenty body like a life jacket, with its light to attract attention, with its whistle on which to blow. But Rev's tied up in her own radically changed world now. Her children need her, and, as with any of us, her children must come first.

It's like a horrendous groundhog day. Angel's flat, the only temporary place the council could find for her, above the William Hill on Midsomer Norton High Street. The unrequited bell. The echoing bangs on the door. The neighbours professing ignorance. Utterly weirdly, it's the same bloody copper who answers our call. He can't believe it's me, either, standing there with my motley crew. But for Blaze, I think he'd probably arrest me – two in one day; I must be up to no good. But he and Blaze know each other from shout-outs. Blaze's presence seems to settle his nerves.

Same fucking battering ram. As he thuds it against her door, my mind's wildly fearful. Women don't generally do violence like men do – it'll be something like an overdose of pills. Maybe she'll still be alive. Maybe a hospital can save her.

The cheap plywood puts up minimal resistance. This time, the bobby tells us all to stay put. We stand at the top of the stairwell – Prof, Zambo, Blaze, Art, a ragged, altered core – our ears straining for any clue from inside, not daring to say a word. After a full-blown eternity, the PC emerges, shaking his head.

Wherever your friend is, he tells us, she certainly isn't here.

I don't know, but this is what I picture.

Angel, her heaps of flesh juddering, her eyes red from weeping, blipping the key to open her Focus with its 1.0 engine, the most power she has ever known. Dropping her handbag on to the passenger seat, and landing herself alongside. Firing the ignition. Driving into the night, with its cloud-obscured moon.

Was she in two minds? Did she head for the pub to start with, half-thinking that she would attend our emergency meeting? I honestly don't know. Maybe she even got there, parked in the Half Moon car park, next to Blaze's pillar-box red MX5. Maybe that was all it took to decide her – that colourful reminder of Royal Mail delivery. It is often something trivial, or left-field, or seemingly random, that flips the points and diverts the train.

As she drove off? As she wended her way through the lanes and carriageways that would lead her to Keynsham and her now decided destination? I guess she was thinking of Merc, and the fragile shoots they had dared to allow to grow. The grief they had shared over their children. Maybe she was going over and over how Merc used to talk about Mark, the pride in his voice, the way it would crack suddenly under the burden of his loss. Perhaps she was going over and over Merc's description of that last agonised visitation, the crossed-armed mother and grandmother flanking the bristling child, screaming his hatred of his cripple dad, their gleeful expressions saying we-told-you-so. Maybe all of that. But much more besides. Running in her mind's eye: pictures of her own two boys, laughing and playing in a sandpit, riding their bikes round the cul-de-sac where she once lived, cuddling up on the sofa for stories, now cruelly dismissive of her, fleeing from her the last time she saw them, completely aligned with their dad. And his mocking barbs after he'd shut them away indoors, standing out there in front of the house, his hands gesticulating, his face contorted by disgust: Look at you! You miserable fat cow. You were shit as a wife, and shit as a mother. You'll never see your kids again.

It will have been difficult driving in that anguished state. Roughly wiping wetness from her eyes, snot snivelling out of her nose. Did she have tissues? Did a big pile of them, scrunched up and discarded, grow on the passenger seat alongside her bag? I'll never know.

I imagine she looked quite a state, standing outside that Keynsham front door. Trembling and slime-streaked and utterly consumed. Who answered? It must have been Merc's ex – perhaps her mother hovering behind, eager to see who was calling at this evening hour. Were they relishing the drama? Were they hoping for a neighbour, an acquaintance, having caught wind of the news? So terribly sorry to hear, it must be such a shock; I mean, I know you'd split up and everything, but even so. Did she open the door, Merc's ex, with a half-smile on her face, expecting unctuous felicitations and a chance to play the poor newly widowed?

All I hope is that the boy, Mark, was nowhere around. That he was safely ensconced in his room.

The first blow must have been one hell of a surprise. The sheer heft of the car jack – the only weapon Angel had at her disposal – slamming into her nose. I picture her standing there, Merc's ex, blood suddenly spurting from her nostrils, any trace of a smile completely erased, struggling to compute this crazed, demented stranger who had appeared from out of the night. Did she know she was anything to do with Merc? Did she recognise her from a glimpse of the fat woman sat outside in the car during Merc's last visit? Even before she'd had a chance to comprehend what was happening, the danger she was suddenly in, Angel will have raised her arm again and brought the steel slamming down with another mighty impact. Fracturing her left cheekbone. Smashing her face in. Only, her face is no longer a face – it's a projection screen. Playing on it: Angel's ex, screaming You miserable fat cow. Shit as a wife, shit as a mother. You'll never see your kids again. The fuckwit judge: I'll jail you for sending your son a card for his birthday.

I guess she went down then, ex-Mrs Merc, dropping like the proverbial sack of potatoes. Perhaps that further fuelled Angel's fury, appearing as though she was trying to hide her face. It will have been the blows to the back of the head that did the most damage. The mother didn't try to intervene, I guess quite sensibly. She ran back inside and summoned the police. By the time they got there, Angel was spent, sat staring blankly at the neat privet hedge, her mind irretrievably scrambled, beside the body of her insensate victim. Neither of them would ever speak again.

Me

THESE DAYS, I'M in the Cloth Road Artists. Painters, sculptors, ceramicists, glass-blowers, the whole shebang. Entry requirements: doing something in the visual arts, and living in any of the towns and villages in this narrow belt of West Wilts and East Somerset that once upon a yester-year had a thriving textile trade. It's how Harri and I met. She works in porcelain, her studio's up a rickety staircase in an outbuilding on the Stowford Manor estate – vases, lamp stands, and graceful forms that have no actual function. As white as a field of virgin snow, smooth as Egyptian cotton, the most sparing use of deep indigo giving definition and signature. She's not much over five foot. She wears an oversized blue boiler suit, heat-proof gloves and welder's goggles when she's firing, blonde hair tied back, wisps escaping round her temples. I fell for her gradually – it took me a long time to find confidence again in whom I might choose. A long time to trust once more in what other people elect to show to the world. It took time for her, too, after her own journey. You'd like her. Your sister does. Maybe one day you will get to know her, too.

I'd all but given up on my art making its mark. Maybe that was what it took – a letting go. I'm still surprised by what some of my stuff fetches in Bristol, London, Manchester, Edinburgh. Bizarrely enough, Madrid. Enough for me to take on a job-share at the unit. I won't leave, though, not till I retire. It's my muse. I've given up abstracts, landscapes, still lifes. These days I do portraits. Of the lads that come to me for therapy. Any that consent, that is, but hardly any refuse. It must be weird for them, so out of kilter with their lived experience – dysfunctional, abusive, neglectful attachment figures; children's homes; young offender institutions; prison. But it's like I'm giving them a present – they who never get gifts for birthdays or at Christmas. Someone taking an interest. Wanting to paint their faces. Someone believing they're a fit subject for art.

I never thought they'd be commercial. Certainly not among the folk with the money to buy stuff. It just goes to show. What it is: I've become practised at capturing them – cracking and discarding the layers of Russian doll till I get to the shrivelled child at their heart. You can make them out, those tousle-haired reception kids in their shorts and spandex polo shirts, hovering mirage-like somewhere in their embittered, angry, time-hardened faces. I think that's what moves the buyers, the dealers and collectors. Glimpsing the human. The vulnerability in tempered steel. Maybe the But-for-the-grace-of-God of what might have been. With the governor's permission, I give each of them a sitting fee. For most, it's one of the few times the world has sent anything their way.

I don't see much of the others any more. Prof was devastated by what happened. She left the group, and the group soon disbanded. She retreated into her books and papers, resolving to focus on theory and let others take on the practical work. She's still active on the secret forum – I see her posts from time to time. She's back in her home country, she landed some academic post in Rotterdam or somewhere. Could be she's an actual Prof these days. Her younger daughter came back to her, last I heard. The older two are still in the UK, but they have both left their father's home now, and with their growing independence they've started responding positively to her DMs.

Rev was tied up for months on end, helping her two deal with the fallout. She got in touch ages later and we went for a drink at the Half Moon. Her son and daughter had turned around incredibly fast, and were counter-rejecting the father – understandable, and it was how he'd taught them to relate, but not what Rev, me, or any of us would want. Rev's challenge – the challenge for us all – is to help our children learn to manage the interpersonal stuff with boundaries and dialogue, not by cutting off and propagating further abuse. Rev's euphoria at them coming back had been quickly sobered by the realisation of the mountainous terrain still to travel. So much pain, confusion, hurt; though at least they could now know her love. She was too preoccupied to talk much about Merc, or Angel, and what had befallen them on our watch. It saddened me at the time. But she's all heart, Rev. No lack of compassion. It was just exhaustion from what else was on her plate.

Zambo started to make headway with his boys, too. Tentative, secret meetings for milkshakes and Nandos. It was going well, they'd met up a half-dozen times, then one of them let something slip and suddenly their mother knew. She retaliated with a midnight flit. First thing Zambo knew, his boys were in Kentucky, somewhere only she, with her dual nationality, could go. Three thousand miles. Zambo might have stopped her with an injunction, if he'd had but time. But the world is so small now, there's no difference pinging emails from five or five thousand miles away. He retreated to Cape

Town, works for one of those big wine companies that mass produces stuff that looks like it comes from a single vineyard, only it doesn't. We chat on the forum sometimes, mainly about cosmology and quantum mechanics and shit. He lives in the hope that, some day in the future, one or both of his lads will be tempted by the brais, the surf, and the African sun, and will come to seek their father.

Blaze. I felt a responsibility. Even though there was no group any longer, I was his buddy, his mentor, so we kept meeting up for a while. But things petered out. He couldn't resist the pull of war. He won one battle – got his name cleared and the contact order restored. You'd think there'd be consequences for those making false allegations, perjuring themselves in court, but there aren't. The fuck-wit judges see it as so much rough trade, and are glad just to get out the other side. So he's locked in sequential returns to court every time his ex breaks the order and refuses to allow the kids to come. He wasn't able to entertain our strategy, what Rev calls dripping the love in, what Prof terms waving from this distant shore. Far less able to embark on the long road to forgiveness. Last drink I went with him, he'd managed to persuade a judge to get psychological evaluations done: on his ex, him, both of the children. It won't get him anywhere, I doubt. It's still too early here in the UK – the concept of what's being done to his kids has yet to catch on. His battle will rage a good while yet. I don't know how it will unfold. I think of his twins, though, pale-faced and shocked by the shells that continue to rain down. But I don't criticise. We each of us have to find our own path, the way our conscience dictates we fight for our children. It was not Blaze who declared the war.

I saw your sister through to the end of sixth form, spending half her time with me, half with Mummy. A strange partitioned existence for her, two lives across a divide. Periodically she would waver – just as you once wavered – especially in the run-up to you leaving for university, when I guess Mummy renewed her campaign to win her for her own. It would alarm me, seeing the same signs in her as I used to see in you, but somehow she always managed to resist it, prevent the splitting. You're different personalities. Plus she never had the attachment trauma you did – you sat on your two-and-a-half-year-old bottom at Chatsworth Road, your beseeching arms sinking as Mummy appeared to reject you. The reverberating insecurity in your primary attachment. In succumbing to the pressure you experienced, in supplying Mummy with all she seemed to require, in stepping into your golden child role, you actually shielded your sister, let her off the hook. There looked to be some scapegoating – times she would recount how mean you'd been to her, you just a puppet on Mummy's strings – but by and large you seemed able to resist that further descent into lording it over your sibling as well. I tried to create a world in which she could talk about Mummy and you, but on the whole you remained on the other side of her wall. She made it to her gap year travels with her attachment relationships ragged but intact. There'll be less for her to repair as life unfolds.

I have made my own amends. I managed to restore some semblance of a relationship between Ma and your sister, so she at least has one grandparent that she's known. Gerry was brilliant: during the months I was fighting for my life, he was on the phone every week, bolstering me up, cheering me on. I was still mired in that pervasive shame that comes from false allegations: you know you're innocent, but you feel the weight of judgement and opprobrium from all around. Smoke and fire, soot and flame. Stevie, you fuckwit, Gerry said, I've known you since you were born. You're fucking weird in all sorts of ways, but I know a pile of horseshit when I see one. In an unexpected way, me going through such trauma seemed to repair the schism that had opened between us after Pa died. I went up to stay with him the Christmas Mummy declared war: he took me out for a beer, leaving Gaby at home with their boys. Gerry, I told him, I'm sorry for cutting you off like I did. He looked at me, gave me a grin, and said: Forget it, you moron. You were trying to keep everything together, that's all. You did what you had to do.

Mark, my old art school mate, was just as forgiving. Roared with laughter when I told him about the pass he'd supposedly made to Mummy that time. But he got it, how the accusation manifested itself to me as a double-bind – junk my friend if I wanted to keep my kids – how I'd felt I had to walk a precarious tightrope to keep the family together. It was as though everything was suddenly normal again, talking it through with him, and him being so amused. It was though everything I used to believe about the world was proved to have been right all along.

And Julie, with her new partner, Greg. Tall guy, neat beard, works as a risk assessor. How great to see her back on track, after the hammer blow of losing her man. She wouldn't even let me apologise. Just looked at me and said: you've been through a nightmare, we both have. But we're out the other side. And with a fierce hug that contained all our histories and the losses we've known, that was that.

I needed to track down Barry Rimmer. The little runt I used to beat up on, whose wrists I would redden with Chinese burns – stranded at their house after school, the lad with the

#deaddad, waiting for his Ma to come home. Google's fucking useful. I made a pilgrimage, back to home turf, struck as ever by the strength of everyone's accents – and how diluted my own is after years of living down south. Barry's taller than me now, must be over six foot. He works at Everton, on the catering staff, running a bar in the VIP suite, even though he's a lifelong Liverpool fan. We went for a coffee at Stanley's on Great Howard Street. It was weird meeting this man who used to be Barry, trying to see the little kid. And there was tension there, coming from me as much as from him. Not knowing how he'd react. We took our flat whites over to the table and I told him: I wasn't sure you'd even remember me. Oh, yeah, he said, I remember you all right. I fucking hated you. You were a right cunt back then. I nodded, and I told him: I know, that's why I wanted to see you. To say I was sorry. He looked at me for a silent second, then did his own nod. And said he appreciated it; that it was good of me. We left it at that, and fell into sharing stories about the old days instead, of growing up on the Wirral. And it turns out he married Samantha Carrigan, who everyone thought was incredibly fit. Runt gets supermodel. They've got two kids, two girls, one at uni, one at drama school. He's done all right for himself, has Barry. We parted as friends.

I've got my life straight, put right the things that needed righting. Everything but you.

But that is the power of forgiveness. That is how things should be done.

Is this how, one day, it will be for you?

Getting together with Harri has shown me just how much effect the years with Mummy had – the constantly distort-ed, ever-changing reflections coming back from her hall of mirrors, twisting and corrupting what it meant to be me. Harri has proved a straight-backed looking glass in which, once again, I get a consistent picture of myself. Shocking to begin with, to be honest. Paralysing fear of expressing a contrary view. Incapable of articulating my own needs. And so trepidatious sexually. It's taken ages – we've been together four years now, and I'm still a work-in-progress – but bit by bit I'm rediscovering myself, regaining my confidence, learning to trust again that two people can respect and honour and enjoy each other without it being about power and control. And gradually I'm relearning that my value lies in who I am, not in what I do to shore up and contain another person's ultra-fragile ego. It's who I used to be, back in my early twenties, in the relationships I had then. Chisel blow by chisel blow I was resculpted – so insidiously, so incrementally, that I didn't notice it happening; like watching children grow. Thanks to Prof, Rev, Zambo, thanks to Harri – thanks even to Art – like a much-despoiled painting, I am gradually being restored.

It will be both different and similar for you, I imagine. The way it seems to me: you were still being formed these past seven years, you will have no reference points to look back on, no anchors to steady you in the storm. But I hope that, as you become ever-more independent, molded and melded by other influences – friends, tutors, colleagues – as you learn to trust the faithful reflections that come back from their mirrors, you will gradually discover what it truly means to be you.

Me and You

ACCORDING TO ZAMBO, you are no longer, physically speaking, the daughter I once knew. Every atom, molecule, cell, and tissue of your fourteen-year-old self will have long since been metabolised, excreted, exchanged, and resynthesised during the course of these seven years. In terms of pure substance, you are someone new. But iron filings in a magnetic field. Beams of electrons spraying moving pictures in a cathode ray. What is the force that sucks and patterns so much matter and energy into the being called You? What was unleashed, what narrative fired its unstoppable engines, when the conception occurred that would lead to you?

Is there a Platonic form that exists outside spacetime? – Zambo again.

If so, what charts prescribe its direction, the course it will take as it navigates life?

Prof would say you're the sum of your experiences. Born with certain characteristics – developed even in utero – but otherwise a blank template to be shaped by your every lived moment. She would see you as melded and molded by hierarchies of relationships, both for good and for ill. Straightened or bent on the anvil of your primary attachments; nuanced by other influences – friendships, relatives, teachers, club leaders; education, reading, travel – as you grow. Engraved by successions of triumphs and reverses, loves and losses, aptitudes and areas-found-wanting, times of industriousness and languid interludes. All played out against a predictable march of developmental psychology: the evolution of adult, independent, critically thinking you. And like us all, you will have your shadow side, those parts of your self for which you feel shame. The capacity to hurt, reject, be self-centred – addicted, even. How much you split these off and project them on to others. Or how much self-compassion you can find – integrating and containing them as just one facet of multi-faceted You.

But in all that. In all that swirling, often contradictory amalgam of influences – what is it that helps us to choose? How do we know what it is to live a right life? What is the nature of the compass that guides us? Is it no more than just what feels good?

Rev would say you're a soul. That in the very heart of your being is an unchanging unique kernel. Mortal or immortal, the debate still rages – I doubt that, till death, we'll ever know. But whichever way that particular cookie might crumble, Rev would see you as one more crucible in which the eternal conflict between opposing kingdoms is joined: love and hate, good and evil – the waxing and the waning of the moon. It's a neat kind of story, Rev's – giving us an origin for morality, no less – something neither Prof's nor Zambo's accounts can explain. And for Rev it is God, if you ask Him, God who will show you the way.

The one-sided conversations we've had these past seven years – my monologues, your silences. All too easily, I realise, I fall into trying to explain you to yourself. Forgive me, please. It's borne of love. To me, you will never cease being my daughter, the child I held just minutes after you were born. Fiercely determined. Fragile to criticism. Loving of animals. Bright as a button. Sporting aspirant. The girl who dangled upside down, thighs clamped round my waist, blonde hair spooling on the ground, looking at the world upside down. The young teen who, while still wavering in the storm raging around you, phoned her dad to hear his pride at some physics test result. The netball-passing interlocutor of a thousand current-affairs chats. The girl cycling alongside me down country lanes. My daughter, incapable of stopping your face crumpling as I drove off to the Peaks and you were unable to come. The half-pint two-and-a-half-year-old sat beside me, waiting for burgundy cars with Daddos Old and New. Watching the world go by.

You are half-Mummy, half-me – genetically speaking, of course, but in a whole lot of other ways besides. Yet have you been taught – coerced, even – to hate, revile, cast out and keep buried one half of your history and ancestry? And in the process, is that how you have come to feel about that side of you, too? Even as you stand posing with schoolmates on prom night, your hands are clenched, and your smile gets nowhere near your eyes. You walk around trying to deal with the implied assertion that one half of you is bad.

Whoever you are, I'd like to believe I know you. That email – with its callous, mummified rhythms. I dwelt in it for ten days or so, letting the paralysing punch to the solar plexus, and the all-too natural anger, slowly subside. Then I wrote back, expressing my understanding, and declaring my faith in the real you, the You that I believed would one day come through.

Whatever you think of Prof's model, it has much power, and there are certain gloomy things that it predicts. Do you, like so many of her YouTube testifiers, find it scary and hard to let people get close? That said, do you feel compelled to help others, and do you measure your worth by how much you please them, not by who you are? The prospect of becoming a doctor, healing the sick – does that satisfy something in your core? Maybe you have had – will have – relationships with well-balanced people; you might even have fallen in love. But deep down inside, is there something flammable that will not ignite? If so, then one day you may meet someone, a pitiful poor-me victim, and you may find yourself falling helplessly in empathy with their plight.

Do you recognise this version of yourself, this portrait? Or would you tell me I've got it all wrong? Got *you* all wrong. What about this, then: in your twenties, or thirties, or forties or beyond – perhaps because of the disintegration of that relationship, and all the heartache it brings – at one point you might begin to reappraise the events of your earlier life. What you thought of as you rescuing your fragmenting Mummy might come to be seen in multiple lights. Did she devour you to shore up her own existence? In containing her emotions, were you also duped into unwitting roles? In one, did you become a sharp-bladed dagger, plunged again and again into your father's heart, a weapon of hate and revenge? In another, might you have played the silent witness for Mummy's latest victimhood – every fresh rescuer who entered her ambit be-guiled? What else could possibly explain a child so ruthlessly rejecting their father, other than that which Mummy claimed about him must be the truth?

Even as you wrestle with these possible new-found insights and the feelings they provoke in you, one other thing, more terrible than them all, might threaten to engulf you. The secret knowledge that, at the time – dare I suggest this? – becoming Mummy's golden child once again felt oh so good.

If the burden of your realisations are too great then you might continue to defend yourself by splitting, projecting all that you recoil from in yourself on to those that you want, in fact, to love. If this is the case, relationships will fracture; there'll be deep hurt and misunderstanding. But you've been taught how to deal with those, haven't you? By cutting them off for good. Your life risks becoming a trail littered with broken loves and lives.

These gloomy prophesies – how I pray fervently that they won't come to pass. I'm no soothsayer, and I have no right to foretell your future. For all I know you will find your Prof, your Rev, your Zambo, and they will help you understand and exorcise the past. Or maybe it will be through Art that you will find your peace. Who knows? Certainly not me. Only you.

Whatever. What you should be sure of: I love you, whoever you are. I understand, as much as anyone can, what you went through. And if ever it's forgiveness you seek – even long after I am gone – then you have my absolution, absolutely. You were only trying to keep your world from disintegrating. You were only doing what, at the time, you believed you had to do.

SIX

Watching the World Go By

F ROM HALF A mile away, atop his tower on St Aldate's, Old Tom sounds the hour. Three sonorous bongs reach my ears.

Je me rends. Rendez-vous?

I stop work and look up Chatsworth Road, with its watchful ranks of Victorian terraces, as though expecting to see you coming. There's a squat elderly woman walking her Bichon Frise on an extendable lead, a couple of lads with skateboards, no one else in sight. What did I think, that you'd turn up on the dot, punctual after all this time?

Seven years. Rev comes to mind. A biblical number. Seven days of creation. Seven years of famine. Seven times seven signals the year of jubilee. I do my best to guard against magical thinking. Just as likely you will take eight, nine, ten years, maybe longer. If ever. Prof often cites twenty-five as the average age at which full adult critical thinking is attained. That would be eleven years, by then.

A memory: in a pub in London with Mark and some other mates, back when I was twenty-four, twenty-five. I don't know what brought it on that particular evening, but I can still recall standing there, hand curled around my pint, feeling bizarrely disconnected from the banter and the chatter. An unpleasant realisation that our days of youth were all but gone. Was that my first real intimation of mortality? I don't think so. Pa dying. The nights I would lie awake, my child-mind trying to grapple with the knowledge that one day I too would die. But it was about then, in my mid-twenties, when the charmed conveyor belt that had ushered me through art school, then out doing casual jobs while I tried to create a reputation for myself – Stevie Buchanan, fine artist – abruptly dropped me off its end. It was going to take years to make a breakthrough with my work, if ever I were to do so. I guess it was the onset of Prof's adult thinking. Time to find something proper to do.

The woman draws near me. Her dog, with its snow-white hair and fountain tail, comes to sniff at my feet. She gives a sharp command and a yank on its lead. I smile as she passes. She looks undecided for just a moment, then walks on without a word.

I figure I'll give it a couple of hours at least, even till dusk begins to fall. You might be busy, tied up in lectures. And it could take a lot of to-ing and fro-ing to pluck up the courage to come. In this day and age, with our lurking suspicions: what could possibly justify a middle-aged man sitting on a wall for that length of time? And in a quiet residential area, too, just round the corner from an outstanding nursery school. I raise my arm, bring the pastel back into contact with the paper, and begin to work on my sketch again.

Cars pass at intervals. None is burgundy. I glance at each – why did I think you'd necessarily arrive on foot? Maybe you've got your licence now, perhaps you've bought a run-around, and figure you'll do a drive-by before anything else. Or you might come by bike, helmeted, a scarf across your face, pedalling then freewheeling, and, with a casual glance, checking me out.

A removals van vavooms by, creating a minor slipstream.

My paper ripples. Suddenly, it's as though I'm sucked side-ways, but I'm not. My body's still upright. I'm flying free.

I'm surprised, it takes a moment to adjust. I float myself backwards, gently, like a kid in a rubber ring. On the wall below, artist's easel in front of me, I am sitting frozen, my hand holding the pastel up to the paper, my eyes gazing into the distance as though trying to discern what it is they see. Crew cut hair. Faded jeans. The leather jacket you so loved, scuffed and dulled now with the passage of the years. I drift upwards, above the rooftops, peering casually through the veluxes and dormers of the ubiquitous converted lofts and the lives they contain. It feels like an age since I was airborne. I think of my stolid walks through this city, sensing your renewed disengagement, my soul unremittingly earth-bound, my feet made of clay.

A current thrills through me. My weightlessness can mean only one thing. The Tacoma Narrows Bridge is buckling and yawing again.

Like an Apollo off the launchpad, I thrust upwards, gaining speed. I overfly dog-woman, way down on the pavement, her pet jigging along in front. Their shadows. Little and large. Up over Hinksey Park, where I used to bring you and your sister to the swings. The lake. Frozen one winter. Me sending chunks of ice skimming across its solid surface, the glacial percussions making scintillating otherworldly sounds.

I start to search the clear blue of the afternoon sky. North, south, east and west. There is no sign of you. But you must be coming. Nothing else can be powering my flight.

That thought. The acceleration takes my breath. An incred-ible surge, propelling me like a thunderbolt. Gingerly, I reac-quaint myself with my manoeuvrability, the merest intention sending me left then right. I hurtle along the course of the Thames, a couple of eights crabbing the water like bizarre pond-skaters below. It takes just seconds to reach Iffley, the lock gates like pinball flippers waiting to flick narrowboats up and down stream.

I put in an arcing turn, screeching up the Cowley Road. A thousand take-aways. Jumbles of house-shares. Studentsville. Maybe you live round here. But there's no trace of you if so. On over St Clements. The Plain. The Angel and Greyhound Meadow.

Angel. Merc. Mark with his #deaddad. His #braindamaged-mum. Angel, mute, rocking on her narrow bed in Southall, women's version of Broadmoor. Her boys, the #madmum lies peddled by their father so grimly made to come true. Prof, Blaze, Zambo; the thousands on the secret forums nationwide, worldwide. So many children, so many parents, so much pain. So much pain. Even Rev with her two – reunited, but it'll never go away. How do they deal with what one parent's done to them, unwittingly, or maybe even deliberately, teaching them not to love, but to hate? On over Magdalen, deer in the deer park, dipping down to race the length of Longwall Street. My fear: that when you finally grasp it, the pain and rejection will simply go the other way. That your life will be blighted by disconnection, estrangement, whichever way this pans out.

Left up Holywell Street, on past the music rooms, cornering hard round the curved Sheldonian. Understanding. Forgiveness. They're the only remedy. All the crap, all the loathing and self-loathing – if we try to not deal with it, to box it away, top nailed down tight, we may bury it safely out of sight. But not out of mind. It will remain gnawing away at us, corroding our souls, to be cast out repeatedly but ineffectually, like tenacious evil spirits, projected on to anyone who by word or deed accidentally jemmies up the corner of the lid.

I dive like all knowledge through the great courtyard of the Bodleian. Swoop like a swallow beneath the Bridge of Sighs. If ever you come back to me, that's what I would wish to pass on. Understanding. Forgiveness.

I barrel straight upwards, college spires clutching vainly at me as I shoot past. Up into clearer air, the fumes and particulates staying fogged beneath. I imagine you asking: Do you forgive her, then? That is so hard. It's one thing to forgive someone who is sorry, another to forgive an eternal victim who is always done to, and can never conceive that they themselves could do anything wrong. That, perhaps, is what you yourself may have to contend with – in your twenties, thirties, forties or beyond – if ever you try to confront her. Gaslights may flare. The truth that exists inside her head. It had nothing to do with her: it was the courts, the judges, the social workers, the lawyers. It was you. It was what you wanted; she was merely doing your bidding. Even as you challenge her with memories, will you find that everything was deniable, re-interpretable? Things you clearly remember: will she swear they never took place? Perhaps she will be angry that you could even suggest such things. If you're anything like me, you'll begin to doubt yourself, doubt your recollections, feel your grip on reality start to slip. But I have found my understanding. So, yes. It took so long – there was all the damage and destruction – not just to me; to your sister, and especially to you. But I understand and I forgive. Like Merc, like Angel; by no means everyone manages to wax the moon.

I slacken my furious pace, begin to cruise at altitude.

Oxford is spread like a toy town below. The cars like corpuscles in its arteries. The parks, quads, and meadows that allow this city to breathe. North, south, east and west. You are nowhere to be seen.

My energy dissipates, my velocity slows further; how wrong I have been. This abrupt flight, I was sure it meant you were coming, but as so often before, waving from this distant shore, I am ahead of myself. Ahead of you.

I swing over north Oxford, the huge Edwardian houses of the Woodstock and Banbury Roads. And face up, once again, to reality. Beth comes to mind. A junior doctor, just like you will be, late in her twenties, on a forensic psychiatry rotation. Attached to the unit. Allotted a half-day to spend with me, to learn about art therapy. A personable lass. I got her to do one of my exercises, drawing the hairstyles she'd had at various stages of her life. She found it funny to begin with, but soon settled to the task. It often opens up reflection, memory. The ponytail she'd worn at the age she was when her parents split up. The asymmetric bob she'd had when her father died. Liver riddled with cancer. Do you miss him, I asked. A dismissive shake: he wasn't a nice man. She told me, as though in a confessional, how he'd ill-treated her mother, cleared out the house and left them with nothing once he'd gone. How her mother had to go crop picking just to make ends meet. I didn't go and see him again, she said, her voice dropping, not even when I heard he was terminal.

Maybe it was true, what Beth had been told – maybe it was the stuff that actually happened. Or maybe it was only true in the head of her mum. Either way, I didn't go there. Too late. The damage done.

Will you be like Beth, progressing through your training,

your post-graduate studies, unshakable in the myth of your #dodgydad. That is what happens to some. The emptiness of the sky, the unbroken blue, tell me that, still now, that must be the case for you.

But. All of a sudden, a realisation. I've been assuming I would encounter you here, up in the crisp autumn air. How wrong, how wrong. My rediscovered capacity for flight – it may still mean you have decided to come.

I drop like a kestrel, down towards the city again. Hurry, hurry. Carfax, St Aldate's, Folly Bridge. I can picture you standing there, beside your immobile father, increasingly worried, shaking my shoulder, calling Dad, Dad, Dad. The movement causing the pastel in my stiffly extended hand to repeatedly scuff the paper. I streak down the Abingdon Road, my slipstream aquiver, racing to get back inside myself. Sharp right, and there ahead of me: the watching-the-world-go-by wall.

My easel has gone.

You're not there.

Neither am I.

Or, rather, we are.

I have travelled in time.

I hover, helplessly fascinated, watching us. A dad and his half-pint daughter, sitting side by side, two dollies on his lap. A car takes the corner. An old Allegro. It's burgundy. The Daddos go mad, leaping and squealing. Burgundy! Burgundy! My cod-ventriloquist's voice. You're laughing, you're ending yourself. It's the funniest funniest sight.

The pain, it's unbearable, twisting and wringing me from inside to out. Blindly I shoot heavenwards – one thousand, two thousand, three thousand feet. On and on like a space-exploring mission. I have, I have to be free. Eight thousand, nine thousand, ten thousand feet.

Finally, eventually, the pain begins to subside. The deafening thunder abates. I slow, stop, then levitate. The air is rare here, thin; I have reached incredible heights. Even the curvature of the earth has become apparent. Brown-green land, gun-metal sea, wispy clouds. I can make out the edge of the continent, across the strip of the channel, where Romania and Italy have become the first to recognise in law the phenomenon that has happened to you. Far away, on the opposite side of this globe, Brazil and Mexico, which have also legislated to make it a criminal offence. But it takes so long. So long. Years even to settle on a name, a label to describe the process of poisoning a child against their mum or their dad. Implacable hostility. Pathogenic parenting. Transgenerational attachment-trauma transmission. Domestic violence by proxy. Strange to think I should have become a subject of domestic violence – me, capable Stevie B. It is violence, though: subtle, incremental, deniable, but violence all the same. Even stranger that you should have been used as the weapon to assault me. My Achilles heels.

Names, names. Gradually, those in the know have settled on parental alienation. I gaze down on our benighted planet, imagine the countless Profs, Revs, Zambos – even Arts – working to spread this new understanding. How these concepts take years, decades, to begin to take hold. We're so complacent. Oh, sure, we know all about those pop stars, cartoonists, coaches, clergy, TV presenters, politicians, DJs – knobbing young kids throughout the ignorant seventies. We shake our heads in wonder at how no one could see what they were up to – that they were able, audaciously, to hide in plain sight. We're oh-so-much wiser than all those erstwhile authorities - the bishops, the inspectors, the managers, the police - who dismissed the accounts of those who dared to blow whistles. It just can't be true. That stuff doesn't happen. It must just exist in their fantasists' heads.

I start to glide, soundlessly. Far below, off to the east, along the flight path into one of the London airports, jumbos are strung out, their headlights glittering like rare precious beads. At some point, it will catch on in Britain, we will wake up and recognise what's being done to thousands of kids. Too late for you, though. And too late for me. And would it have helped, to have criminalised Mummy? Probably not - she needed reams of help, not a sentence. It might sober the lawyers, though; prevent them playing their sickening game. And give pause to the judges, the social workers - the unwitting colluders. The people whose job it should have been to stop it happening to you. But the day will come. The day on which, when a child coldly rejects, people assume not that there must be something very wrong with the outcast parent, but ask instead: what might be going on with the other one?

My spirit has quieted, the sheer tranquillity of the troposphere. I steepen my angle and start to descend. Names. I am Art. I am Stevie, Stevie Buchanan. Once upon a time I was Steve. Steve to Stevie. I thought it marked the start of my new life. But I see now that it didn't. Only once I'd created a family of my own, faced the terror of losing them, and then lost them for real - and survived. Only then could Steve rest in peace.

Only then could I truly be Stevie.

Art.

Me.

You changed your name, too, so I heard from your sister,

back when you went into sixth form. You adopted a contraction, a popular short version. That decision; I think I understand: was it one way you could start, ever so gently, the process of prising yourself free? No hint of abandonment of Mummy. No suggestion of rejection. The beginning of the ongoing, snail's-pace progress in discovering what it means to be you.

What is this utter yearning, undimmed within me, this unquenchable drive to see you? A memory, from that years-ago visit to Mummy's childhood home, before she cut Ted and Gloria out of her life. Daylight, the morning after that private home movie view. Coming outside into the crisp Yorkshire air. Ted in the yard, the cacophony all around. Him, separating lambs to be turned into meat. Hefting them aloft with fearsome power and dumping them behind a line of hurdles. The frantic, panicked bleating between the ewes and their young. Piercing cries, shredding the soul. This utter yearning, it is as ancient as nature herself. The need to know that my child is all right.

There is no sound here, nothing but the susurration of the wind. The stage you are now, it's a time of natural detachment, perfectly normal not to give the folks back home a second thought. We parents, we never own our children, we only ever have them on loan. To start with, we do everything for them. But the course of a childhood should be a masterclass in letting go. We debated a lot – Prof, Rev, Zambo and me – how long to carry on. How long to keep dripping the love, to keep waving from this distant shore. Some of our clan never stop, through thirties and forties and beyond. Till death do us part. But there comes a point where a child becomes truly an adult, responsible for writing the story that has become their own.

That fuck-wit bearded judge, bless his soul. The one thing he did do - ripping me away from your sister, from you - was to grant me one hour, as long as I wasn't alone. Your grandma, hot-footing it down from the Wirral. The four of us gathered in quavering jollity in the lounge at Drake Avenue. Christmas tree all set up ready for the big day that would not now happen. Me telling your sister, you, that come what may - come what may, I will always be your dad. I will always be there for you.

I saw that register in your eyes. In the merest inclination of your head.

Perfectly normal not to give the folks back home a second thought. But they're there, our primary attachments, running through us like a wick through a candle flame. Yours with Mummy: from what I saw, inherently insecure. Golden child, outcast, golden child once more. But then, in that second enmeshment, what made you so precious was not who you are, but what you could do for her.

Yours with me? I have kept that promise I made. I keep it still. You will look back and always know that your daddy never abandoned you. But maybe it's time to rest this aching arm. Maybe it's time to leave the rest with you.

※

I've done with thundering, hurtling, screeching. My descent is as soft as a sycamore seed's. Drifting down to re-enter myself: to pack up my easel, stow my pastels and putty rubbers, get to my feet and recede. Oxford swims serenely up to greet me, opening her streets like arms widened for a welcome embrace. The confluence of the Thames and the

Cherwell like an arrow, pointing to Grandpont where my body awaits.

Just for a second there's a lurch. A figure, standing next to me, alongside my easel. But I quickly make out it's a man, balding head like a holy monk in aerial view. Not you.

Back inside myself, I keep my movements slow. I turn my head to look at him.

I said, he says. I said, I can't work out what it is you're drawing.

I let my hand fall to my lap, pastel stick in my fingers, its dust pigmenting my skin.

I know, I say to him.

He huffs, then turns away, and sets off up Chatsworth Road.

I wonder how long he's been stood there, peering in the direction of my gaze. Scrutinising the houses, the trees dotting the grounds of the nursery school, then comparing it with the work-in-progress on my A2. How long did he wait, reluctant to disturb an artist in his reverie, before clearing his throat and interrupting, and asking what's the connection between the two?

It would have taken a lifetime to explain. I shake my head and lift my hand again. My sketching is swift, efficient, honed by the decades I've spent practising my art. In fifteen, twenty minutes, it's finished. The picture I've done for you.

I knew better than to come on your birthday. That, I know, you will have spent with Mummy - probably through choice, but certainly because you felt obliged. So I left it a week before proposing this trip to the watching-the-world-go-by wall. This drawing is yours. My birthday gift for twenty-one-year-old you.

Will you recognise yourself as that baby, just eight or nine months old? The look of delight I've captured on your podgy face. Your hair wisping about you. Your little body flying absolutely free.

And will you recognise those hands as mine? The pigment staining on my fingers. The palms cupping gracefully, with creases a fortune teller could read. Hands that never stray far from you. Hands that, as gravity asserts itself and you begin to fall, are there to catch you again.

I had hoped you would come. I had dreamed, in the smallest of hours, that I would hear your footfalls, look up to find your willowy beauty, hear your cry of 'Da-ddy!'. I had craved the chance to give you your present in person.

But no matter. That is what life is like on this distant shore. Back home, I will roll up the paper, slide it into a cardboard tube, take it to the post office in Hinton, and buy stamps with which to send it to you. I have no address, and if I post it c/o Mummy I have no faith it will get through. But in a few months' time, your sister will return from her travels. I rarely ask anything of her in connection with you. But this will be an exception.

Will you look at it? Who knows. Maybe you will put it in a cupboard somewhere, or the bottom of a drawer, furled in its cardboard coffin. But maybe at some time, later in your twenties, or your thirties, forties or beyond; perhaps when you've had children of your own, and know how precious they are to you. Maybe then you'll find that dust-gathered artefact, slide the paper out, and look back across the years at me and you.

I stand, and sling my canvas roll-bag over my shoulder. It feels lighter now for some reason, and I do a double-take to check I've put the easel in. But I have. I begin the long walk back up Chatsworth Road. My heart is leaden. I have no stomach for staying over. I will head back to Somerville, create some fiction for the bemused porter, collect my belongings and catch a late train home. Back to Harri. My cottage. The Cloth Road Artists. The life I have for myself. A Facebook post will soon come from Guatemala or wherever it is your sister has got to by now.

I pass our old house. The same memory: how I decorated the ceiling of the room that was your nursery. Pale blue, with fluffy white clouds, so that during the day it resembled the sky. And how I stuck numerous stars across it, made of a translucent plastic that glowed in the dark. So that when you woke in the night, you would still have the sense of the heavens above you.

I wonder if subsequent owners have over-painted it, burying it beneath new layers of white. Or whether it's like that still. I glance up at its window, but it's impossible to tell.

I'm still there, teetering on my step ladder, paint brush in hand, pot of cheap blue emulsion slung over the crook of my elbow, when a raucous squeal jerks me back. A bike, completing its brake-juddering stop right in front of me. The young woman cyclist landing a hasty foot on the pavement to steady herself. Looking up to see her stranger's face. Hearing her voice.

Daddy?

You.

Acknowledgements

I AM INDEBTED to Phyl Thorpe and Jane Stewart, who generously shared their experiences as practising art therapists during the course of my research. I couldn't have created the character of Stevie Buchanan without them. Thanks also to Phil Saul for making the introductions.

My friend and fellow writer, Martyn Bedford, provided a characteristically astute appraisal of an earlier draft of the novel, as well as unstinting encouragement and support.

Thank you to Robyn Whitaker for Sree and André; to Jo Roth for the well-timed comment about flight; and to Hilary Arden, Simon Crouch, Alex Wade, Sue Whitaker, Jason Cowley, and Bridget Whitaker, all of whom made invaluable contributions.I am also grateful to many people I cannot name: the parents and grown-up children who shared their experiences of parental alienation during the writing of this book - in person, and via the closed web communities into which I have been welcomed.

Parental alienation causes serious harm, but it is as yet poorly understood and frequently unrecognised. Among this novel's readership there will be people who realise for the first time that there is a name for what they themselves experienced. For anyone interested to learn more, I can recommend Dr Amy Baker's seminal *Adult Children of Parental Alienation Syndrome: Breaking the Ties that Bind*. Dr Richard Warshak's *Divorce Poison* is also very informative, as is *Understanding*

Parental Alienation: Learning to Cope, Helping to Heal by Karen Woodall and Nick Woodall from the Family Separation Clinic in London. Karen Woodall's blog (karenwoodall.wordpress.com) and the website of Dr Nick Child (www.thealienationexperience.org.uk) are excellent online resources.

I am fortunate indeed to have such fantastic publishers in Jen and Chris Hamilton-Emery, together with the whole crew at the mighty Salt. My agent, Jonny Geller at Curtis Brown, has given much support over the years, and I'm also grateful to Jonny's eternally capable assistant, Catherine Cho.

NEW FICTION FROM SALT

SAMUEL FISHER
The Chameleon (978-1-78463-124-6)

KERRY HADLEY-PRYCE
Gamble (978-1-78463-130-7)

BEE LEWIS
Liminal (978-1-78463-138-3)

VESNA MAIN
Temptation: A User's Guide (978-1-78463-128-4)

ALISON MOORE
Missing (978-1-78463-140-6)

S.J. NAUDÉ
The Third Reel (978-1-78463-150-5)

HANNAH VINCENT
The Weaning (978-1-78463-120-8)

This book has been typeset by
SALT PUBLISHING LIMITED
using Neacademia, a font designed by Sergei Egorov
for the Rosetta Type Foundry in the Czech Republic.
It is manufactured using Creamy 70gsm, a Forest
Stewardship Council™ certified paper from Stora Enso's
Anjala Mill in Finland. It was printed and bound by
Clays Limited in Bungay, Suffolk, Great Britain.

CROMER
GREAT BRITAIN
MMXVIII